MORE PRAISE FOR CHINA BAYLES AND *THYME OF DEATH* . . .

"AN APPEALING CHARACTER . . . a good addition to the growing list of female amateur sleuths."
—***Booklist***

"A NOVEL TO SAVOR . . . I LOVED IT!"
—**Susan Dunlap,**
author of *Death and Taxes*

"LIVELY AND ENGAGING."
—***Fort Worth Star-Telegram***

"A PLEASING ADDITION TO THE GROWING SHE-SLEUTH POPULATION."
—***Rockland (ME) Courier-Gazette***

"FANS OF STRONG WOMEN DETECTIVES WILL BE DELIGHTED TO MEET CHINA BAYLES . . . I'm looking forward to hearing more from Susan Wittig Albert."
—**Maureen Reddy, author of *Sisters in Crime: Feminism and the Crime Novel***

"COLORFUL CHARACTERS . . . A wreath of (bay) laurel goes to Susan Wittig Albert in this, her debut into the mystery game."
—***Western Wake (NC) Herald***

China Bayles Mysteries by Susan Wittig Albert

THYME OF DEATH
WITCHES' BANE
HANGMAN'S ROOT
ROSEMARY REMEMBERED
RUEFUL DEATH
LOVE LIES BLEEDING
CHILE DEATH
LAVENDER LIES
MISTLETOE MAN
BLOODROOT

With her husband Bill Albert, writing as Robin Paige

DEATH AT BISHOP'S KEEP
DEATH AT GALLOWS GREEN
DEATH AT DAISY'S FOLLY
DEATH AT DEVIL'S BRIDGE
DEATH AT ROTTINGDEAN
DEATH AT WHITECHAPEL
DEATH AT EPSOM DOWNS

Nonfiction books by Susan Wittig Albert

WRITING FROM LIFE
WORK OF HER OWN

A China Bayles Mystery

SUSAN WITTIG ALBERT

BERKLEY PRIME CRIME, NEW YORK

THYME OF DEATH

A Berkley Prime Crime Book / published by arrangement with Charles Scribner's Sons, an imprint of Macmillan Publishing Company

PRINTING HISTORY
Charles Scribner's Sons edition published 1992
Berkley Prime Crime edition / March 1994

For information address: The Berkley Publishing Group,
a divsion of Penguin Putnam Inc.,
375 Hudson Street, New York, New York 10014.

Visit our website at
www.penguinputnam.com

ISBN: 0-425-14098-9

Berkley Prime Crime Books are published
by The Berkley Publishing Group,
a division of Penguin Putnam Inc.,
375 Hudson Street, New York, New York 10014.

PRINTED IN THE UNITED STATES OF AMERICA

20 19 18 17 16 15 14

Acknowledgments

I wish to acknowledge the contributions of the following people: Mike Ellison, Texas Poison Control Center; Mike Cleckler, Cleckler Firearms, Leander, TX; Connie Moore, The Herb Bar, Austin, TX; Peggy Kelley and William Fly, who furnished legal background; and John Webber and Patty Craig, who offered valuable editorial comment. I also wish to thank Anita McClellan, without whose dedicated efforts and patient encouragement this book might not have been published, and Susanne Kirk, Executive Editor of Scribners, for her energetic support of this project.

Most of all, I am grateful to my husband and partner, William Albert, who provided technical underpinning, plot thickening, and editorial sharpening, and computer consulting, at all hours of the day and night.

Author's Note

This novel is set in the imaginary Texas town of Pecan Springs, which includes such fictitious elements as the campus of Central Texas State University and the Pecan River. Readers familiar with the central Texas hill country should not confuse Pecan Springs with such real towns and villages as San Marcos, New Braunfels, Wimberley, or Fredericksburg, or CTSU with local universities. The author has created the fictional characters and events of this book for the reader's pleasure, and intends no connection to real people or happenings.

CHAPTER 1

If I'd known how the week was going to turn out I would have sent it back first thing Monday and asked for a refund.

But Monday morning fooled me. It was the kind of day that thrills members of the Pecan Springs Chamber of Commerce right down to the pointy toes of their cowboy boots. The blistering Texas summer was fading fast, the cedar elms were coppery against a crisp blue sky, and as I came down the flagstone path to the street I was grinning. After two-plus years in Pecan Springs, I was still grateful for having escaped Houston with most of my sanity and some of my youth. I'd spent what seemed like an eternity there, give or take a few centuries, in a law firm that specialized in protecting the constitutional rights of bad guys—mostly *big* bad guys who had the wherewithal to pick up the tab for an expensive defense. At the weathered age of thirty-nine, I'd sold my yuppie condo-with-sauna and moved to Pecan Springs, Texas, population fifteen thousand, not counting the tourists and the students at Central Texas State U. I'd put my savings into a century-old stone building that housed an herb shop with the clever name of Thyme and Seasons Herb Company. Everybody in the law firm knew I'd gone nuts. Me, I knew I'd gone sane. I'm not saying I believed every second that I was doing the right thing, far from it. But I'd elbowed my way up the ladder and the view from the top wasn't pretty. I'd seen enough of the shadow side of justice to last me for the rest of my life.

Thyme and Seasons fronts on Crockett Street, a couple of blocks from the town square and a dozen blocks from the CTSU campus. Pecan Springs is a picturesque town, halfway between Austin to the north and San Antonio to the south. People who think that Texas is nothing but sagebrush and prickly pear flats are always surprised to see the cedar-blanketed Edwards Plateau that rises west into the hill country, and the flat fertile farmland that spreads east to the Gulf Coast. West, too, lies the chain of highland lakes, strung like silver charms on the silver bracelet of the Colorado River, where Dallas and Houston money comes to play. Ten miles from town there's Canyon Lake on the Guadalupe River, the site of several luxurious vacation communities, and the lovely San Marcos River rises from Spring Lake and winds crystal clear beneath massive cypresses and sycamores. While Pecan Springs may not be endowed with big-city cultural riches like opera and ballet, I personally prefer to live in a green and beautiful place, with blue lakes and limestone hills within biking distance. And after fifteen years of risking life and limb on the I-10 into Houston, simply not having to drive to work every morning is something to feel cheerful about over breakfast.

Today was my day off. The shop was closed, and I was headed next door to the Craft Emporium, a rambling Victorian mansion that houses a jumbled warren of tiny craft shops, antique booths, and boutiques. As I opened the stained-glass front door, Gretel Schumaker was hanging a fresh batch of hand-dipped candles in the front window of what was once the parlor. She was surrounded by her craft—a forest of scented candles in dozens of shapes and hundreds of shades.

"Hi, China," Gretel called. She is blond and sturdily buxom, like her mother and German grandmother, who also make candles. It's a family enterprise. "Hey, you got lavender oil? Mom wants to dip a batch tomorrow."

"Sure," I said. "Stop by and knock at the kitchen door in an hour or so, and I'll get it for you." I live behind the shop. As far as the neighbors are concerned, that means I'm never closed. Sometimes that's a nuisance. Mostly, though, it's okay.

Because I was on an errand, I only nodded at Peter Dudley, who was fussily dusting Depression glassware in what used to be the mansion's dining room and is now his upscale antique shop. If you do more than nod, you're lost. Peter's fund of gossip is only rivaled by that of Constance Letterman, who owns the Emporium. Peter wears a dark toupee that covers his bald spot, open-necked white shirts with the sleeves rolled up, and pastel slacks. He's a rare treat in Pecan Springs, where everybody's into jeans, tee shirts, and cowboy boots, which is exactly what I was wearing today. My tee shirt announced that behind every successful woman was herself.

"If you're here to see dear Constance," Peter said solicitously, putting down a Fiesta Ware pitcher as if it were the Hope diamond, "you've just missed her. She's gone to the newspaper."

"Thanks," I said, and kept going, up the grand staircase that climbs to the second floor. I was on my way to Violett's Doll House, a tiny shop, squeezed, appropriately, into the mansion's old nursery and crammed floor to ceiling with dolls, each one uniquely and individually handcrafted by Violett Hall.

Violett herself is shy and sweet-faced, with a cupid's-bow smile and brown hair fringed in Mamie Eisenhower bangs and curled over her ears in tight, tidy rolls that Peter affectionately calls "cootie garages." She's lived all of her fifty-something years in Pecan Springs, keeping house and caring for an invalid mother who died several years ago. When Violett wasn't nursing Mrs. Hall or mothering the multitude of cats and birds she dotes on, she was sewing stuffed cows and plaid pigs and checkered chickens for the First Baptist Church Holiday Bazaar and the Public Library Baked Goods and Craft Sale. After Mrs. Hall died, Constance talked Violett into renting the mansion's nursery and making a business out of her hobby. It seems to have worked out, for her soft, pudgy dolls and stuffed animals have been featured in several newspaper and magazine articles, and her customers come from as far away as Little Rock. She can't be turning a huge profit (nothing in the Emporium does *that*), but Constance says that Violett's Doll House always pays its rent on time and Violett probably clears enough to feed her pets and keep a roof over their heads. She's fanatical about her animals. One purpose of my visit was to bring her the herbs she'd ordered, tincture of echinacea and goldenseal to treat a cat's ear mites, and the tincture of marigold and myrrh that she uses to fight her foot fungus. It must have been bothering her. I noticed that she'd switched to sandals, a departure from the usual sensible loafers that went with her neat A-line skirt and the tidy white round-collared blouse she wore buttoned up to the throat. Violett's outfits always reminded me of schoolgirls' uniforms.

I wasn't the only person in the shop. Violett was tending to a pair of well-dressed female tourists, themselves doll-like, one with improbable blue hair and the other with equally improbable red, both heavily made up and pants-suited. While I waited, I looked around. My other reason for coming was to find a gift for Jo Gilbert. Today was her fifty-ninth birthday, and she needed some cheering up. Jo had breast cancer.

I glanced over Violett's dolls and stuffed animals. Jo is too firm and no-nonsense to go for something frilly. But I happened on a red calico goose wearing a defiant look in her black eye. That rebellious eye reminded me of Jo. Jo is an organizer. She organized Pecan Springs' small chapter of NOW under the upturned noses of the Junior League. Then, in the teeth of widespread community apathy, she organized the drive to hack Pecan Springs Park out of a willow thicket. Most recently, she had organized the Anti-Airport Coalition, which opposes the regional airport that the cities of Austin and San Antonio are considering building on a site seven miles outside of Pecan Springs, on the other side of the proposed high-speed rail line. I grinned at the stuffed goose. The only thing it needed to make it perfect for Jo was a sign saying FUCK THE AIRPORT!

I tucked the goose under my arm and turned around to see the blue-haired tourist lean over the counter and pick up a plump-faced pink bear wearing a strawberry-print apron and a pink straw hat with a wreath of strawberries around the brim. "Look, Maxine," she cried. "It's StrawBerry Bear! Isn't she simply precious?"

"StrawBerry Bear!" Maxine cried, clapping her hands. "My little granddaughter's been asking for her!"

Never having been a mother myself (never having even *wanted* to be a mother), I know next to nothing about what turns kids on these days. But even *I* know that StrawBerry Bear is enormously popular with the four-to-eight crowd, almost as big as Big Bird himself. I know this because StrawBerry Bear just happens to be the brainchild of Jo's friend, Rosalind Kotner.

Roz's life has to be your all-time Cinderella story. Until she hit the big time with StrawBerry and the spin-off books, clothes, and toys that came when the StrawBerry Bear Kids' Klub ratings topped the chart, Roz lived here in town in Jo Gilbert's spare room, pretty much hand-to-mouth, like any other would-be actress stuck in a small Texas town. But that was back then, five, six years ago. Now she lives in New York, where she tapes her weekly TV show in front of an audience of adoring kids, and masterminds her sprawling empire of StrawBerry Bear spin-offs. And poses for magazine covers, like the latest *People* magazine, where she was perched on a pyramid of pink stuffed bears, with greenbacks spilling everywhere. The cover story was all about how many millions of StrawBerries had been sold and how many millions of dollars Roz stood to rake in over the next few years. It's an impressive achievement for a woman who came out of the Texas boonies with only a stuffed bear and what turned out to be a blockbuster idea.

But Maxine's granddaughter was not destined to receive this particular bear. "I'm sorry," Violett said matter-of-factly. "It's a . . . it's not for sale." She took the bear out of Maxine's hands and stowed it under the counter.

Maxine pouted. "That's really too bad," she said. "Everybody's out of them. Even Toys 'R' Us has had to back order. I can't persuade you to—?"

Violett smiled. "Let me show you Missy Prissy. She's a sweet little lady with a pink ruffled apron and pink booties. Maybe she'll do instead."

Apparently Missy Prissy did, for in a few moments Violett had rung up a sale and Maxine and her blue-haired friend were on their way out.

I put my goose on the counter. "I thought Jo Gilbert might like this for her birthday," I said. "And I've brought the tinctures you wanted." I gave her the package and began to count out the money for the goose.

"How is Jo?" Violett asked.

I gave an evasive shrug. Actually, Jo had seemed depressed lately, maybe because the Anti-Airport Coalition was running into a full-scale flak attack from the local paper, the *Enterprise*, which seems dead set on turning Pecan Springs into an airport suburb. Or maybe because of her birthday. I get depressed on birthdays too, even though I've only gotten as far as forty-two. But at least I'm still counting. I'd probably be a lot more depressed if I got to number fifty-nine and my doctor told me it might be the last. After a mastectomy and chemotherapy, Jo's cancer was spreading.

"I understand her daughter's staying with her," Violett said. She put the herbs in her purse and counted seven dollars and forty-two cents out of the register.

"That's right," I replied. Jo's daughter Meredith is a CPA from Dallas. She had come down for a few weeks' visit.

Violett gave a long, expressive sigh. "I hope she isn't thinking of giving up her career to nurse her mother. That would be a terrible sacrifice."

"I think it's only temporary," I said, and then wished I hadn't. If Jo's doctor was right, it might be *very* temporary. When I left, Violett was putting a new doll on the shelf to replace Missy Prissy.

I couldn't help smiling as I went back down the grand staircase and out the front door of the Emporium, thinking fondly of Violett and her dolls, and Gretel and her candles, and Peter and his Depression dishes.

Ordinary people doing ordinary things. The beginning of a slow week in a small town.

As I said, Monday morning fooled. Me.

That afternoon I went out to the herb garden to plant a row of garlic bulbs along the fence. The old two-story building I live and work in was originally built by a German stonemason who knew his business so well that every piece of square-cut limestone still fits snug and true. It sits back about ten yards from the street on a deep, narrow lot that goes all the way to the alley. I've planted herb gardens front and back, more to attract customers than to grow a substantial crop, and I spend a couple of hours a week messing around there, digging, planting, composting, and trying to improve the rock-hard caliche soil.

A lot of people ask me why I got out of law and into herbs. I have a stock answer: plants don't argue. They also don't lie, cheat, connive, or hit below the belt. That's true, of course, but the real answer is more complicated. The first part of it is that I left law because I stopped believing in the partnership between justice and the legal system. I also left because the practice of law was changing me into somebody I didn't like very much, somebody more arrogant, more competitive, more cutthroat than I knew myself to be. If I stayed in much longer, I knew what I'd become—a carbon copy of the senior partners in our firm, four men who lived for their work, whose lives were empty of anything else.

I got into herbs (this is the second part of the answer) because when I was a kid I was crazy about growing things. It was a trait I inherited from my father's mother, who had what was probably the finest herb garden in New Orleans parish. I inherited Gram's name, too. China Bayles. I've also developed a stock answer to "What a weird name," which I hear a lot. I tell people I was named after my grandmother, who was conceived in Shanghai during the Boxer Rebellion.

That's a lie. I have no idea where Gram was conceived. When I was practicing law, I used my initials to obscure the fact that I was a woman. Now that I'm growing herbs, I've gone back to China. It feels right.

People also ask me why I went into law in the first place. The truth is that as a child I wanted to become a botanist. But my father, failing to beget a son, expected his only child to wear his boots, as they say in Houston, where I grew up. And that was fine with me. I was impressed by his power, and I wanted to be as much like him as possible. I certainly *didn't* want to be like my mother, passive and purposeless. So I went to U.T. law school, stiff-armed my way into a tough field, and set about the serious business of showing my stuff and making a lot of money in the process. Did that please my father? I doubt it. He didn't invite me into *his* firm. But it was the only way I knew to get his attention.

Still, I was somewhat schizoid. While part of me wanted to be the wealthiest and most successful woman lawyer in Houston, another part still wanted to be a botanist. So while I was doing law, I was also growing herbs, as many as I could fit into the custom-built window greenhouse in my condo. When things got to the point where I knew I had to quit the firm, I didn't have a burning ambition to do something else. But plants were what I knew and enjoyed, and I thought the herb shop would allow me to make a kinder, gentler living. I pay my dues to the Bar Association because it's not a bad idea to have a backup in case the business goes bust. But even though I can take a few cases if I need to, it hasn't been necessary.

The business is in the black, although barely.

I was finishing the row of garlic bulbs and was about to divide a thick clump of silver-gray, velvety lamb's ears when Ruby Wilcox came around the house. Behind her was Meredith Gilbert, Jo's daughter.

I straightened up. The front of my stone building is divided into two shop spaces. Thyme and Seasons takes up one space. Ruby Wilcox rents the other for The Crystal Cave, Pecan Springs' only New Age shop. She's tall, over six feet in the spiky heels she sometimes wears. Her orangy-red hair is an Orphan Annie frizz, and her wide, spontaneous grin and the gingery dusting of freckles across her nose take ten years off her forty-three. She was wearing black ankle-length stretch pants, black three-inch heels, and a green cotton tunic that matched her contacts. (Her eyes are naturally hazel, but she says that the tint was only twenty-five dollars extra and what the hell?) Our working arrangement is exceptionally handy, not only because The Crystal Cave's rent shores up the mortgage payments, but because Ruby and I often cover for one another, so that neither of us is irrevocably tied to her shop. Even if you love what you're doing, some days a one-person business feels like a one-ton albatross.

Ruby plopped down on the white-painted iron bench at the edge of the spearmint bed and dropped her shopping bag. Meredith, in a black boat-necked tee and trim-cut khakis that gave her an athletic look, sat down beside her. Like Jo, Meredith has clear gray eyes, a strong jaw, and dark, wiry hair cut short and brushed straight back. The firmness of her facial structure is matched by a no-nonsense posture and challenging directness that borders on the brusque and quick-tempered. With Meredith, as with Jo, what you see is what you get.

The fact that Meredith is a lot like her mother probably explains why I like her. When I moved to Pecan Springs, Jo became a kind of surrogate mother for me. She fed me, she introduced me to the right people, she offered straight talk when I needed it. My connection to my own mother is strained, to put it mildly, and Jo filled an empty place in my life. The fact that Meredith and Jo are alike also probably explains why they don't get along all that well. They both have a certain wariness about connections and a fierce sense of privacy, characteristics that don't allow them to open themselves to real intimacy. And neither suffers fools gladly. But that didn't keep me from loving Jo and liking Meredith a great deal.

"What're you planting?" Ruby asked. She kicked off her heels, stretched out her long legs and rotated her feet at the ankles, first one way and then another. Ruby is very flexible. She does yoga.

"Garlic," I said. I grow as much as I've got room for and buy lots from a nearby grower. Customers like garlic braids, and the dried flower heads make great wreath material. "I have a birthday present for your mother," I told Meredith. "How is she?"

"Birthdays have never been Mother's thing," Meredith said matter-of-factly. "She's been a little down lately, thinking about . . . well, you know. And money could get to be a problem. She doesn't have very good insurance coverage, and if things get bad—" She shrugged. "But her new hobby is cheering her up some."

"New hobby?" I asked.

"Bird watching," Ruby put in.

Meredith nodded. "No matter how rotten she feels, she tramps out every morning with her bird book and a pair of binoculars. You've got to admire her spirit."

"That's because she's on the Path," Ruby said cheerfully, rotating her feet in the opposite direction. Ruby is a believer in New Age alternative therapies, in which she is also something of an expert. She helped Jo put together a "wellness program" that includes a sugar-free, fat-free diet, weekly visualizations, daily meditations, and hourly affirmations, all designed to help Jo's ailing immune system triumph over the invading cancer cells. The Healing Path is what Ruby calls it, the Way to Wellness. "Mystical claptrap" is what my friend Mike McQuaid calls it. The AMA probably has several other names for it. I didn't care. I just hoped that whatever Ruby and Jo were doing, it would at least give Jo some sense of control over what was happening to her body, and some release. I cared for Jo too much to hope that her days would be extended at the cost of pain.

"What have you two been up to all day?" I asked, snipping the seedheads off a lanky dill plant. Dill is wonderful, but it's terribly invasive. If I let it go to seed, it's everywhere. I can visualize the whole world, dilled.

Ruby reached both hands high in a stretch, breathed in deeply, then bent over and grasped her toes. "Buying clothes," she said in a muffled exhale. "We drove to Austin."

"Find anything interesting?"

Ruby straightened up, breathed in, and reached for her toes again. "An orange and black top," she reported on the exhale. "Matching stirrup pants." Where clothes are concerned, Ruby has a flair for the weirdly dramatic. She's especially impressive when she's costumed to teach the tarot and astrology classes that are regular events at the Cave.

Ruby is my best friend, but our personal styles are distinctly different. Where she tends to the flamboyant, I lean to the plain and serviceable—jeans, tees and sweatshirts that feature various ecological and feminist exhortations, sneakers and cowboy boots—and I wear my straight brown hair in a short, swinging cut that does absolutely nothing to disguise the wide streak of gray at my left temple. I confess to owning a few shirtdresses and some tailored skirts and blouses, leftovers from my power-dressing days, but that's it. Costuming myself in lady lawyer clothes—monochrome copies of men's suits—was one of the career requirements that I gave up with immense relief, along with acting and talking as much like a man as possible. It had gotten to the point where I felt like I was cross-dressing when I put on anything with a ruffle. To look at me now, you probably wouldn't say I'm a lot more feminine, at least not in a conventional sense. But I'm free to be what I choose, which is somewhere between the two.

"I got a blue Dallas Cowboys jogging suit and a pair of running shoes," Meredith said. She pulled the shoes out of her sack. "Sears had them on special. Nifty zig-zag tread, huh?"

"Nifty," I said. "You'll make tracks in those shoes. The mark of Zorro."

Ruby did another stretch. "There you have it, Meredith. The verdict. Once a lawyer, always a lawyer."

"Up yours," I said pleasantly.

Ruby grinned. "Once a lawyer—"

Meredith clasped her hands behind her head. "Have you ever been sorry you left the law, China?"

"Never," I replied firmly. For a lot of years, I'd let my career define all aspects of me, the personal as well as the professional. It had given me an identity even a man would be proud of. For the first few months after I left I'd felt loose, unmoored, like a boat drifting in a crosscurrent with a nasty surface chop. There'd been plenty of guilt about not living up to my potential, betraying the cause, selling out—accusations that some of my feminist acquaintances had unloaded on me. But the guilt sloughed off and the unmoored feeling had faded as I learned to live in a different way. Now I felt as if I were growing roots instead of being tied to an anchor.

"Ask me if I regret leaving my career," Ruby said.

Meredith and I laughed. Three years ago, Ruby had divorced Ward, her husband of seventeen years, who had done the classic number and fallen for his secretary.

Ruby pulled her legs up under her in a full lotus. "I'm serious," she protested. "Who says that being married and raising a kid isn't a full-time career?"

"I'm sorry, Ruby," Meredith said. "Sure, marriage

is a career." She grinned. "The trouble is, the ladder has only one rung, the pay's rotten, and seniority doesn't count."

"Still, leaving wasn't easy," Ruby said. "I mean, everything went, everything. *Poof,* like smoke. The nice house, the car, the country club—all gone."

"You could have gotten temporary support," I reminded her.

Ruby lifted her chin, eyes glinting. "Would you take money from a turkey like that? Jeez, and the girl's only a couple of years older than Shannon." Shannon is Ruby's and Ward's daughter. She's a sophomore at U.T., and dear to Ruby's heart. Ruby closed her eyes meditatively. "But I have to say that getting out was worth it. No more bullshit, no more wondering whether he's sneaking around, no more—"

"Money," I said. "No more money. When you leave your career, the paychecks stop."

Meredith picked a sprig of spearmint. "I guess I'd miss the money," she said thoughtfully. "Taking a pay cut would be tough. But I don't think I'd miss Dallas—the traffic, the noise, crime. I live in a nice suburb, but a woman from my neighborhood was kidnapped from a convenience store only three blocks away, and my apartment's been broken into twice. I bought a gun a while back."

"Oh yeah?" Ruby asked with interest. Ruby is addicted to mysteries starring such gun-toting private eyes as Kinsey Millhone and V. I. Warshawski. She says that in her next life, maybe she'll have her own agency. Ruby Wilcox, P.I.

Meredith nodded. " 'The great equalizer,' my NRA

instructor calls it. I hate to say it, but a gun makes the only argument some people understand." She looked at the pink rose climbing the stone wall of the garden, its blossoms blushing in the sun. "To tell the truth, I've been thinking of quitting too. Cashing in, pulling up stakes, finding a small, peaceful town—like this, maybe."

Ruby gave an approving nod. "I'd think a good accountant could pretty much make a living anywhere doing taxes. If you're not out to make a killing, that is."

"Voluntary simplicity," I offered. "You definitely have to be into voluntary simplicity. I've got a book I'll be glad to loan you."

Ruby grinned at me. Money—mostly the lack of it—is something we talk about fairly often. Although I checked out of law with a hefty chunk of change, there's no regular paycheck coming in. Leaving the law definitely meant scaling back.

"Maybe voluntary simplicity wouldn't be so bad in a place like this," Meredith said. She glanced at her watch and stood up. "Gotta go, guys. I have to do some grocery shopping and stop at Adele's to pick up a chocolate cake for Mother's birthday. I know it's not on her diet, but I don't think a piece of cake will hurt her." Adele runs Sweets for the Sweet and bakes absolutely the best cakes in the world. "Mother and I had a little fuss this morning. I thought maybe one of Adele's masterpieces might pave the way for our making up."

"I haven't wrapped Jo's present," I said, "but you

can take it anyway." I went into the house to get the calico goose.

When I brought it out, Meredith smiled at the Fuck-the-Airport! sign I'd made for the goose. "Cute," she said.

After Meredith had gone, I turned to Ruby. "I've got a couple of salmon steaks I was planning to bed down in lemon butter and dill. Want to stay for dinner?"

"Offer I can't refuse," Ruby said promptly. "I'll put on my new outfit."

I laughed. "Fine by me," I said, "but there's only the two of us, unless you want to call somebody." Since her divorce, Ruby's dated quite a few guys. But lately, she's gotten more discriminating. She says she's looking for a man who's on the Path. It's a word that Ruby always says with a capital letter.

Ruby shook her head. "Just you and me, babe," she said, and flung her arm across my shoulder. "Can't I dress up for my best friend?"

"No problem," I said, "as long as I don't have to." I yanked a handful of dill for the sauce. Back in Houston, I didn't have time for cooking, and not a lot of time for eating, either. Or maybe food just wasn't on my priority list. But since I chucked it all, eating is right up there, with cooking just behind it. I could become a blimp without even trying. I sweat off the calories at Jerri's Health and Fitness Spa a couple of times a week, and I ride my bike instead of driving my car. Pecan Springs is the kind of town where you can do that.

Ruby followed me into the kitchen. The last owner of this place, a clever young architect, renovated the entire building. He had his studio where the Cave is now, and his wife ran the herb shop. They lived in the back, where I live, in four large, bright rooms—kitchen, living room, bedroom, guestroom/office. The walls are built of stone, and the rough pine ceilings are supported by beams hand-hewn from massive cypress trees that once grew along the San Marcos River. A nifty place. There's a stone cottage out back, too, equally nifty, that used to be a stable. It sits vacant except on the rare occasions when I have a weekend guest.

Ruby went into the bedroom and changed into the translucent orange-and-black bat-sleeved top and mottled orange-and-black stirrup pants. She looked like a six-foot-tall Monarch butterfly. She fluttered onto a bar stool in the kitchen and began to paint her fingernails an orangy-red that matched her top. Ruby's nails are so long and artificially perfect that they give me an inferiority complex, even though I personally wouldn't have them. Mine are serviceable, but they always look like they've been grubbing for worms, which isn't far wrong, since I do a lot of digging in the dirt.

While Ruby polished, I put two potatoes in the microwave for baking, lit the broiler of my wonderful old Home Comfort gas stove, made lemon butter, and set out cobalt blue plates on the pine table that's the pride of my kitchen. Its top is scarred, even scorched where somebody must have set down a hot stewpot. But it's rock-solid and big enough for chopping herbs, making wreaths, mixing potpourri, and eating—all at once. The rest of the kitchen is like the table: designed for real cooking, not just for storing processed food until it's time to add water, heat, and serve. The green-and-white enameled stove is older than I am but marvelously dependable, and there's an elbow-deep double sink and an extra sink for washing herbs and salad plants. The big refrigerator is often stuffed full of fresh herbs, and dried herbs and braids of garlic and peppers hang from the ceiling, along with my collection of copper cookware.

The salmon was ready in fifteen minutes. Ruby and I were just starting to eat when the phone rang. I reached for the kitchen extension.

Meredith's voice was carefully calm and controlled, but it vibrated like a plucked string. "China, you've got to come over."

I looked at the pink salmon swimming in lemony-dilly butter on my favorite plate. "Right now?"

"Yes, now." I could hear her sucking in her breath, panic edging through. "It's Mother. She's dead, China."

"Jo's dead?" I asked blankly.

Ruby's fork rattled onto her plate. "Dead?" she echoed, her green eyes huge in a face suddenly gone white. "But she can't be! We meditated together this morning, and she was fine! How could she . . . I mean, so quickly—"

"There's a bottle of pills on the table," Meredith said, "and a note." Her voice broke. "It looks like she committed suicide."

"Suicide!" I exclaimed.

"No!" Ruby wailed, fluttering her butterfly arms. "She wouldn't! She *couldn't*! She was on the Path!"

CHAPTER 2

Jo Gilbert had been a handsome woman, upright and indomitable, with a stern, graying distinction. But she wasn't handsome and indomitable now. She was sprawled on the sofa in front of the fireplace, her head lolling loose over her left shoulder, left arm dangling, fingers curled limply, legs spread. She was boneless, a sack of sagging flesh gone loose and chill in the undignified abandon of death.

I looked at her waxy face, firm mouth half open, eyelids closed over eyes that had stopped seeing. Then I looked away again. I'd been called to the death scene too often by panicked clients who wanted a shield between themselves and the law. I'd grown a callus over the place where death shocks and wounds, to the point where I had been able to kill someone myself once in self-defense. But I wasn't that person any longer. The callus had softened and the pain seared through, jagged, abrasive, as caustic as lye. This was Jo, a woman

I cared for as much as—no, *more* than—I cared for my mother. Suddenly, I realized that, I had been anticipating a longer death, with time for goodbyes, not this hasty, ungraceful exit that robbed me of the chance to tell her I loved her. It made me angry, somehow, as if Jo hadn't had any right to leave unexpectedly, to catch me off guard and vulnerable this way.

Beside me, Ruby made a whimpering sound and turned her face away. "I don't believe it."

Bubba Harris, Pecan Springs' chief of police, was bent over the coffee table in front of the sofa. On the table was a copy of *Birds of North America* and a pair of binoculars. Beside them was a water tumbler, an empty bottle of over-the-counter sleeping pills, an empty Smirnoff bottle, and a quart jar of something called Hot Shot Texas Style Bloody Mary mix, a quarter full. There was also a piece of torn-off notebook paper. I couldn't read what was written on it.

Bubba straightened. "Looks to me like she downed a handful of pills and chased 'em with the booze," he said. He scowled, looking down at Jo's sprawled body. "Bad combination. Good way to do yourself in. Painless."

Bubba Harris, who has been chief for at least a decade, is a good old boy in his early fifties, slow-moving and slow-talking, with a Lone Star Beer belly that rolls out over his Lone Star belt buckle. His brown hair is going gray and he sucks on an oversize cigar—never lit—that dwarfs the other features in his jowled, meaty face. Unfortunately, I can't look at Bubba without thinking of Jackie Gleason in *Smoky and the Bandit*. But underneath Bubba's overstuffed, rednecked exterior, there's a steely hardness that comes from a longtime, sure-fisted control of his town. In Texas, only one serious crime in every five is cleared by arrest. But the police in Pecan Springs clear something like four out of five, according to my friend McQuaid, a former Houston homicide detective who now teaches in the criminal justice department at Central Texas State University. Bubba's in charge and he knows it. So does almost everybody else.

Bubba glanced up. It took him a minute to place me, but when he did, his cigar twitched and he pulled his dark brows together in a heavy frown. When I opened the shop, we'd had a discussion about whether selling medicinal herbs amounted to practicing medicine without a license. I pointed out my sign, which read, "I am not qualified nor does the law permit me to diagnose or treat your medical problem." This is an issue these days, and I aim to be clear on it. I'm glad to sell people what they ask for or refer them to reliable texts. But that's where I have to draw the line, and that's what I told Bubba. It probably isn't too often that he comes up against a five-foot-six hundred-and-forty-pound female who knows the law and talks back. He remembered me. And he knew that I was a friend of Jo's, too.

Ruby also talks back. "It wasn't suicide," she said emphatically. Her voice was pitched too high and she swallowed, making an effort to bring it down a notch. "Jo wouldn't kill herself."

Bubba rolled his cigar from one side of his face to the other and regarded Ruby. "Accident, you figure? Could be she didn't know what would happen if she mixed pills and booze. But what about the note?"

"What does it say?" I asked.

Bubba bent over and looked, not touching it. " 'I'm sorry about what I said. It wasn't what I intended. Please forgive me.' "

Ruby bent over and looked too. "It's not signed. And it doesn't say who it's to."

"Her handwriting?"

Ruby straightened up. "I don't know," she said doubtfully. "Maybe."

"We'll check it out," Bubba said. He switched his cigar to the other side of his mouth. "Looks like suicide to me."

"No," Ruby said. "I mean . . ." She waved her arms, an agitated butterfly. "I mean, Jo Gilbert was working to *heal* herself. She didn't like medicine. She especially didn't like sleeping pills. She wouldn't have taken any, much less enough to kill herself."

Bubba's brows came together. "The lady was terminal, wasn't she? Seems like what I heard around town."

"She had cancer," Ruby admitted. "But she'd never give up. Never." She gulped and turned helplessly away from the loose bundle of cooling flesh. "Never."

I looked down at the empty pill bottle on the table. Like Ruby, I didn't want to believe that Jo could have killed herself. But there was a part of me that was trained to assess evidence and draw valid, verifiable conclusions. Like it or not, that part had to admit that the worsening pain of cancer or the fear of being a helpless burden on her daughter and her friends might have pushed Jo into doing something otherwise unthinkable. A handful of sleeping pills, a couple of strong Bloody Marys to wash them down, might have seemed the most reasonable way out of an altogether unreasonable illness. She'd been depressed lately, and today was her birthday. Perhaps it had seemed a symbolic day on which to bring her life to a close.

"Well, then, mebbe an accident," Bubba said. "Say she took a few pills, had a drink, got dopey, took a few more. It's happened before."

"But she wouldn't take the pills in the *first* place," Ruby insisted.

Bubba shrugged. "We'll see what the J.P. has to say." I made a face. In Texas, a justice of the peace is required to attend and rule on all suspicious deaths, although most aren't trained for the task.

He jerked his head toward the kitchen. "The daughter's back there. Whyn't y'all see if she needs anythin'. I'll call Watson's Funeral Home to come and take care of bidness." That's the way all good old boys pronounce "business" in Texas, even the ones who've promoted themselves into gov'ment bidness and gone to Washington. I used to wonder whether they'd admit me to the club if I took to saying it. When I realized I was tempted to test out the theory, I knew it was time for a career change.

Bubba turned to the telephone. Ruby and I had been dismissed. I gave her a little shove and we went down the dark hallway toward the back of the house.

Meredith was sitting at the oilcloth-covered table in Jo's pleasantly old-fashioned kitchen, her head on her folded arms. The room was dusky and a red enameled teakettle chirruped merrily on the gas stove. A white cake carton sat on the yellow formica counter, beside a box of birthday candles and the calico goose. I turned off the teakettle and turned on the light over the sink. One end of the fluorescent tube glowed, the other flickered fitfully. Jo had been meaning to replace the ballast.

Ruby bent over Meredith. "Meredith," she said in a whisper, "I'm so sorry."

"Yes," I said, low. But sorry didn't cut it. Sorry didn't begin to describe the sadness and loss I felt, standing in Jo's familiar yellow-painted kitchen, her birthday cake and Fuck-the-Airport! goose on the counter, while the funeral home was coming to handle the "bidness" of taking her body to the Adams County Hospital, where some doctor would cut her up and tell us what killed her. But what else was there to say?

Meredith raised her head, stricken. "I didn't even know she *had* any sleeping pills."

"And I never saw her take more than one drink," Ruby said.

Meredith leaned against Ruby. "She had a bout with hepatitis once. She always went easy on booze. The last time I saw that Smirnoff bottle, it was better than half full." She paused. "I didn't know she had any of that Hot Shot stuff, either. She liked to drink it for breakfast. She said it woke her up. But we ran out, and the liquor store was out of it." Her pale face looked pinched and blue under the flickering fluorescent light and her cheeks were furrowed with tears. "But it's the pills that bother me. She must have bought them just for . . . this."

Ruby looked shocked. "Jo? Buy pills?" She shook

her head firmly. "She was into self-hypnosis. She refused to take anything chemical to knock her out or cut the pain. She wouldn't use pills."

I opened the cupboard where Jo kept the cups, neatly hung from hooks. I couldn't see where all this denial was getting us. Jo's dying left a cold, empty place where something alive and vital had lived. But evading it wouldn't bring her back. "So what about the note?" It certainly looked to me like a suicide note.

Ruby shook her head stubbornly. "I don't know. But Jo wouldn't take the easy way out. For her, cancer was the lesson she had to learn in this life. She wanted to *confront* it, learn from it, not escape from it. That's part of healing."

I took three cups from the cupboard and set them on the counter. When Ruby talks like this, I always feel uncomfortable, like an atheist at a prayer meeting. Maybe it's because I haven't started down the Healing Path. To do that, Ruby says, I'd have to give up my anger at Leatha, my mother. I've mellowed some since I left the law, but I'm not ready to give up my anger. It's been part of me for so long, I'm not sure who I'd be without it.

Ruby reached for Meredith's hand. "Your mom had the courage to choose her own way," she whispered, "and a marvelous strength of will. Her next life will be something special."

I measured peppermint tea into the teapot and poured boiling water into it, wondering if Ruby realized that her remark could go both ways. Jo had the courage and will to commit suicide, if that's what she decided.

I looked at Meredith. "What about that note?" I asked again.

Meredith rubbed her eyes with the backs of her hands. "We had an argument this morning. You know, mother-daughter stuff. It wasn't really earth-shaking, but I guess it was bad enough to make her want to apologize before she—" She shook her head, the tears coming again. "Oh, God, I couldn't live with myself if I thought our argument was what pushed her into this."

I looked at Meredith. "You're *sure* there weren't any pills in the house?"

She shook her head numbly. "Last night I couldn't sleep. I'm not into self-hypnosis, and I don't have Mother's thing about chemicals. I asked if she had any. She said she didn't." Her face twisted. "She must have got them this morning. Or she lied."

"Listen, you guys," Ruby said urgently, "I came over yesterday afternoon and Jo and I did our regular yoga and meditation together. I'd have known it if she was thinking of something like . . . this. But she was fine." She closed her eyes. "She was *fine*," she repeated fiercely, as though she herself were responsible for the balance of Jo's mind.

Meredith looked at me, her gray eyes shadowed. "But there is something odd, China. There was somebody here today. While Ruby and I were in Austin."

I got up and turned on the hanging light over the table and flicked off the fluorescent. I hate those stupid things. Even when they're working right, they make people look like day-old corpses. They always remind me of the light in Leatha's kitchen and the washed-out blue of her face when she'd been drinking. "Who?" I asked. "Who was here?"

"I don't know. I came in the back way, because I had Mother's cake and your present and I wanted to surprise her. Then I went into the living room and found . . ." She paused and swallowed, reaching deep inside for control. A moment later, calmer, she went on. "Just as I came into the room, I got a whiff of perfume. I'm sensitive to smells, but I couldn't identify it. Something exotic."

"I didn't smell any perfume," I said.

"Not now, you wouldn't." Meredith rotated her shoulders wearily and Ruby got up and moved behind her, kneading her shoulder blades with the tips of her fingers, to save her orangy-red nails. "It was just the barest whiff. It was gone the second I opened the door. And then I found Mother, and the paramedics came and tried to revive her, and when they said she was dead they called that awful policeman who smells like damp cigars." She made a wry mouth. "Thank God he isn't *smoking* the damned thing."

I frowned. From the look of it, Jo had to have taken the pills soon after Meredith and Ruby had left this morning. But acccording to Meredith, she didn't have any to take, and no Bloody Mary mix. Had somebody else brought the pills and the Hot Shot? A speculative question, no clear-cut answer. I'd been taught in law school to go for the most obvious, least debatable answer first. And the most obvious answer was that Jo had put Hot Shot on the grocery list and lied to her daughter about not having sleeping pills. It wouldn't be the first time a mother lied to her daughter.

"I'm not trying to say Mother didn't do it," Meredith said. "She'd been down for the past few weeks. Who wouldn't be, with the cancer, and the pain, and the bills. She was pretty depressed."

Ruby's lips tightened. "Will you knock off the depression shit? Sure, she was frustrated at not feeling better. But she wasn't the kind of woman who'd kill herself over a little pain. And not over a few bills, either."

Meredith straightened her shoulders and fished a tissue out of her pocket. She blew her nose with the grim determination of someone who's decided not to cry anymore. "You're right, Ruby," she said. "Mother and I weren't close, even after Daddy left and there were just the two of us. But at least I know her that well. Mother hated to give in."

"What was he like, your dad?" I asked, realizing I didn't know much about Jo's life. She'd moved to Pecan Springs from the South Side of Chicago fifteen years ago, that much I knew. But that was all.

Meredith shrugged. "Typical blue-collar, patriarchal. He worked in the mills and he didn't want her to work. He thought she should stay home and take care of me and cook his meals and iron his work clothes and pack his lunch bucket."

"Wow," Ruby said incredulously. "Jo was married to a man like *that*?"

Meredith laughed. "Until the summer I was fourteen. That's when they divorced. I remember them arguing about the ERA, and about women coming over to the house to organize a chapter of NOW. And once Dad got really ticked off because Betty Friedan came to

Chicago and Mother took me to hear her. Then one day he packed up and left and there were just the two of us." She blew her nose again. "I thought we'd be closer after that, but it never happened. Oh, Mother was good to me. She made a good home and all that." She smiled mistily. "She even baked cookies. But I always had the feeling she took care of me because she was doing her duty, not because she found a lot of joy in it. I hope that doesn't sound too awful," she added. "Maybe she wasn't really like that. Maybe that's just *my* stuff."

I touched Meredith's shoulder. The Jo I knew and loved had been reserved, sometimes remote, but it was hard to recognize her in Meredith's description. Still, I knew what it was like to want a mother and find her missing.

"I think it was just the old mother-daughter thing," Ruby said. "My mother won't stop telling me what an idiot I was to let Ward get away. And she *still* keeps after me about finding another husband to take care of me."

Meredith shook her head. "It was more than that. Even when we lived together, I didn't know her. And these last fifteen years—" She raised her shoulders and let them fall, a despairing gesture. "When I was a senior, my grandmother died and left Mother some money. She gave me enough to pay my college tuition for four years. She took the rest and moved down here and bought this place. When I got the job in Dallas five years ago, I thought she'd be pleased. But she didn't even want me to *visit* her, for God's sake. It was like I belonged to a part of her life that was over, being married to Dad, being a housewife, even being a mother. She didn't want anything—even me—to remind her about it." She put her head in her hands. "And now this. She was a mystery. A total mystery."

I understood something of Meredith's despair, but in a different way. My mother's drinking had kept me from knowing her. But even at seven, I had understood why she did it. My father's law practice was the most important thing in his life. She was a poor second. Nothing—not a huge house in University Hills or a white Cadillac or a generous allowance—could compensate her for his loss. Not even her daughter. Nothing but the booze.

But it wasn't just her alcoholism that made my mother unknowable. It was the nearly overwhelming idea of *mother*, a woman who was me and yet not-me, from whom I had somehow, by some complicated and tricky maneuver, to separate myself. I wondered whether any of us ever really knew our mothers, yet whether we could ever be successful in knowing ourselves apart from them.

Meredith raised her head and took a deep breath, as though unloading her feelings had made her feel better. "But things were improving between us," she said fiercely, trying to convince herself. "She was down, but it didn't have to do with *us*."

"Well, sure," Ruby said comfortingly. "There was the airport, and Arnold Seidensticker. She had plenty else on her mind."

Arnold Seidensticker is the owner and publisher of the *Enterprise*, Pecan Springs' weekly newspaper. The Seidenstickers and several hundred other German immigrants had settled the area in the 1840s. They'd brought their German customs and their culture, which is a large part of the charm of the area today. Most of the other immigrant families died out or diluted themselves through marriage or moved on. But for over a hundred and fifty years, the Seidenstickers remained the town's leading citizens. That's what made Arnold Seidensticker think he had a mandate to promote Pecan Springs as the site of the Austin–San Antonio Regional Airport, a complex that was supposed to rival the Dallas–Fort Worth airport in terms of air traffic and the flow-through of dollars. Jo and the Anti-Airport Coalition were all that stood between him and success.

Meredith smiled a little. "Mother was plenty ticked off at that guy, all right. She said if she ever got to the point of hiring outside muscle to keep the airport out, he'd be at the top of her hit list. You know Mother's temper. And I wouldn't blame her if she did. Seidensticker was a pain in the ass."

That was Jo, all right. She liked to surprise people with her South Side tough talk, and she had a temper that matched her mouth. I had the idea that Meredith was a lot like her in that respect, too.

"But she was feeling better about the airport lately," Meredith went on. "She wouldn't tell me what it was all about, but I think she'd discovered something—something she hoped would keep the airport from going through."

Ruby scowled. "That's another reason I don't think she killed herself. She'd never abandon the field to Arnold Seidensticker. It would give him too much satisfaction. And without her, the Coalition's likely to fizzle. She was the main energy behind it."

"It wasn't Arnold Seidensticker who was getting to her the last week or so," Meredith said. "It was somebody else. Somebody named Roz. No big deal, I guess. But her phone calls definitely upset Mother."

"Roz?" Ruby asked. "Rosalind Kotner, the one who does the StrawBerry Bear shows?"

"That's the one. Mother said she used to rent her a room. Do you know her?"

Ruby shook her head. "I've seen her on TV once or twice. She looks like Alice in Wonderland with good legs."

I had to smile at that. When I'd seen the show, Roz was wearing a short pink pinafore with a flirtatious white eyelet flounce, white stockings, and black patent-leather slippers, her hair in girlish blond ringlets.

"I've met her," I volunteered. "She stayed in my guest cottage once when she was visiting and your mother was having the house painted." I didn't add, although I might have, that Jo Gilbert and Roz Kotner struck me as an oddly assorted pair. Jo was older, and her reserved grace threw Roz's coy, kittenish cuteness into high relief. And Roz liked the spotlight. Whenever she was around, Jo sat back and let Roz capture all the attention.

Ruby came back to the subject of Jo's supposed visitor. "China," she said, "if somebody else was here this morning, would there be fingerprints?"

I picked up the teapot and poured three cups of peppermint tea. "If there are, Bubba will find them. He may look like a dumbass, but McQuaid says he's plenty sharp." As an ex-cop, McQuaid ought to know.

"What'll he do?" Ruby asked, reaching for a cup.

"He'll check the bottles and the glass and the note for prints, and dust the coffee table and other likely places. He'll get a handwriting expert to verify that Jo actually wrote the note. He'll ask you and Meredith what time you left, when you got back, that sort of thing. The medical examiner will do an autopsy and establish cause and time of death. The report, along with the death certificate, will come out in a few days. It may or may not settle the question of how she died." I put a cup down in front of Meredith. "There are things you need to think about, Meredith. Funeral arrangements, notifying family, stuff like that. Is there anything Ruby or I can do to help?"

Meredith stood up. "Mother made that part easy, at least," she said. She got up and left the room. A moment later she was back with a large folder. She opened it and took out a sheaf of papers.

"Instructions," she said. "It's all here. Mother expected to get well, of course, but she made plans in case she . . ." She took a deep breath. "She was determined to be in charge either way." She gave a small, hurt-sounding laugh. "I suppose she didn't trust anybody else but herself to make decisions. Certainly not her daughter."

"You see, China?" Ruby challenged. "That's what I mean. Jo wanted to be in charge. She wouldn't do a thing like . . ." She shook her head, then got up and went to the counter and started fooling with the cake.

"Yeah, I see," I said. Suddenly I felt very tired. What I saw was that it was pointless to argue with Ruby.

From her point of view, suicide didn't seem consistent with Jo's character. But from a different point of view—the idea of Jo wanting to take control of her life, and her death—it was entirely consistent. And, although it didn't seem very likely, I had to admit that it might even have been an accident. Unless Bubba or the medical examiner turned up something definitive, we'd probably never know exactly what happened.

Looking as if she were glad to be doing something constructive, Meredith began going through Jo's papers. "She wants to be cremated as soon as possible, no funeral, just a memorial service. She suggests Pecan Springs Park. There's also a copy of her will here—her lawyer helped her rewrite it last week—and a list of her assets."

"Last week?" I asked.

"She just wanted to be prepared," Ruby said defensively. "In case."

I turned to Meredith. "Relatives?"

"Lucille, mother's sister. She lives in Hawaii, so I guess we could have the memorial service on Thursday. That'll give her time to get here."

"Want me to call Roz?" I asked. "They were friends a long time. She'll probably want to come."

"Whatever," Meredith said. "I don't care."

Ruby turned away from the counter with Jo's birthday cake, alight with fifty-nine candles arranged in tight circles. There was a single candle in the middle. She set the lighted cake on the table in front of us.

"One life ended, its lessons learned," she said, her eyes on the blazing candles. "I think we should honor this day by singing 'Happy Birthday.' "

I wasn't sure how I'd feel if a bunch of my friends got together and sang "Happy Birthday" when I was dead. But I didn't say anything. The three of us joined hands around the table and sang. Thinking of Jo, my eyes blurred with tears and my throat hurt.

"Rest in peace, Mother," Meredith said. She squeezed her eyes shut. "I hope you didn't do it because of me." Then she took a deep breath and blew out the candles. But the one in the middle somehow escaped. It still burned brightly, and for a long time we sat in silence, hands linked, watching its steady flame.

CHAPTER 3

"So Ruby gave Bubba a hard time, huh?" McQuaid asked. It was Wednesday evening, and he'd come over for dinner. He sat down in the rocker, propped his feet on the antique milking stool, and took a long pull on his Lone Star.

"She doesn't think Jo killed herself," I said.

McQuaid shoved a shock of dark hair out of his eyes and leaned back comfortably. "Yeah, well, my money's on Bubba. He may act like a hick, but there's nothing wrong with his head."

Cops are like that, even ex-cops. Brothers under the skin. McQuaid may take a few cheap shots at Bubba just for fun, but he accepts his competence as an article of faith. Me, I'm not so accepting. I was on the other side of the fence for fifteen years, remember? It was my business to question cops' judgments. Often the best way to do my job was to prove that they hadn't done theirs. It was an adversarial relationship I haven't grown out of, and probably never will.

But there's nothing adversarial about my relationship with McQuaid, even if he is—was—a cop. He's a big man, six feet, one-ninety-plus, with the broad, well-muscled shoulders and thick thighs of an ex-U.T. quarter-back, which is one of the things he did before he joined the force. I have a large kitchen—they made them large, back when children came by the dozen—but when McQuaid walks through the door, it shrinks. When he's around, there's never enough room. My body becomes tinglingly aware of his body, and I find my eyes lingering on the white scar that runs diagonally across his tanned forehead, where some crack-crazy doper slashed him with a knife. On the twice-broken nose, the lived-in face that's seen plenty of action in its thirty-five years. I find myself thinking high-voltage thoughts, bedroom thoughts. It feels like somebody's turned the heat up.

I pulled my attention away from McQuaid and back to the subject. "The M.E. got his report out in record time."

McQuaid glanced at me. "What'd he come up with?"

"What Bubba expected. Jo had taken enough of those pills to kill her, and the alcohol contributed to the toxicity. Cause of death, cardiac arrest brought on by an overdose of barbiturates. Approximate time of death, noon."

"Prints on the pill bottle?"

"All hers. She could have bought it at any drugstore."

"When's the memorial service?"

"Tomorrow. Jo's sister Lucille is coming from Honolulu. I called Roz Kotner's office in New York yesterday and left a message that Jo had died. I haven't heard whether she's coming."

McQuaid nodded. "How's Meredith?"

"Hanging in there. She's staying on in the house a few weeks, trying to decide what to do. She's on leave, but she's thinking she might not go back."

Actually, I thought Meredith was handling Jo's death better than Ruby was. Ruby was still vehemently insisting that it wasn't suicide. It wasn't an accident, either, she said, which didn't leave much of an alternative.

I bunched another handful of spinach leaves on the chopping block and picked up my knife. I was making herbed spinach-cheese lasagna, with three kinds of cheese and my own tomato sauce, with plenty of fresh parsley to offset the extra garlic McQuaid loves. I cooked the garlic the way I usually do, by putting a couple of cloves into the skillet with the onion I was sautéing. When the onion's done, I use a fork to mash the cloves. Too many people make the mistake of mincing the garlic first, which makes for burned garlic and a bitter-tasting dish.

McQuaid usually comes for dinner once a week or so, depending on his university schedule and what's happening with his son. Brian is ten. McQuaid is a divorced single parent. I met him back in Houston, on a pro bono case where I argued for the defense and he was the prosecution's chief witness. My client had shot her husband seven times. The jury returned a not-guilty verdict after I pieced together a history of persistent abuse and battery. After all, there's a limit to the number of times a woman can accidentally fall down the stairs. McQuaid is one of the rare cops who care more for justice than the law. He'd tried to convince the D.A. that they couldn't make a murder charge stick. I wasn't surprised when he appeared in the shop one day to tell me he'd left the force to teach at CTSU. I've been trying since then to convince myself that this is just a comfortable friendship with some exceptionally fine sex thrown in.

Brian is a big reason why I'd like this relationship to stay where it is. Brian's a sweet kid. He's got his father's blue eyes and crooked smile and persuasive charm, and there's an elfin quality to him that hooks me whenever I'm around him. But I'm pretty negative about motherhood. Between my mother's alcoholism and my father's workaholism, my childhood was what Ruby would call definitely toxic. Given the scarcity of healthy parenting models in my life, I'm skeptical about my ability to be an adequate mother.

And another thing. I'm not on the career track any longer. McQuaid is. He started his Ph.D. at Sam Houston State while he was on homicide detail with the Houston P.D. In a few months he'll finish his dissertation and have the credentials to move to an associate professorship in a big-time criminal justice program somewhere. But I'm no more eager to be a faculty wife than I am to be a mommy. I like living alone in my four stone-walled, cypress-beamed rooms, surrounded by my herb gardens. I like being in business for myself. I like Pecan Springs.

The trouble is, I also like McQuaid. Given this conflict, I've carefully built up my defenses, avoiding any topic with long-term implications—say, past the next two or three weeks.

But tonight I was feeling less defensive than usual. Maybe it was the thought of Jo's body sprawled on the sofa, reminding me that life is beautiful, brief, and fragile. Or maybe it was the laugh crinkles around McQuaid's ice-blue eyes, or the Bach concerto he put on after dinner, or the champagne we poured to toast the completion of chapter four of his dissertation, which is called "Organization and Training for Small-City Law Enforcement." Whatever it was, even though dessert was still on the table and the dishes weren't washed, I found myself on the bed in McQuaid's arms with his mouth urgently searching mine, my defenses crumbling. McQuaid had his hand on my right breast, inside my unbuttoned blouse, when there was a knock at the kitchen door.

"Let 'em knock," McQuaid muttered, kissing my throat. "There's no law says you have to answer."

For a moment I yielded to his kiss. Then the knock came again. I pushed him away and struggled to sit up. "It might be Meredith. Maybe she needs to talk or something."

"Helluva time to *talk*," McQuaid said.

"I'll make it quick," I promised. I yanked my blouse on and buttoned it up.

But it wasn't Meredith. And I couldn't make it quick.

The woman who stood on my back step was a petite, dusty-blond woman in her late thirties with china blue eyes, a nose that turned up perfectly, and a Barbie-doll smile carefully outlined in two tones of pastel pink lipstick. She wore a classy pink crepe suit with padded shoulders and a pink jewel-neck silk blouse. The woman was Roz Kotner.

"Hello, China," she said.

"Hello, Roz." I groped for my top button and wished I'd glanced in the mirror after I'd wriggled out of McQuaid's clutches.

"I didn't have time to call." Roz spoke fast and breathlessly, with the same wispy little girl's voice I'd noticed on TV. It was impossible to tell if it was her real voice or the product of years of performance aimed at six-year-olds. It made me feel like an elderly tourist in Munchkin Land. "I was in San Francisco when my secretary finally reached me with your message, and I just jumped on the plane and came, without thinking what I'd do when I got here." Her voice wavered and broke and tears flooded her blue eyes. "I can't believe she's dead. I just talked to her a few days ago, and she didn't seem terribly ill. I didn't expect she'd go that fast. What happened?"

I opened the door wider. "You'd better come in."

As she stepped inside, Roz saw the table set for two and the remains of dinner. I saw her glance at my disheveled hair and put it all together. "Oh, but you have company," she said quickly. "I don't want to intrude."

I closed the door. "Roz," I said, "it wasn't the cancer. It was an overdose of sleeping pills."

"Oh." The sound was small, tentative, a thin wisp

of air escaping through parted lips. "Then she . . ."

"It could have been accidental. Jo wasn't used to taking pills. She might not have known how many. She'd been drinking, too."

"I . . . see." Roz looked down. There was a silence, then, "Her daughter was staying with her?"

"Yes. Meredith. As I told your secretary, there's a memorial service tomorrow. You'll stay?"

"Of course," Roz said. She fumbled in her pink leather bag and came up with a small linen handkerchief. "Jo and I have been friends for a long time." The tears were pooling in her eyes, threatening to spill over onto her cheeks. "But we had . . . well, words, over the phone. About an old matter, very silly and petty, really. But now—" She shook her head and began to sob. "Now it's too late. Now I can't tell her how sorry I am."

I put my arm around her shoulders and guided her to the kitchen rocker. McQuaid came to the door, combing his fingers through his hair, and gave me a questioning look. I shook my head. He frowned mightily, raised both shoulders in an eloquent shrug, and disappeared back into the other room.

I let Roz cry for a few moments. Then I said, as gently as I could, "Look, Roz, there's nothing you can do tonight. You've had a long day and you must be tired. Why don't you let me open up the cottage for you?" Being both a tourist mecca and a college town, Pecan Springs has the usual motels and several nice bed-and-breakfasts. But it was late, and Roz was upset.

She blew her nose. "Would you? I hate to be a bother, but I'd much rather stay here. I have pleasant memories of my last visit. Jo and I had so much fun laughing at—" Tears threatened again. "Of course, I'll be glad to pay."

"It's no bother. And don't even think about paying." I stood up. "There are clean sheets on the bed, but let me get you some fresh towels."

I cast a regretful glance toward the empty doorway. McQuaid never goes anywhere without his briefcase. No doubt he was opening it now, settling down at my desk to grade papers or work on his notes for the next day's lecture. If I hurried, I might get back to him before he buried himself completely in whatever he was doing. Once he got involved with his work, the chances of taking up where we'd left off were just about shot for the evening.

In an earlier incarnation, the guest cottage had been a one-story stone stable. The architect who redesigned the house turned it into a rustically elegant two-room affair (three, if you count the bathroom) with rough-plastered white walls, a skylight, a fieldstone fireplace with a hand-hewn oak mantel, and a terra-cotta tile floor. There's a small bedroom with white-painted French doors that open onto a tiny thyme-bordered patio, and a larger living-dining area, separated from the kitchen by a counter. The windows, old-fashioned casement windows that open out with a crank, are deeply recessed into the stone walls. When I first moved in, I thought of renting the place, but I don't much like the thought of a full-time tenant living in my herb garden.

I turned on the lights and the hot-water heater, plugged in the refrigerator, and put out some fresh towels and some handmade lavender soap. I showed Roz what was in the small liquor cupboard beside the fireplace. "If you want something else, Bart's Liquor Store is across town, on the highway."

"I only drink occasionally," Roz said. She sat down on the small batik-print loveseat in front of the fireplace. "Poor Jo," she said, pressing her fingers to her temples. "It's hard to believe she could do such a thing. But she never wanted to be dependent on anybody. I can see why she might have . . ." Her voice trailed off.

"I know," I said. I had the feeling she wanted me to sit and talk, but I had other things on my mind. I looked around. "Can I do anything else for you?"

Roz thought for a moment. "Jo's daughter—Meredith? I've never met her, you know, and I'd like to. Let me take the two of you out to dinner tomorrow evening."

"I'll have to ask Meredith," I said, moving toward the door. "Tomorrow's not going to be easy for her."

"Of course," Roz said. "Just tell her how anxious I am to meet her. We have so much in common, loving Jo as we did."

"I will," I said. I put my hand on the knob. "Anything else? You'll be all right, here by yourself?"

"Quite all right," she said. She sighed. "I just have to get used to the idea that Jo's gone, that's all. Good night."

"Good night," I said, already on the stoop.

But I was too late. When I went into the living room, McQuaid was sitting at my desk, hunched over a yellow legal pad, taking notes out of *Modern Correctional Practice*. There were two other books on the desk, and his leather briefcase—large enough to be a satchel—was open on the floor beside him.

I came up behind him and put my arms around his neck. "Hi," I said in my huskiest, sexiest voice.

"Hi," he said absently. "Hey, China, when you were in practice, how much did you get involved with community reentry programs? What's your feeling about them? Do they work?"

I dropped my arms with a sigh. I knew the signals. I could forget about sex for the moment.

"Oh, by the way," McQuaid said, putting down his pencil, "I forgot to tell you. Brian will be home at nine-thirty tonight, so I can't stay late."

Maybe it was just as well, I thought. My body might be here, but my mind was far away. With Jo, whose absence was a sad, lonely ache.

CHAPTER 4

I called Meredith at eight-thirty the next morning, Thursday. Lucille had arrived from Hawaii the afternoon before. I figured that the two of them hadn't had a very happy evening, but when Meredith answered the phone, she sounded upbeat enough. I asked if I could give her and her aunt a ride to the park that afternoon.

"Thanks," Meredith replied, "but Lucille rented a car at the airport. You can give me a ride home, though. She's driving to Austin after the service to catch a flight back."

"Sure," I said. "Are you feeling up to dinner? Roz Kotner would like to take us."

"Roz? When did she get here?"

"Last night. She's staying in my cottage."

"Did she say anything about the argument with Mother?"

"Just that it was silly and she was sorry. I think

maybe that's why she wants to take you to dinner. To make amends. How about it?"

Another pause. "Well, I guess," Meredith said slowly. "But let's make an early night of it. Today isn't going to be the easiest day of my life."

At nine I propped open the front door of my shop with the stone figure of Haumea, the Hawaiian goddess of wild plants, that Ruby had given me for my birthday. I swept the walk, hung a large herb wreath outside the door, and lugged a heavy tray of potted thyme and basil and rosemary plants out to the sidewalk to entice casual passersby into the gardens and the shop.

I have a good feeling about Thyme and Seasons. The shop's only twenty by twenty, but I use every square inch. Floor-to-ceiling shelves along the back wall hold jars and bottles of dried herbs, tinctures, salves, and ointments. Herb books are neatly racked in the corner, and shelves on another wall are full of potpourri and potpourri makings. A wooden display case houses essential oils, bottles, and perfume supplies. Other shelves hold various herb products that I make or buy from local craftspeople—gift baskets, vinegars, seasoning blends, jellies, soaps, candles. Handmade baskets are stacked in the corners and spill onto the floor. Dried flowers are everywhere, bunched in jars and hanging from the wooden beams, and braided ropes of red peppers and garlic hang on the stone walls. Compared to my office in the law firm, with its bone walls, designer silk ficus trees, and greener-than-grass carpet, the shop feels natural and homey. It feels *real*.

I dusted the counter, turned on the hot plate under

the teakettle, and got out a tray of herb-cheese biscuits. I serve my customers hot herb tea and a snack during the cool autumn weather, iced herb tea or homemade nonalcoholic ginger beer during the summer.

I poked my head through the door to Ruby's shop to see if she was there yet. The Crystal Cave was dark and silent and smelled of the incense that Ruby burns constantly. She doesn't open until ten. We joke that people who buy crystals and incense sleep later than people who buy herbs.

Roz came through the door five minutes later. She was wearing a soft lemon-yellow top and matching slacks, with a paisley scarf looped with studiedly casual artifice about her throat. She smelled lemony, too—some sort of fruity, citrusy perfume. I told her that Meredith had agreed to dinner.

"I'm glad," she said. She appeared to be looking for something. "China, do you have any garlic extract?"

I was a little surprised. I wouldn't have thought that Roz would be into garlic. It just goes to show that appearances don't tell the whole story, or that garlic has a universal appeal, or both. Probably the latter. Garlic is the most popular medicinal and seasoning herb of all time. I found the extract for her, and a bottle of gel caps.

"Would you rather have gel caps?" I asked. With garlic, a lot of people worry about odor, although the extract has been "odor-modified," meaning that they took out a lot of the smell.

Roz shook her head. "Gel caps are much less effective," she said, with emphasis. "Jo introduced me to the extract. I mix it with my morning tomato juice. I have high blood pressure and an ulcer—it's the show, of course—and the garlic helps both."

I laughed. "It helps almost anything," I said. The world's oldest medical text, the *Ebers Papyrus*, lists garlic as an ingredient in twenty-two remedies for headache, insect and scorpion bites, menstrual difficulties, worms, tumors, and heart ailments. For a long time, people even thought it was a powerful antidote—a "charm against poison," as one seventeenth-century herbalist said.

Roz took the garlic extract and an herb biscuit. She had turned away to look at the gift baskets when Violett Hall came in, wearing one of her modest white-blouse-dark-skirt combinations. "I wanted to tell you that Pudding's ears are *much* better," Violett said.

"Whose ears?" I asked, drawing a blank.

"My cat. The one with ear mites."

"I'm glad to hear that, Violett," I said gently, "but I think it will be several days before you can tell whether your cat really is improved." Healing herbs work gently and reliably, but I hate it when people think they're a miracle cure. I always try to make them understand that herbs work more slowly than modern medicine's silver bullets.

"Oh," Violett said. She looked around. "Anyway, Gretel asked me to pick up some more lavender oil," she added. "She—"

A book in her hand and a smile on her face, Roz moved out from behind the paperback rack. Violett saw her and stopped talking.

Roz adjusted her scarf, looking distinctly uneasy.

Her smile faded as if someone had hit the dimmer switch. "Hello, Violett," she said.

Violett blinked. "What are *you* doing here?" she asked in surprise. And then answered her own question. "Of course, the memorial service." She smiled uncertainly. "But why didn't you call? We have a lot to—"

Roz's eyes flicked to me, as if she were giving a warning, and Violett shut her mouth. Roz stepped smoothly into the unfinished sentence. "I'm sure you weren't expecting to see me. I haven't been able to get back to Pecan Springs very much lately. And of course I'm still trying to recover from the shock of Jo's death. It was so dreadfully unexpected." She took a bill out of her purse and handed it to me to pay for the book and the extract. "Please tell Meredith that I'm looking forward to dinner tonight, China."

Violett leaned forward. "Maybe we could get together," she said. "I think we have some catching up to do. Don't you?"

Roz's nod was almost chilly. "But I don't have time to do it now," she said. "I need to do some shopping. We can talk at the service this afternoon." With a wave to me, she left.

For a moment, Violett stood there, frowning past me as if she didn't see me. "Is there anything else I can get you?" I asked.

"What?" She started. "No, this is fine," she said, taking Gretel's lavender oil. She paused. "Is Miss Kotner staying in your cottage again?"

I nodded. She paid me for the oil and left, looking slightly troubled.

The next hour was busy. I had a big order of books to check in and a solid stream of customers to tend to. One of the TV cooks was doing a show called "The Herbal Gourmet," and it was inspiring people to stock up on dried seasonings they hadn't any idea how to use, as well as pots of fresh basil, parsley, oregano, and marjoram. With almost every order, I sold a copy of *It's About Thyme!*, a great book by Marge Clark.

I had worked halfway through the box of books when somebody else came in. I looked up. The woman was tall, almost as tall as Ruby, her dark hair pulled back into a sleek, no-nonsense chignon at the nape of her neck, lips and nails a rich plum. She wore an elegant gray gabardine suit, a softly tailored and tucked gray silk blouse, and gray leather pumps. She carried a gray suede briefcase, monogrammed with a gold JD. When she saw me on my knees in front of the bookshelf, one eyebrow arched. "Hello, China," she said.

I stood up, uncomfortably aware that my jeans were dusty, my green SPICE-IT-UP-WITH-HERBS tee had a coffee stain on the front, and my hair was hanging in my eyes. "Hello, Jane," I said. Her gray suit reminded me of one I'd paid a fortune for a few years back at Neiman-Marcus. I felt like a scullery maid.

Jane Dorman is Roz Kotner's agent. She's in her late forties, brusque and wittily articulate in the New York style, and impressively competent where money is concerned, at least according to *People* magazine. Apparently, Jane was the financial wizard behind Roz's toy empire. I'd met her once at a barbecue in Jo's backyard, when she came for a visit with Roz. Only once. Jane was friendly enough and she seemed to be enjoying herself, even though she was dressed to the teeth and the rest of us were wearing jeans and sneakers. She was as out of place in Pecan Springs as Maria Callas at the First Baptist choir picnic.

Jane gave me a slight smile. "I was in San Antonio on business when Roz's producer called about the renewal of her TV contract. Since I wasn't sure when Roz would be in New York, I thought I'd catch her here. I phoned her secretary this morning and learned that she's staying in your cottage."

"Sure," I said, blowing the hair out of my eyes. "Just follow the path through the herb garden."

Jane glanced around and curled the corners of her lips in a smile. "Your shop is so charmingly rustic," she said.

"And profitable," I replied, stung. But that was dumb. Jane's idea of profit is more along the lines of the Fortune 500.

She smiled again. "I'm sure," she said, and left me seething, wishing I'd had the sense to keep my mouth shut. I've never been very good with the withering rebuttals that the Perry Masons of the world produce spontaneously. And Jane gets to me. I have the feeling that she basically dislikes all women but herself, and that she doesn't really think of herself as a woman.

Ten minutes and two customers later, I was putting the last book on the shelf. Ruby poked her head through the door that separates Thyme and Seasons and The Crystal Cave. She was wearing a beige safari-style shirt and a denim skirt, with a red silk scarf tied around her head, red hoop earrings, and Birkenstocks. "Hey, it's twelve-thirty. I'm ready to close. When are you knocking off?"

"Right about *now*," I said firmly, pushing Haumea into the corner and closing the door. I penciled a note that said "Closed for Jo Gilbert's memorial service. Open tomorrow at nine," and taped it to the door.

I turned to Ruby. "There's some spinach-cheese lasagna left from last night," I said. "Want some? We could eat out on the back patio."

"Super," Ruby said enthusiastically. Ruby is always enthusiastic where eating is concerned. But anybody who's almost six feet and only one-thirty-five can afford to be enthusiastic about food.

I locked up and we went through the connecting door into my place. I stuck the lasagna in the microwave and found several deviled eggs in the fridge, along with some celery and carrot sticks. We carried our lunch trays out to the sunny flagstone patio under my kitchen window, where the late-blooming butterfly weed was attracting the last of the hummingbirds, tanking up for the long haul to Mexico, where they spend the winter. If you sit out there for lunch in the summer, you'll be barbecued in nothing flat, but on an autumn day like today it was perfect, just the right mix of sun, cloud, and breeze, seasoned with the sweetly pungent odor of the sun-warmed creeping thyme that grows among the paving stones. It was going to be a fine afternoon for a memorial service. Just the kind of day Jo loved.

Ruby and I were unusually silent. When we were finished eating, she leaned back in her chair. "I still don't believe Jo did it," she said testily, as if she were contradicting something I'd just finished saying.

"You've said that before. Several times."

"I'll keep on saying it."

"Well, fine," I replied reasonably. "But I don't know what you think it proves. Bubba says—"

"Piss on Bubba!" Ruby ran her fingers through her frizzy orange hair, making it even frizzier. "Bubba Harris is a grade-A turkey. He doesn't know the least thing about the way people *feel*."

I sighed. "I won't dispute you there. But feeling doesn't have a lot to do with the facts in this case. And Bubba knows plenty about police procedure. All the evidence points to—"

"The evidence could have been planted."

I stared at her. "Planted? By whom?"

"By the person who killed her, of course. Who else would plant evidence?"

I narrowed my eyes. "Let me get this straight. You mean, you think Jo was *murdered?*"

"She didn't kill herself, and she didn't take an accidental overdose," Ruby replied firmly. "That leaves only one alternative, doesn't it?" She shot me a challenging look. "Well, doesn't it? You must have seen plenty of murders dressed up like suicides, back when you were defending crooks."

"Clients," I corrected her. "They might have been crooks before or after I defended them. But *while* I was defending them, they were clients."

Ruby waved a dismissive hand. "Crooks, clients, whatever. Weren't there cases that looked like suicide and turned out to be homicide?"

"Her prints were all over the bottle. And the glass."

"Somebody else could have put them there after she was dead, or unconscious. I've read about it in murder mysteries. In fact, it was in one of the Kinsey Millhone books. The murderer pressed the victim's hand around the poison bottle, and violà! Prints."

"Oh, yeah?" I said acidly. "Then why don't you tell me who you think did all this surreptitious fingerprinting? And while you're at it, P. I. Wilcox, you can also expound your theory of how the pills got into her in the first place. Did somebody pry her mouth open and pour them down her throat? And what about the note? And the motive? Just *why* would anybody want to kill Jo?"

Ruby gave me an injured look. "You don't need to be so sarcastic, China. I was just telling you what I think."

I modified my tone. "Well, who, then?"

"Arnold Seidensticker, for one."

"Arnold—" I stared at Ruby. "You mean, you think that an illustrious city father and the owner of the town newspaper would murder—"

Ruby spoke with dignity. "The owner of the newspaper *and* the chief lobbyist for the airport. He's been courting the developers for months, China. He's spent all his spare time and a big hunk of change trying to convince the City Council that the airport would be good for growth. Jo was standing between him and that airport, and the Coalition was getting stronger every day. He wanted her out of the way. And somebody was in that house, remember? That's what Meredith says."

I frowned. Ruby's arguments made a certain kind of

sense. But Arnold Seidensticker was a cautious, conservative man with an enormous sense of his own and his family's importance. It was hard for me to picture him pouring sleeping pills into a woman who would probably die of cancer before she could do more than set back his schedule by a month or two.

"Arnold Seidensticker doesn't wear perfume," I said.

Ruby sighed. "Well, then, Lila Seidensticker."

I hooted derisively. Lila was Arnold's wife, a skinny platinum blonde with arms like diamond-circled soda straws and a mouth the color of a freshly painted fire hydrant. She was a total dingbat. But Arnold wasn't a dingbat. Nor was he a man to be trifled with.

I leaned forward. "You listen to me, Ruby. Lay off that murder stuff. If Arnold Seidensticker hears you defaming his sacred name, you'll find yourself sued for slander in nothing flat. What's more, there's not an attorney in this town who'd touch your case. And you still haven't told me how you think the murderer got the pills into her. Assuming of course, there *was* a—"

Ruby cocked her head. "Listen," she said. "Somebody's having an argument."

"You bet your sweet bippy somebody's having an argument," I replied warmly. "In my professional opinion, people who go around making unsupported accusations deserve to—"

Ruby gave me a patient smile. "Not *us*, silly. The argument's coming from back there." She gestured in the direction of the cottage. "Listen."

I listened. I heard an angry voice, loud and getting louder, coming from the open window of the guest cottage ten yards away.

"It's Roz yelling at somebody," Ruby said.

"She must be yelling at Jane," I replied. "Her agent. She came to bring Roz her new TV contract."

Ruby raised her eyebrows. "It sounds like Roz doesn't want to sign it."

"—not *going* to renew," Roz was saying, "and that's that. Period. Paragraph. End of script."

I grinned. Roz's voice was strident but clear, no sign of Munchkin breathiness. That answered my question. Roz was definitely a woman of many talents.

Jane's voice was much lower, a steely thread. "You're crazy, Rosalind. Giving up this contract for a man! You've lost your mind!"

Roz laughed, but her answer was knife-edged. "Don't you wish *you* could, Jane? Don't you wish you were involved with the man who—"

"Can that crap," Jane said savagely. "We're not talking about me, we're talking about you. This contract is worth four million dollars! And do you know why? Because *I* upped the ante, that's why! *I* made them sweat. Four million, you're getting. Four *million*!"

"At fifteen-percent agency fees, that's over a half million to you," Roz retorted. "That's what we're talking about, isn't it? You're into me for commissions on residuals at fifteen percent. But that's peanuts compared to what you think is coming, isn't it? When I say no contract, I'm killing the goose that laid your golden egg."

Jane's voice vibrated, low. "I earn my commissions."

Roz paused. I could barely hear what she said next,

but there was no mistaking the accusation in it. "Are you sure you've earned it *all*, Jane?"

"What are you talking about?"

"I'm talking about the royalty account. I'm talking about—"

At that tantalizing moment, before Ruby and I could hear just what Roz was talking about, the open casement slammed. The show was over.

"Wow," Ruby breathed. "I've heard of holdouts, but four *million*?"

"Maybe Jane is right," I said. "Maybe Roz is crazy."

"Maybe she's in love. There was something about a man. And what was that stuff about royalties?"

We weren't going to find out. A few minutes later, we heard the cottage door bang. Jane Dorman stormed down the path, her high heels crunching in the gravel. She looked like a woman who hadn't gotten what she came for.

CHAPTER 5

After lunch, Ruby went home to her apartment to change for the memorial service, while I put the plates in the sink and hunted up my one good basic black, a double-breasted cotton blend with pleated shoulders and long sleeves. But as I pulled it over my head, it seemed to me that black was all wrong. Jo wouldn't have wanted black, especially on such a beautiful day. So I dug in the closet and found a muted autumn green wrapdress and added the gold pin Jo had given me last Christmas. I tucked a sprig of rosemary behind the pin, for remembrance, and ran a brush through my hair. Then I went to back my old blue Datsun hatchback out of the Emporium's garage, which I rent from Constance. My place doesn't have a garage, and I don't like to park on the street and take up customer space.

Ruby had decided against black, too. She was wearing an off-white knit with a blue-green scarf and belt. When she saw my green dress, she grinned and gave me thumbs-up. Then, with self-conscious solemnity, remembering *why* we were all dressed up in the middle of a Thursday, she settled herself in the passenger seat for a silent ride to the park where Jo's memorial service was being held.

Pecan Springs' older businesses—the Grande Cinema (recently restored by the Community Theater Guild), Winn's Variety, Hoffmeister's Clothing Store, the hardware store, the *Enterprise*'s office, the public library, and so on—are arranged in a square around the pink granite courthouse that centers the old part of town. Four streets create the square. Crockett (the street that the shop is on) dead-ends at the CTSU campus ten blocks north, where there is another, smaller business area, mostly fast-food joints, bookstores, copy shops, and boutiques. Robert E. Lee crosses the railroad track and heads a mile east to the Interstate, where two sprawling malls have sprung up in the last couple of years to house Walmart and Albertson's and a four-screen movie theater. LBJ Boulevard extends west past the post office and the bank, where it turns into Ranch Road 1830 and takes off into the hills toward Canyon Lake and the posh Lake Winds Resort Village. Anderson Avenue runs south to the river, lined for four blocks with arching pecans and live oaks and fine old Victorians behind wrought-iron fences. Arnold Seidensticker lives on Anderson, in an immense white house with a two-story columned portico across the front, as do most of Pecan Springs' leading socialites. Anderson eventually runs into Pecan Springs Park, where Jo's memorial service was being held.

Until Jo started the anti-airport campaign, Pecan

Springs Park had been her major civic project. A few years ago, she and some of her environmentalist friends infiltrated the Pecan Springs Garden Club, a namby-pamby group whose most controversial project was planting Japanese iris around the county courthouse. But Jo got herself elected president and set about infusing the club with a sense of environmental urgency. Her target was the Pecan River, where it flowed along the southern edge of town. The river emerges from a small spring-fed lake, flows through the CTSU campus, and eventually through a swampy patch of poverty weed and scrub willows that used to border the old town dump. Jo armwrestled the City Council for control of a strip of land on both sides of the river, including the dump. Then she energized the women of the town (and a few of their husbands) into months of long, hard cleanup work. When that was done, she browbeat the downtown merchants into contributing major bucks for landscaping, including an amphitheater and rose garden. Now the thirty-acre park is one of Pecan Springs' most widely trumpeted tourist attractions. The Chamber of Commerce rents inner tubes and canoes for float trips down the river. Arnold Seidensticker has brought in one of the major golf pros to design a course on the other side of the old dump, adjacent to the park. And Harley Chadwick is talking about starting an upscale development on the other side of the golf course. One thing leads to another.

The park's rose garden was set up with metal folding chairs arranged in neat rows, most of them already occupied. Meredith was sitting in the front row, dressed in a pale beige two-piece dress with green trim, her face carefully blank. Beside her was a plump middle-aged woman in a dark blue suit with a fussy lace blouse whom I took to be Lucille, and on the other side was Mayor Pauline Perkins, brisk and efficient-looking in spite of her thirty extra pounds. I see the mayor regularly at Jerri's Health and Fitness Spa striding determinedly along the treadmill. Reverend Lewis, the Unitarian minister, sat next to the mayor, solemn and self-impressed in a slate-gray suit and tie. Reverend Lewis was new to Pecan Springs and scarcely knew Jo, but no doubt he'd been given a list of appropriate compliments to pay.

If none of the other mourners was wearing black, Roz was. She was sitting conspicuously alone in the second row. I wondered whether she'd just happened to have a black suit, black strappy heels, and black gloves in her luggage, or whether the outfit was what she'd gone shopping for. Her mourning garb gave her a look of fragile composure, which was heightened by her deeply shadowed blue eyes and her blond hair severely twisted into a knot at her neck.

I glanced at the other mourners. Most of the people who counted in the town were there, friends and enemies, arranged on either side of the center aisle like guests at a wedding. On the anti-airport side was RuthAnn Landsdowne, square-jawed and capable. RuthAnn was Jo's chief co-conspirator and current president of the garden club. She was sitting with a large group of women whom I recognized as Coalition members and the half of the City Council that had been brave enough to go on record against the airport. On the pro-airport side was Arnold Seidensticker, his neatly parted brown hair, brown horn-rimmed glasses, and brown suit giving him the look of a tidy brown owl. He was sitting next to his wife Lila, whose platinum hair had a salmon tint that was set off by her salmon-pink coatdress. She looked remarkably bony, and her thin hands as she twisted her handkerchief were like claws. Seated in the same row were Mr. Schwartz, president of Hill Country Fidelity Bank, Harley Chadwick, and several real estate developers whom I recognized by sight. Behind them were those members of the City Council who supported the airport. Bubba Harris, uniformed as usual in tan polyester, stood at the rear of the crowd, nervously twirling his cowboy hat. For the first time since I'd known him, he was minus his cigar.

Ruby nudged me. "Maybe Bubba's here to keep an eye on the Seidenstickers," she whispered. She glanced at them. "Arnold looks like a big toad gloating over a little puddle."

Reverend Lewis was beginning the service. After a lengthy prayer on behalf of the departed, a psalm and an oration I couldn't see the point of, he sat down and Mayor Pauline Perkins got up to deliver the eulogy. I listened thoughtfully, although the person the mayor was describing seemed only tangentially related to the Jo Gilbert I had respected and admired and, yes, loved. Jo's concern for her friends, her stern sense of justice and rightness, her ability to sacrifice everything to a cause she cared for—all the individual characteristics that made Jo a *person* were submerged in the grand scheme of the mayor's recollections, in which Jo, motivated by civic pride and a burning desire to enrich the lives of her fellow citizens, starred as the Prime Mover of Pecan Springs' cultural and environmental renaissance. This praise of Jo's achievements must have proved a bit trying for the mayor. She had to skirt the dangerous territory of Jo's opposition to the airport to avoid offending Arnold Seidensticker, the banker, and the developers, and the half of the City Council that favored the airport. At the same time, she had to recognize Jo's commitment to the Anti-Airport Coalition in a way that would placate the greens, the women, and the Coalition. I was glad I wasn't in Pauline Perkins' shoes.

I glanced at Meredith and wondered whether the mayor's epic catalog of Jo's publicly virtuous life or my own fragmented impressions of a friend tallied at all with the grieving daughter's recollection of her mother. What Meredith knew of her, I added to myself, remembering what she had said about Jo's deliberate efforts to separate herself from her daughter. But what do we ever know about another person? We know only surfaces, facets, impressions—depths elude us. Ruby, beside me, in many ways an enigma, once an everyday housewife, now a believer in such things as the tarot and the I Ching and reincarnation. Roz, across the aisle, another mystery—shallow, silly, famous, and rich Roz, who had somehow been Jo's friend. Do we ever truly know another person, or are we eternally deceived by appearances, posturing, role-playing? For that matter, do we ever know ourselves?

I was still drifting around in these muddy metaphysical waters when Mayor Perkins, clearly glad to have her task safely over, concluded with the triumphant announcement that from this day henceforth the rose garden would be known as the Josephine Gilbert Memorial Rose Garden, a designation that probably wouldn't offend anybody. A women's quartet furnished by the Pecan Springs Choral Club sang *all* the verses of "Amazing Grace," Reverend Lewis blessed us, and the memorial service ended.

Arnold Seidensticker was the first to shake Meredith's hand, murmur regrets, and leave, followed by his nervous, salmon-tinted wife. The rest of the mourners milled around, admiring the roses and discussing Jo's death in whispers. I gave my condolences to Lucille, a short, tearful woman as huggable as a marshmallow. Meredith was thin-faced and hollow-eyed but controlled. She seemed to be bearing up well enough as Mayor Perkins introduced her and Lucille to one after another of Jo's dearest friends and enemies.

While I was waiting for Meredith to finish meeting the town's dignitaries, I watched Roz, who was getting as much attention as Meredith. That wasn't especially surprising, since a great many people obviously recognized her and wanted to get StrawBerry Bear's autograph for their children. She signed with a flourish.

After a few minutes I saw Constance Letterman, the Craft Emporium owner, bumping her way through the crowd of autograph seekers. Constance is small and round and perky, with a small pink nose and pink cheeks, and she wears her brown hair permed in tight fingertip curls.

Constance seemed even shorter and rounder than usual today. She was wearing a brownish-orange tent dress that made her look like a ripe pumpkin, an effect that was heightened by the trailing leaf-green scarf around her short neck. In addition to owning the Emporium, Constance also writes the society column for the *Enterprise*, an honor conferred on her, no doubt, because she is Arnold Seidensticker's first cousin. Today, I guessed, she was doing research for her column.

Constance came up to Roz and pumped her hand eagerly. She reached into her capacious canvas bag and pulled out a steno pad and pen. I wondered what she would write about Jo's memorial service and how she would fit Rosalind Kotner into the story. But whatever her angle on Roz, there wasn't much of it. After a thirty-second conversation, Constance tucked away her pad and pen, extended a fat hand, and said good-bye.

A moment or two later, Violett Hall came over to Roz. She was wearing a serviceable black skirt and neat gray blouse and jacket, and her Mamie Eisenhower bangs were sprayed flat against her forehead. Her face was flushed and her smile was eager. Roz seemed less eager to see Violett, but Violett planted herself in front of Roz, still smiling, and began to talk. I couldn't hear what she was saying, but the more animated she became, the more strained and uncomfortable Roz seemed. After a few minutes of this odd exchange, Roz nodded nervously, as if agreeing to something she wasn't exactly pleased about, and Violett walked away with the air of someone who has accomplished her mission.

I was distracted by several members of the garden club wanting to reminisce about Jo, and when I spotted Violett again she was talking to Jane Dorman. I was surprised to see Jane. I had supposed that, PO'd as she'd been over Roz's refusal to renew the contract, she'd head straight for the airport. But maybe a four-million-dollar deal was too sweet to lose without a fight. Or maybe she'd stayed especially for the memorial service. After all, she'd once been Jo's guest. I was also surprised to see Jane actually bending over to listen to Violett. I wondered what Violett Hall could have to say that would command Jane Dorman's attention for more than thirty seconds.

Roz also seemed surprised to see the conversation. Her jaw tightened and she watched with a nervous frown. A few minutes later, she brushed off the last few autograph seekers and made her way over to Jane and Violett, who stopped talking when they saw Roz coming. The three stood together in an uncomfortable tableau, then Violett detached herself and walked away. Roz went in a different direction, and Jane came toward me.

"China," she said brusquely, without preamble, "I'm in a jam. The Chrysler I rented at the airport has some sort of ignition problem, and the tow truck is coming to get it. I have to make a five-thirty flight back to New York. Could I impose on you—?"

"I'd be glad to," I said, "but Lucille, Jo's sister, is headed back to the airport." I pointed her out, standing next to the mayor. "I'm sure you can ride with her."

Jane nodded her thanks and went toward Lucille, her gray heels digging little round holes in the turf. I was about to go over and speak to Meredith when I saw Ruby talking to Bubba. It looked as if she were in her confrontational mode. I stepped closer, wanting to listen but definitely *not* wanting to be involved.

"You have to look *deeper*," Ruby was insisting. "You can't be content with the way things seem on the surface. This is obviously a very complicated case."

Bubba's mouth twitched as if he sorely missed his cigar. "There ain't anything deeper to look into," he said. He gave her a shrewd, narrow-eyed look. "A'course, Miz Wilcox, if you're holdin' onto information—"

Ruby sniffed. "I've already told you what I know—that Jo Gilbert didn't commit suicide. What about the person who was with her the day she died?"

Bubba shrugged and hooked his thumbs in his belt. "Not enough," he said, shaking his head. "Not near enough. So the daughter smells perfume. So what? Why, the mayor wears perfume, and half the City Council." He grinned. "Hell, mebbe the *whole* City Council, for all I know."

Ruby glared at him. "I just want you to be aware that as far as I'm concerned, this case isn't closed, not by a long shot. Jo Gilbert was beating the pants off Arnold Seidensticker and his developers. If she'd had another month to get the greenies and the no-growthers together, Seidensticker could've kissed his airport good-bye."

Bubba paled visibly, and I did too. "Hey, hold on there," he began. "You're not accusin' Mr.—"

"I'm not accusing anybody," Ruby replied, much to my relief. "I'm telling you that there's more to this matter than meets the eye. I know there's been foul play here, and when I find out—"

"Well, that's good, Miz Wilcox," Bubba said. "When you find out what it was, you tell me, and we'll *both* know." He jammed his hat on his head and marched off to his squad car—in search, no doubt, of his cigar.

I shook my head. This time, at least, Ruby had the good sense not to libel Arnold Seidensticker. But what would she say *next* time? I went over to Ruby and was on the point of cautioning her about it when RuthAnn Landsdowne joined us. Her dark brown hair was cropped in a severe pageboy and she was wearing low-heeled burgundy pumps and a burgundy suit with square shoulders that gave her the solid, rectangular look of someone who could be counted on to carry the flag. Her jaw was working, her eyes were red-rimmed in her plain face, and she was sniffling into her handkerchief.

"Such a sad affair," she said with a sigh. "Jo and I did so much good work together. I had such respect for her. And now . . . this." She blew her nose hard. "And to think that I was *there* that day. I could have—"

Beside me, Ruby stiffened. I frowned. "You were *there*?" I asked. "At Jo's?"

"About eleven-thirty," RuthAnn said painfully. "Just about the time she—" She broke off, shaking her head, and the tears threatened again. "If only I'd gone in. I might have *saved* her!"

I made the obvious answer, but it held no comfort. "You couldn't have known."

RuthAnn wiped her eyes. When she spoke, she was clearly making an effort to control herself. "The Coalition was holding a meeting at three that afternoon. Jo said she had something important to tell us—some reason or other why the airport couldn't be built." She smiled a small, wavering smile. "She said she was ninety-nine percent sure we could sabotage it. I asked her how she knew, but all she'd say was 'A little bird told me.' " The corners of her mouth trembled. "Jo didn't make a lot of jokes. That one sticks in my mind."

"So what *did* you do?" Ruby asked.

"I wanted to go over the agenda with her. But there wasn't any answer when I knocked, so I left. She didn't show up at the meeting, and when I called to find out why, her daughter said—" Her rectangular shoulders shook, seemed to lose their solidity. She choked up. "You'll have to excuse me," she said, ducking her head, and hurried away.

Ruby turned to me. "Are you thinking what I'm thinking, China?"

I sighed. "I'm thinking that it was a damned shame that RuthAnn Landsdowne didn't put one of those capable shoulders to the door and break it down. She's right. She might have saved Jo's life."

Ruby frowned. "Yes, that. But I'm thinking that she must have just missed—"

"Ruby," I said, "*stuff* it." I was having a hard enough time dealing with my own sadness without having to listen to Ruby's imaginative theories. If she wanted to express her grief by composing a bunch of weird scenarios, that was fine. But I didn't want to hear them.

"But China," Ruby said, "don't you see how—"

Roz interrupted us. "It was a lovely service, wasn't it?" she asked breathily. "And it's wonderful to know that Jo was so deeply loved."

Roz's remark was so stickily sentimental that it didn't warrant response. I looked in Meredith's direction. The crowd around her had thinned out, and Mayor Perkins and the women's quartet were saying their good-byes. "I'm about ready to take Meredith home," I said. "Do you know what time you'd like to go to dinner?"

"Perhaps we could ask Meredith," Roz said. "I haven't met her yet."

Meredith acknowledged the introduction without special warmth. Roz didn't seem to notice. She spoke for a few moments about her friendship with dear Jo and how much she was looking forward to getting acquainted with Jo's daughter. Meredith listened, nodding politely. After a few moments, we agreed to dinner at six-thirty, and Meredith turned to me. "I'm ready to go home, if you and Ruby are."

Roz smiled graciously. "I'll see you this evening," she said, and turned to give an autograph to Reverend Lewis's wife.

Ruby and I drove Meredith home, not saying very much. Meredith asked us in for a cup of tea, but her invitation didn't carry much conviction, and I knew she wanted to be alone. I let Meredith out and headed for Ruby's apartment complex, which is on Ferguson, about three blocks from the shop. Ruby rented the place on a month-to-month with the idea of finding something permanent. But it's been a year and she hasn't started looking.

We were almost there when Ruby broke the silence. "I was listening to my Inner Guide this afternoon," she said thoughtfully. "During the memorial service."

I sighed. Ruby has been reading the books on channeling that she stocks in her shop, and lately she's begun to get messages from her Inner Guide. It's really her right brain speaking, she tells me. Her intuition. That's what channeling is all about—becoming more intuitive.

"You see, your left brain, the logical brain, is always chattering away," she had said. "The noise is so loud you can't hear your right brain. You've got to shut up the left brain so you can pay attention. Then your Inner Guide can get through."

"How do you do that?" I'd asked sarcastically. "Stuff a pillow in one speaker and turn up the volume on the other side?"

But I couldn't disagree with Ruby about the importance of intuition. I'd had a few hunches of my own from time to time, especially when I was working on a difficult case. Whether it was my Inner Guide communicating or (as Ruby had said when she read my horoscope) the fact that my Moon was in Pisces with Neptune just a few degrees off my Gemini Ascendant, listening usually paid off. This time, I had an intuition about what *her* intuition was about. I was right.

"Arnold Seidensticker did it," she said. "I'm positive."

I sighed again as I pulled the Datsun into the parking lot of the Enclave, Ruby's upscale apartment complex. The Enclave is faced with weathered gray cedar and has a cactus garden out front featuring a homicidal-looking prickly pear and a handsome saguaro cactus planted in a pool of pea gravel. Some landscaper probably stole it from the national monument west of Tucson. Shoppers who see a large saguaro for sale ought to inquire after its pedigree—although that doesn't guarantee they won't be lied to.

I turned off the ignition. "Ruby," I said, "for God's sake, will you lay off Arnold Seidensticker?"

Ruby turned an anguished face toward me. "I *can't* lay off, China! Not when Jo is dead, and nobody knows who, or why, or how, or—" She bit off the words. "I already know who," she said, narrowing her eyes defiantly. "Did you hear RuthAnn say that Jo had found a way to stop the airport? Obviously, Arnold Seidensticker killed her to keep her from revealing it. I intend to nail him. Are you going to help, or do I have to do this on my own?"

"Me?" I yelped. "You want *me* to help *you* try to pin a murder on Arnold Seidensticker? You've got to be out of your mind!"

Ruby put her hand on the door handle. "I thought we were friends." Her voice sounded small and hurt. "I mean, really *friends*, China."

"We are," I said firmly. "But I'm not into suicide pacts. Anyway, it's *your* Inner Guide who's throwing Arnold Seidensticker's name around. My Inner Guide hasn't spoken up yet." There was a tragic mystery behind Jo's death. But it wasn't the mystery that Ruby wanted to make it into, something that a little part-time sleuthing could solve. The mystery had to do with the kind of person Jo was, with those inner, hidden depths that we never truly know.

Ruby shrugged, resigned. "Well, then, I guess I'll just have to solve this on my own."

I leaned forward urgently. "Listen, Ruby, I venture

to say that I've been around more criminals than you have. I've got a pretty good sense when it comes to knowing who's capable of what kind of crime. I'm telling you that Arnold Seidensticker just isn't the type to kill somebody. But he *is* the type to get very upset if he catches you throwing spitballs at the sacred Seidensticker name. He wouldn't stoop to something as crude and vulgar as poking nasty pills down your gullet, but he might not be averse to a little mannerly arm-twisting in the courts. If I were you, I'd be careful."

"I'll do what I have to do," Ruby said icily, picking up her purse. When she got out of the car, she slammed the door so hard that my ears popped. At 110,000 miles, my little Datsun is still drum tight. Not a rattle anywhere. When you slam the doors, it pops your ears. Top that, General Motors.

Trying not to think just what kind of trouble Ruby could get herself into playing Kinsey Millhone, I drove back to my place, changed into my jeans, poured myself a glass of hibiscus tea, and pulled up a chair to the desk in the kitchen where I keep my computer. It was time to do some bookkeeping chores and find out whether Thyme and Seasons Herb Company was going to allow me to buy groceries this month. It was a job that held my attention completely.

Almost.

I was distracted by an occasional vision of Ruby being accosted by Arnold Seidensticker's high-priced lawyer and slapped with a big-time libel suit.

I was distracted by a phone call from McQuaid, asking me about the service and reminding me that he was coming over for dinner tomorrow evening. It was his turn to cook, and how about shrimp gumbo?

I was distracted when I glanced out the window and saw Violett Hall walking quickly down the path that led to the guest cottage. She moved with purpose, like a woman with an important mission.

I was distracted for the last time when Violett left the cottage ten minutes later, head down, shoulders hunched, chin flattened against her chest. Whatever her mission had been, she looked as if she had just been shot down.

CHAPTER 6

A little before six I changed into a blouse and denim skirt, still puzzling over what was going on between Roz and Violett. But whatever it was, it wasn't high priority with me. I had plenty to worry about with Ruby, who could get herself into serious trouble if she went around sullying Arnold Seidensticker's good name. I was betting she wouldn't turn up anything connected with Jo's death, because all my legal training and experience told me that Seidensticker, conservative and smart as he was, wouldn't risk killing a woman who was going to die in a matter of months. But Ruby might be able to dig up some dirt on him, or he might think that's what she was doing. Depending on the dirt, that could mean trouble for Ruby.

At six, I went to the cottage to pick up Roz for dinner. There was a red Buick Century parked in the alley—her rental car, I assumed. I knocked at the door. Roz opened it with a glass in her hand. Her blond hair was loose to her shoulders and she was wearing a short, silky black thing that hit her at midthigh, open to reveal scanty black briefs and a black bra. There was an unmistakable aura of my best scotch about her.

"Come in and sit down," she tossed over her shoulder as she headed for the liquor cupboard. "I'll fix you a drink." Her words were slightly slurred.

I shook my head. "No, thanks. Meredith will be waiting."

Roz poured herself another drink. I noticed that the bottle had been substantially diminished and made a mental note to buy another—*after* she'd left. If she was going to guzzle the stuff at that rate, she could buy her own.

Roz tossed her hair back with a petulant gesture and gulped her drink. "Meredith can wait until I'm damn good and ready." She held up the bottle, gauging what was left. "That may not be for a while."

I frowned. When I'd left Roz after the memorial service, she'd been fine. It was safe to assume that her visit with Violett had changed her mood as much as it had changed Violett's.

"The golden goose," Roz muttered, flinging herself on the loveseat.

"What?" I asked, startled.

"The goose that laid the golden egg, goddammit," Roz said morosely, staring into her scotch.

I was no wiser than I was before. All I knew was that StrawBerry Bear was on her way to a good drunk.

Roz heaved a sigh, as if the explanation were too much trouble. "They all want a ride," she said thickly, "but do they want to pay the fare?" Pounding her fist on the arm of the loveseat, she answered her own question. "Shit, no. They just want me to keep on laying golden eggs so they can keep on lifting them." She waved her drink, spilling most of it. "Mother-fucking sheep in wolf's clothing."

I couldn't help smiling. This was not the demure, Barbie-doll creature who had shown up on my doorstep in her pink suit and her sweet childish voice or the grieving friend struggling for composure at the memorial service. This was a half-naked profane broad spilling drunken metaphors. Which one was real? Who was the authentic Rosalind Kotner?

But it was time to get the show on the road. I reached for the phone and dialed Meredith's number. When she answered, I explained that Roz and I had been held up. It might be closer to seven when we got there, but we'd make it as quickly as we could. Meredith was annoyed, but agreeable.

"What'd you do that for?" Roz asked irritably, when I hung up the phone. "I said she can wait."

I headed for the coffee maker. "Get in the shower."

Roz chugged the rest of her scotch, stood up unsteadily, and took a step toward the liquor cupboard.

"Unless you want to call off the dinner tonight," I said to her back.

Roz turned. Her black robe, wet with spilled scotch, clung to her breasts, surprisingly full for such a small-bodied woman. "You think I'm drunk."

"No, but I think you're getting close. You can chug-alug scotch on your own time. If you want to go to dinner with Meredith and me tonight, I suggest that you get in the shower."

Roz came closer. "Says who?"

"Says me," I replied firmly, filling the coffee maker. "You can shower or you can drink. You can have dinner with Meredith and me or you can drink. Your choice."

She looked at me again, measuring. Then she laughed with throaty good humor, to show she'd enjoyed the volley and didn't resent briefly retiring from the court. She went to the shower. When she came back fifteen minutes later, wearing the lemon-yellow top and slacks and paisley scarf she'd worn that morning, she was almost sober. And she no longer smelled of scotch. She smelled of the lavender soap I'd put in the shower. Just the same, I decided I'd drive. If Roz got picked up on suspicion of DWI, she'd probably want me to be her lawyer. I've never gotten a kick out of defending drunks, especially famous drunks.

Roz spoke in my Datsun, on the way to Meredith's. "I don't want you to think I do this all the time."

I shrugged. "How much you drink is your business."

"It's just that . . ." She stopped and looked out the window. "You have no fucking idea."

"Probably not," I agreed, wondering what we were talking about.

Roz gave a harsh, bitter laugh. "You couldn't begin to guess how many people sponge off me. There's no fucking end to it. Producers, directors, agents, coaches, business managers, accountants . . . next week I'm having the auditors in."

I didn't doubt that show business was no business in which to find true love and happiness. It was probably a lot like the legal business—full of arrogant, greedy people glad to take their bite and then some. And it wasn't any fun to keep looking over your shoulder, wondering who was going to slip it to you next. If that was why Roz had turned down the contract, I could certainly sympathize. I might even applaud. But I didn't particularly want to listen to her chorus of complaints. So I just gave a non-committal "hmm." Luckily, we were almost at Meredith's, and there wasn't time for any more confidences.

The back seat of my Datsun is cramped, but there's room for a short-legged passenger or a long-legged one who can hike her knees to her chin. Meredith was the latter. She climbed in, we exchanged greetings, and started off.

"Mm-mm-m," Meredith said appreciatively, sniffing. "Lavender."

"Lavender?" Roz asked.

"The soap I put in your shower," I explained. "I made it myself, out of the lavender that grows along the path. The scent might be a little strong."

"I have a sensitive nose," Meredith said, and fell silent.

Roz wanted to go to the Spanish Courtyard, an upscale restaurant overgrown with a fake jungle of ferns and philodendrons, which featured an imitation mariachi band with too much tambourine. McQuaid had brought me here a few months before, and we'd since crossed it off our list. I hoped we'd finish our dinner and be gone before the mariachis showed up.

Meredith still displayed the reserve she had shown at the memorial service. But Roz was an entirely different person than she'd been an hour earlier. The tough, surly talk had vanished, along with the boozy incoherence. She was smiling and empathetic, warm and cordial, and solicitous of both Meredith and me. She made tactful inquiries about Meredith's plans, paid generous compliments to me, and told cute, funny stories about Jo.

"I'm sure you know, Meredith," she said, leaning forward, "what an absolutely marvelous letter writer your mother was."

Meredith added another dollop of sour cream to her chicken flautas. That's what I had ordered too. They were the best item on the menu. "Actually, no," she replied, not looking up. "Mother hardly ever wrote."

"Well, she wrote to me," Roz said, undaunted. "But of course I was her closest friend. I have boxes and boxes of her letters." I saw Meredith frowning at her flautas. I winced. I had the sense that Roz's harping on how close she'd been to Jo must be hitting a nerve. But Roz didn't seem to notice. She waved her hand. "They're such *marvelous* letters, simply crammed with witty, insightful little vignettes about the people here."

I bit down on a smile. I wondered what witty, insightful vignettes Jo had offered about Arnold Seidensticker.

"To tell the truth," Roz went on, "I've been wishing I had the letters I wrote to her. Before I leave, I'd like to get them, if you wouldn't mind."

"The only papers I've found are related to Mother's projects," Meredith said. "The park, things like that."

Roz sipped her wine. "I could help you hunt."

Meredith pulled herself up, offended. "That won't be necessary," she replied sharply. "When I get a chance, I'll look through the papers again. If there's anything that concerns you, I can mail it."

Roz looked as if she wanted to press the issue, but Meredith was clearly in no mood. It was time for me to change the subject.

"We've been talking about everything all evening but *you*, Roz," I said brightly. "Both Meredith and I are *dying* to hear all about your life in New York." I wondered if my tongue would freeze to the roof of my mouth before it uttered any more such ridiculous nonsense.

Maybe Roz decided she wasn't going to get anywhere with the letters and might as well drop the subject. Or maybe she just plain took the bait. Whatever it was, she gave us both a smile.

"Actually," she said, "I do have something to tell you. It will be announced in Washington and in Los Angeles early next week, but I'd like you to be among the first to know."

"Know what?" I asked.

Roz pushed her plate away. "I'm leaving show business."

"Leaving!" Meredith exclaimed, genuinely amazed.

I was surprised too. From the argument Ruby and I had overheard, I'd assumed that Roz was refusing to sign only one contract. I hadn't suspected she was giving up the whole works.

Roz nodded. "I'm selling everything to Disney."

So *that* was what was behind Roz's refusal to sign the contract! She was selling out! But why hadn't she told Jane? I was sure she hadn't—at least, not in the conversation I had overheard. Then a thought hit me.

Maybe Roz hadn't told Jane because there was nothing in it for Jane. Roz had negotiated the deal secretly, leaving Jane out of the picture, which would no doubt frost Jane mightily when she found out. Not to mention losing Roz as a client, which—depending on how many other four-million-a-year clients she represented—could carve a hefty chunk out of her annual take-home.

"But why are you leaving?" Meredith asked. "I thought things were going your way."

Roz's blue gaze was candid. "They certainly are. But I'm tired of performing. I'm tired of people taking advantage of me. And there's the money, of course."

"How much?" I asked curiously. "If you don't mind telling us."

"I can't," Roz said. "That's part of the agreement with Disney. It's quite a nice sum, though—enough to make it worth my while." She gave us a smug smile. "But I have another reason for retiring."

Meredith and I traded glances and waited. Finally, when our silence was beginning to seem impolite, I asked, "And what is that?"

Roz toyed with her glass. "The truth is that Howie has this idea—old-fashioned, to be sure—that a Senator's wife doesn't belong in show business. But then, Howie is a little old-fashioned. It's what makes him so special."

"Howie?" I asked.

"Howard Keenan has asked me to marry him," Roz said, and waited triumphantly for our reactions.

I sucked in my breath. "Howard Keenan?" I *was* surprised. Blown away, in fact. Stupefied. Roz Kotner was reeling in the biggest fish in the pond.

Meredith was shocked too. "*Senator* Howard Keenan?" she asked incredulously.

Everybody knows Howard Keenan. He is one of the most powerful members of the U.S. Senate. Fiftyish, handsome, sophisticated, he is also heir to the fabled Keenan oil-and-gas empire, which extends from the sands of West Texas to the sands of Saudi Arabia. With every Mid-East war and rumor of war, the Keenans pump up more barrels of petrodollars. But more to the point, Senator Keenan has recently been mentioned as the most likely Democratic presidential nominee in the primaries, and smart money says he'll be the people's choice. Incredible as it seemed, if Roz held on to her big fish through the white water of the primaries and the deep dives of the presidential election, she could end up as the nation's First Lady.

There was a long silence. Finally, I spoke. "Congratulations," I said lamely. I picked up my wineglass. "To Senator and Mrs. Keenan," I said. With some reluctance, Meredith joined us as we tipped our glasses together. Roz told us the story.

She had met Howie at a New York cocktail party. (Howie doesn't drink, of course. He's a deacon in the Southern Baptist Church, which looks askance at wine and women. Song is acceptable as long as it begins with Holy-Holy-Holy.) They had carried out their courtship in secret, away from the media's prying eyes but under the watchful gaze of the senior Mrs. Keenan, Howard's mother, whose staunch morals qualified her as chaperone. After their wedding, which would take place during the upcoming Congressional recess, there wouldn't be time for show biz. Instead, Roz would be busy with her new assignment as the Senator's Washington hostess and co-campaigner.

"Anyway," she added delicately, "Howie doesn't think it's seemly for me to stay in show business—given the upward momentum of his political career, that is."

It was on the tip of my tongue to point out that—seemly or not—one recent show business president had ridden his upward momentum right into the Oval Office. And never even unsaddled his horse. But Ronald Reagan wasn't a deacon, and some people might suggest that there was a difference between "Do it for the Gipper" and "Let's all do it with StrawBerry Bear." Not to mention Roz's legs, up there on the screen where Baptists and non-Baptists alike could get an eyeful. I knew several Southern Baptists who were exceedingly moralistic about women's bare legs—in public, that is. A little leg in private was a different matter.

I thought back to the fragment of argument I had heard that morning. Now I understood why Roz was able to shrug off a four-million-dollar contract. Even the Disney sale must be small potatoes compared to the Keenan treasure chest and a stay in the White House.

Roz's announcement was the high point of the evening. We'd already said everything there was to say, and Meredith was still clearly angry. What's more, the mariachis were warming up. So when the waiter brought the dessert cart around, we turned down his blandishments, Roz paid the tab, and we left.

We dropped Roz off at the cottage and then I drove

Meredith home. The drive was silent until we arrived.

"There's still plenty of Mother's birthday cake left," Meredith said. "Come in and have some."

I'd already said no to dessert, but I had a fondness for Adele's chocolate cake—it's worth the cost in calories—and Meredith seemed to want to talk. Meredith cut two generous slices of cake. "I lied," she said, putting mine down in front of me with a thump. "There might be some letters. I found a couple of boxes when I was going through Mother's closet."

"Might be?"

Meredith handed me a fork and sat down. "The boxes are taped up, and I didn't open them. There's a note on top. It says that you're supposed to have them." Her tone was corrosive. "It's the same old thing, isn't it? Mother could write hundreds of letters to some friend in New York, but she did everything she could to keep her daughter out of her personal life." Her mouth wrenched with bitter irony. "In the end, all she left me was a lousy three-line note."

I touched her hand in silent sympathy. "I'll take the boxes when I leave," I said. With Meredith feeling this way, it was better to get them out of her way.

Meredith pulled her eyebrows together in a resentful scowl. "I just don't get it, China. I can't fathom what Mother saw in Rosalind Kotner. The woman is totally arrogant and egotistical." She flung her fork down. "What makes her think she can come over here and poke around in Mother's papers?"

I tried to make a joke out of it. "Watch it. That arrogant, egotistical woman may be our next First Lady."

Meredith made a gagging noise.

"Anyway," I said more seriously, "just because we think she's egotistical doesn't mean that your mother saw her that way. Maybe Roz showed Jo a different side."

"Maybe. Or maybe Roz Kotner, ego and all, appealed to a part of Mother I never knew." She put her hands up to her face. "Oh, God, China, I thought it would get better. But it doesn't." Her voice dropped, grew ragged, barely controlled. "I know she wouldn't want me to miss her, but I do, damn it."

I took her hands across the table. "I know," I said. It wasn't enough, but there wasn't anything else to say. Meredith's grief, her anger, went so deep that words couldn't reach it.

"If only she'd let me *in*," Meredith whispered, fighting tears. "If I'd known what was going on with her, maybe I could have helped."

"But you didn't know. You can't blame yourself for that."

Meredith pulled back her hands and clenched them into tight balls of fists. "I don't blame myself," she cried roughly. "I blame *her*. Oh, God, China, I *hate* her for what she did!"

Then the tears came, as fierce and hard as a flash storm. I got up and rubbed her shoulders awkwardly, not as well as Ruby does it. But it seemed to help, and after the storm had passed, she wiped her eyes.

"Thanks," she said wearily. "I just can't seem to get over being angry. I want to love her, but I can't. It gnaws on me all the time." I sat down again and we finished our cake in silence.

When we were done, Meredith brought me the boxes. There were two of them, old boot boxes, tied together, their lids taped. I stuck them in my hatchback and told Meredith to call if she needed anything. When I got home, I left the boxes in the car. There was nothing pressing about Jo's old letters, and I was too whacked to fool with them. It had been a very long day.

So I poured a brandy, climbed into a steamy bubble bath, and gave myself over to some serious philosophizing. Jo Gilbert was dead. Roz Kotner was about to trade her ruffled pinafore for the Keenan millions and a shot at the White House. The way was clear for Arnold Seidensticker to get his regional airport.

There was no justice in the world.

CHAPTER 7

I was awakened early the next morning by a call from McQuaid. His pickup had started making an ominous noise the day before. "It's the water pump," he told me. "If you're not going to be using your car today, can I borrow it?"

I agreed, so the first hour of the morning was spent following McQuaid's blue Ford pickup to Hank's Auto Repair, waiting while Hank filled out the paperwork, and stopping for breakfast. Maria's Taco Cocina is crowded into the front half of a small frame house on Zapata Street, behind a bare-earth yard dotted with truck tires, painted white and filled with dirt, transformed into flower beds. Inside, the tables are covered with red-checked oilcloth and surrounded by mismatched kitchen chairs. Each table has its own bouquet of plastic flowers. Ours were neon pink and citrus yellow roses, stuck in an empty Del Monte ketchup bottle. Maria, a squat Mexican lady with snapping black eyes and a renowned culinary talent, makes extraordinary breakfast tacos with chorizos and eggs, seasoned heavily with cumin and chili peppers and rolled up in a chewy flour tortilla. They're so good that nobody cares that the stainless doesn't match, the plates come from the Salvation Army thrift store, and the napkins are paper. After we'd pigged out on three of Maria's tacos and two cups of her fine Chilean coffee, McQuaid dropped me off to open the shop and took my car to the campus, promising to bring it back that evening when he came for dinner.

I was writing copy for the first issue of the newsletter I'm planning when Constance Letterman came in. She was wearing a pair of wine-red polyester slacks and a matching boat-necked jersey top with a wide green stripe that went around the neck and down both arms. She looked like a beet. A round, happily boastful beet.

"Ms. Kotner agreed to let me interview her for the *Enterprise*," she said, leaning on the counter. "I'm goin' to write a feature article on her." Constance has a sharply nasal East Texas twang.

"That's great, Constance," I remarked, straightening a stack of herb calendars on the counter. She must have hit Roz up for an interview during the brief encounter I'd seen at yesterday's memorial service.

Constance regarded me hopefully. "I thought maybe you'd come too."

"Me?" I asked, surprised. "Why would you want me to barge in on your interview?"

" 'Cause you know Ms. Kotner better than I do. With you there, maybe she'll feel looser, more like talkin'. We might get into more . . . well, intimate territory."

I wasn't quite sure about the intimate territory, and I certainly didn't count myself one of Roz's friends. But after seeing her virtuoso performances over the past two days, I couldn't help wanting to see more. After all, someday soon I might be watching the woman waltz the first waltz at the Inaugural Ball—on television, of course.

"All right, I'll go," I said, and Constance beamed. I put my head through the door into The Crystal Cave, where Ruby was waiting on a well-dressed young professional woman who was choosing a tarot deck. I waggled my "I'm stepping out for a minute" sign and Ruby nodded that she'd cover for me. Constance and I headed out the door and down the path to the cottage.

Roz was dressed to meet the press in a pair of silky cream-colored slacks and a creamy silk blouse topped with an elegant strand of pearls. She was on the phone with Jane's office in New York, but she hung up immediately.

"Jane's taking a few days off to drive up to her cottage in Vermont," she said. She turned to me. "She left a message for Meredith, China. She thought Jo's memorial service was quite impressive—the fact that so many people came, I mean." Roz supplied us with coffee, picked up the tomato juice she'd been sipping (heavily laced with garlic extract, no doubt), and led us out to the tiny patio outside the cottage bedroom, where we pulled white wicker chairs around the small white table. The air was heavily scented with thyme. Bees were busy among the violet-colored blossoms.

Constance took a professional-looking tape recorder out of her voluminous carryall, checked the batteries, and set a mike on the table. "Now, Ms. Kotner," she said, wreathed in smiles and fluttering like a middle-aged groupie, "tell us *ever'thang*!" East Texans have a wonderful way with their *ings*. *Thing* always comes out like *thang*.

Roz arched her eyebrows. "Everything?"

"Oh, dear, yes!" Constance gushed with avid enthusiasm. She took out a steno pad and a pencil. "In Pecan Springs, we're proud of your rise to stardom. We like to feel that maybe we've had a teensy part"—she held thumb and forefinger a fraction of an inch apart to show how much "teensy" was—"in your success story."

I had no idea that Roz Kotner had risen to the stature of a Pecan Springs' folk heroine. As far as I knew, this wasn't even Roz's home town. It was just the last place she'd happened to live before she became famous. But I could understand why Pecan Springs might take a proprietary interest in her. After all, how many of its former citizens had ever made the cover of *People* magazine perched on a pile of pink bears?

Roz gave Constance a kindly smile. "Well, then," she said, "perhaps it's appropriate that the word go out from Pecan Springs at the same time it goes out from Washington and Los Angeles. But I *will* have to ask you to hold the story until you have clearance from me."

"Sure," Constance agreed eagerly. She leaned so far forward that I was afraid she might tip over, even though her chair was anchored by her ample beet-colored behind. "What story?"

Roz glanced at me approvingly. "I see you haven't mentioned it," she said. I shook my head and she turned back to Constance.

"I'm leaving the entertainment field," she said. "I've sold my corporation to Disney."

And then, before Constance had time to recover, Roz dropped bombshell number two.

Constance's eyes grew round in her round, flushed face, and her chair teetered dangerously. "*Senator Keenan!*" she exclaimed. "Lord sakes!" Then, remembering herself, she burbled through profuse congratulations, tripping over every other word, with anxious glances at her tape recorder to make sure it was still running. This was clearly the biggest scoop of Constance Letterman's journalistic career.

Ten minutes later, when Constance had asked all the questions she could think of, she stammered grateful thanks, turned off her recorder, and dashed off—straight to the *Enterprise*, I'd bet, to write her story.

I said my good-bye and was following Constance out the door, when Roz stopped me. "China," she said, putting a beautifully manicured hand lightly on my arm, "what do you think I can do to persuade Meredith that there's no harm in letting me look for my letters? With all the details of the memorial service and settling her mother's estate, I'm sure that a few old scraps of paper aren't a high priority for her. It might be months before they're found, and I'd really like to take them back with me. God knows when I'll get to Pecan Springs again."

I hesitated, thinking of the boxes in the back of my car, which was parked in a CTSU faculty lot. For a moment, I considered telling Roz that if anybody had the letters, I was the one. But I decided against it. Time enough to tell her when I knew for sure what was in the boxes.

"I'm afraid Meredith is like Jo when it comes to making up her mind," I said apologetically. "She can be pretty stubborn."

"I see," Roz said. Then she dismissed the matter with another wave. "Oh, well, they're just old letters. Not at all important. I suppose I'm being too sentimental."

I glanced at my watch. "I'm sorry to have to run," I said, not sorry at all, "but I'm scheduled to give a lecture to the Friends of the Library this afternoon, and I have to get my act together."

I went back to the shop to tend customers and sort out my notes and locate the slides I'd taken of the summer's herb garden. It was twelve-thirty when I finished. I'd planned on asking Ruby to keep an eye on things, but she was late getting back from lunch so I called Laurel Wiley, who is usually available to take charge of both shops. Laurel is a regular student in my herb classes and a friend of Ruby's, too. She's good backup for times when Ruby and I both are gone. I changed into a green corduroy skirt and green print blouse, and then Mrs. Culpepper, the president of the Friends of the Library, came to pick me up.

The lecture, which was held in the small library auditorium, went well. I enjoy talking about herbs, and the Friends of the Library are a receptive audience. But

I had the sense of something wrong, something out of kilter. It didn't take long to figure out what it was. I missed Jo. When I first opened Thyme and Seasons, she was the one who had encouraged me to get out and talk to community groups.

Jo wasn't there. But Lila Seidensticker was, her thin neck and arms glittering with Seidensticker jewelry. I hoped fervently that Ruby's sleuthing was running into a dead end. I wasn't sure what would happen if she actually turned something up—not that she would.

The lecture over, I went back to the shop. Business had been slow, according to Laurel, maybe because the weather was so beautiful. The afternoon sun spilled a rich, burnished gold over the autumn trees, and the temperature was in the low seventies. Ruby hadn't gotten back yet. Lured by the fragrance of the roses in the herb garden, I left Laurel behind the counter, took my shears and went out to the bed along the alley, behind the cottage. Sweet Annie—*artemisia annua*, called Qing hao by Chinese herbalists—grows hip high there, golden brown and fluffy, with its own unique spicy-sweet fragrance. Right now, it was at a perfect stage for wreath-making. Wreaths are big holiday sellers in the shop. I buy dozens on consignment from various local craftswomen, each of whom has her own unique way of combining materials. But I manage to devote a few October and November evenings to weaving dried flowers and seedpods and grasses into bases made of sweet Annie or artemisia. I'm always surprised when I see how beautiful my wreaths are. I spent so many years lavishing all my creative energy on legal briefs and courtroom arguments that this kind of creating is sheer joy.

The sweet Annie patch borders the cottage. The afternoon was warm, so the windows were open. When the telephone rang inside, I knew I'd be able to hear every word of Roz's conversation. The honorable thing, I suppose, would have been to pick up my basket and leave. But I didn't do the honorable thing. I kept on cutting sweet Annie right where I was. After all, it *was* my garden, and if I let this batch of ripe stuff stand, it could get rained on.

The truth was, Roz's opening line, after her breathy hello, had caught my attention. "I'm sorry, but as I told you, it's all over. It's out of my control now. I can't give you anything more."

I froze, bent over the sweet Annie. Who was Roz paying?

There was a silence while the person on the other end of the line responded. Then Roz laughed, a light, careless laugh, but nervous, pitched just a little too high. "Yes, but who's going to believe you? There's no proof. And even if there was, it doesn't matter. It was my talent that brought it off, and I'm getting out."

Another silence, as Roz listened to the caller. Then: "If that's what you think, you're mistaken. I gave you money only because I felt sorry for you—not because I owed you anything. But things have changed. If you push this, the only thing you'll get out of it is a lot of trouble. Do you understand?" She slammed down the receiver.

I finished cutting and went back to the shop, where I paid Laurel and sent her home. Then I bunched my cuttings, climbed up on the stool, and hung the bunches from the rafters. As I worked, I kept thinking about the phone call. Could someone be blackmailing Roz? I thought back to her bitter comment the night before about directors and producers and agents and coaches, all wanting to get something from her. No wonder she wanted to bail out of the business. Washington politics probably looked like patty-cake compared to the games she'd been playing.

I was hanging the last bunch when Ruby came in. She was wearing a 250-watt grin and her frizzy red hair stood up all over her head, practically snapping with electricity.

"I know you said you didn't want to help," she said. "But will you at least *listen*?"

I climbed down from my perch and carried the stool behind the counter. "Don't tell me you've been playing detective."

Ruby's face darkened and she turned away. "Okay, don't listen. When the whole thing is over, you can read it in the newspapers."

I closed my eyes briefly. I knew this was something I didn't want to know. But I had the feeling that if I didn't know it, I'd probably be sorry. "Ruby," I said to her back, "give me a dollar."

Ruby fished in her shoulder bag for her billfold. "What do you want it for?" she asked suspiciously. She found one and handed it to me.

I put the dollar into my skirt pocket. "You've just hired me," I said with a sigh. "As your lawyer."

Ruby's grin came back. "You mean, you're going to help?"

I sat down on the stool. "Help, bullshit. I said I'd listen, and anything you say is privileged communication. But that doesn't mean I'd aid and abet you in anything stupid. It also doesn't mean I'd go to court for you if Arnold Seidensticker slaps you with a libel suit. You'll have to find another lawyer for that."

"It's no libel, it's the truth," Ruby said earnestly. She leaned both elbows on the counter and lowered her voice. "Lila Seidensticker takes sleeping pills."

"Big deal," I said, folding my arms. "Ninety percent of the adult population of Pecan Springs has probably popped pills at one time or another."

Ruby looked over her shoulder to make sure that nobody was listening. She did it strictly for effect, because there was nobody else in the shop.

"She takes the *same* sleeping pills that killed Jo."

I raised my eyebrows. "So? Divide the ninety percent of the population who've taken sleeping pills by the number of nonprescription brands on the market, and you'll find out how many other people take the same sleeping pills that killed Jo." I put on my stern look. "But I'm curious. Just how did you manage to find out what brand of pills Lila uses? And please don't tell me you bribed her maid."

Ruby shook her head. "No, nothing like that. I just followed her."

"You followed her!" I squawked. "Ruby, you've got to be careful! People *notice* you." This is true. At six-feet-something in her heels, with Orphan Annie hair and green eyes and a loose-jointed grace, Ruby is eminently noticeable. People *enjoy* noticing her.

"I was careful," Ruby insisted. "I followed her at a

distance, so she wouldn't see me. I probably wouldn't have done it at all," she added, "except that I saw her having lunch. The opportunity kind of fell into my lap, so to speak."

"Where did you follow her *to*?"

"Peterson's Pharmacy, on the square. That's where she bought the pills. I hung out at the magazine rack. Then I followed her to the library and then I quit. I didn't think I'd learn anything at the Friends of the Library meeting."

"You might've," I said. "It was a good lecture. The woman who talked really knows her herbs."

"Actually," Ruby said, looking down, "I went to the courthouse. I was hoping to get a lead on whatever Jo had discovered that was going to keep Seidensticker from building his airport. I thought it might be something about the land title."

"And what did you find out?"

Ruby brightened. "That's where I really hit the jackpot," she said. "China, Arnold Seidensticker has quietly bought up all the land where the airport's going to go—*if* the Anti-Airport Coalition fails, that is," she added significantly. "Which it very well might, now that Jo isn't around to push it."

I frowned. "You mean, he owns it directly? In the Seidensticker name?"

"Well, no," Ruby admitted. "An outfit called the Landmark Corporation owns it. But Arnold owns a lot of Landmark Corporation stock. I know, because I read it in the paper a while back. If the corporation sells its land to the airport authority, Arnold is bound to make a pot of money." She frowned. "But whatever Jo discovered, I don't think it has anything to do with the title. The site belongs to Landmark, free and clear. You see, China? He's got it all. Means, motive, and opportunity."

It sounded like Ruby had been watching "L.A. Law." "And just how many other shareholders do you suppose the Landmark Corporation has?"

"I don't know," Ruby said. "Why?"

"Because if your logic is accurate, every single one of them had exactly the same motive. And any one of them could have walked into Peterson's Pharmacy and bought those same pills."

Ruby's jaw set stubbornly. "I still think Arnold Seidensticker did it. He stood up in front of the last City Council meeting and said he wants Pecan Springs to have that airport and that he'd do anything to make sure it happens."

"I know," I sighed. "Motive and means—right? But what about opportunity?" My pause was heavy with irony. "I guess you've figured out how he talked Jo into swallowing nearly an entire bottle of sleeping pills."

"Well, I—" Ruby began.

"Did he do it at gunpoint?" I asked, piling on the sarcasm. "Or did he just say to her, 'My dear Ms. Gilbert, I really think it would be extremely helpful if you took these pills so my corporation and I can make a cool five or ten million dollars on this airport deal'?"

Ruby looked at me. "Have you ever heard of a Mickey Finn?"

"Yeah, sure, but—"

"Well, what if Jo didn't actually *take* the sleeping

pills? What if Arnold Seidensticker, or maybe Lila Seidensticker—one or the other or both—ground up the barbiturates, enough to kill her, and dissolved them in Jo's drink. That spicy Bloody Mary mix probably masked any off taste. She wouldn't have known what she was swallowing."

"I see the logic," I said slowly. "But I *can't* see Jo Gilbert inviting Arnold and Lila Seidensticker—either one or both—to her house on Monday morning to share a friendly Mickey Finn. The last I heard, Jo and Arnold weren't on speaking terms, much less drinking terms. And if the Seidenstickers—one or both—were going to do it, they'd have to bring the ground-up sleeping pills with them, slip them into her drink, and shake it up. It isn't something you can do in front of your intended victim without raising at least a suspicious eyebrow."

"Maybe they doctored the mix at home and brought it with them," Ruby suggested helpfully. "That way, all they had to do was add the vodka."

I shook my head. "Look, Ruby, I hate to dampen your enthusiasm, but you haven't answered my objection. Do you *really* think Jo agreed to have a drink with Arnold Seidensticker early Monday morning?"

Ruby gave a discouraged sigh. "I guess I'm a little weak on opportunity," she admitted. "But I'll figure it out. It'll just take a little more snooping."

I reached into my pocket and pulled out the dollar. "You've just fired me," I said, handing it to her.

"But what about our privileged communication?"

I shrugged. "So you went into a drugstore to hang out at the magazine rack," I said. "There's no law against that. And you went to the courthouse to consult a public record. That's your right as a citizen." I gave her a sternly cautioning look. "But you'd better be careful with the snooping. Arnold Seidensticker probably has eyes and ears all over this town." I grinned. "Speaking of ears, want to hear some interesting news?"

Ruby was looking disgruntled. "Yeah, I guess."

"The reason Roz didn't sign the contract Jane was pushing was because she's sold out to Disney."

"Sold out!" Ruby exclaimed. "No kidding!"

"No kidding. And the reason she sold out is that Howie"—I slipped into Roz's breathy stage voice—"doesn't think it's seemly for a Senator's wife to be in show business." I dropped back into my own voice. "Howard Keenan, that is."

Ruby's eyes bulged. "Howard Keenan? As in *Senator* Howard Keenan?"

"You got it."

"But he's up for the nomination . . .. I mean, he might be . . . I mean . . ." Ruby gulped. The gingery freckles were standing out all over her face. She spoke in an awed whisper. "My God."

"Yeah," I said thoughtfully. "I wonder if she'll do the Oval Office over in pink."

Before Ruby could reply, a pair of customers came in. I greeted them with a smile. "What can I help you with today?"

Without a word, Ruby turned and went into The Crystal Cave. A moment later, I smelled the special incense she always burns when she's upset and needs something to soothe her spirit.

By the time I waited on the two customers, answered a phone question about the toxicity of *aconitum vulparia*—wolfsbane—and put the finishing touches on next week's newspaper ad, it was five-thirty and time to close for the day. McQuaid was coming for dinner. It was his turn to cook, which meant that I didn't have to buy any groceries. But I was out of his favorite scotch, and I needed to knock the rust out of my knees, and McQuaid had my Datsun. So I hopped on my bike and headed for Bart's Liquor Store, over on Converse, about a mile away. I'd had a bike when I lived in Houston, but I probably rode it once a month, maybe less. Riding in the city's high-density traffic, I felt the way one of Custer's men might have felt as he topped the hill and saw what was coming. Now, I take short rides two or three times a week and longer rides on Monday. I'm not in terrific shape—actually, I'm sort of average in the creaks and groans department—but I'm working on it. The bike helps.

I was almost home with the scotch when I saw a woman getting into a dinged-up old brown Duster that was parked on the street behind my shop. There was something about the set of her shoulders that reminded me of Jane Dorman, but elegant Jane wouldn't be caught dead looking like this woman, with her shapeless brown sweater and limp shoulder-length hair.

I glanced back once more, and nearly wiped out. Sarita Gonzales stepped off the curb right into my path. I grabbed for the brakes, and she jumped back with a shriek. Sarita is a handsome Hispanic woman with large brown eyes, a wealth of brown hair, and a ready smile that shows bright white teeth. She's a fourth-grade school teacher and the wife of Rogelio Gonzales, pastor of the Guadalupe Methodist Church. The church is my neighbor, a few doors down, and Sarita and Rogelio live in the parsonage on the other side.

Sarita grinned when she saw that I was the one who had nearly run her down. "Hey, China," she said, "where you goin' so fast?"

I stopped and leaned a foot on the curb. "Just on my way home," I said. "How've you been, Sarita? How's Rogelio?"

Sarita's face went sad. "We heard about your friend Jo Gilbert. She was a good person, and such energy. I know you're going to miss her."

"Thanks," I said. I was grateful for her simple and deeply felt sympathy. "I hear the church is getting ready for another sale next weekend. How about if I make a few more of those big herb wreaths for you?" I'd donated several to the church bazaar in the summer, and they'd been a hit. "And I just got in a new batch of epazote—I'll package some of it." My Hispanic customers buy epazote to flavor their ethnic dishes, those who don't grow it themselves. You can find epazote in almost every garden on the east side of Pecan Springs.

Sarita's smile was warm and genuine. "*Muy bueno.* You're a good neighbor, China. You need anythin', you let me know, *comprende*?"

"Thanks," I said again, and rode home feeling good. In all the years I lived in my Houston condo, the only interaction I had with the neighbors was when we had a problem. Here, everybody's a friend. Sometimes it feels like we live in one another's pockets, but this was one of the days when there didn't seem to be anything wrong with that.

After I got home, I put one of Ruby's spacy New Age tapes in the cassette player and climbed into a hot bath laced with sweet almond and lemon grass oil. I lay back in the tub and let the heat and the aromatic fragrance soothe me. It had been a hell of a week and tonight was my night with McQuaid. I was looking forward to it.

Little did I know.

CHAPTER 8

I dipped a tortilla chip in McQuaid's secret-recipe jalapeño salsa, which is so hot it nearly takes your head off, and settled back into the kitchen rocking chair. "So what did you tell Patterson after he said *that*?" I asked lazily.

It was nearly seven, the events of the week were rapidly fading in their importance, and I was feeling relaxed. I had a tangy margarita in one hand, a crisp chip in the other, and an admiring eye on McQuaid, who was putting the finishing touches on his tasty-looking gumbo. He was tasty-looking too, in jeans and a red plaid shirt with the sleeves rolled up. He was in the middle of an involved story about his run-in with the department chairman over next semester's teaching assignments.

"I told Patterson it was time Hawkins moved over and let somebody else teach the graduate intro course," he said, tasting the gumbo and adding another jolt of

Tabasco sauce. Hawkins is senior man in the criminal justice department. He'd had the introductory graduate course sewed up for years, assuring himself of a steady flow of graduate students. "I told him if he couldn't guarantee the course next spring—fall at the latest—I'd start looking for another job."

I licked salt off the rim of my glass. "Kind of ballsy, wasn't it?" I asked, carefully casual. "What will you do if Patterson tells you to get your résumé together?"

McQuaid put the mixing bowl and eggbeater into the sink and ran water into it. "Not ballsy at all," he said, drying his hands on the crocheted potholder Aunt Mildred sent me last Christmas. "I'm holding the cards."

I twirled my glass, not sure I liked the direction this was moving. "Got a good hand, huh?"

"Yeah, a real good hand." McQuaid pulled out a kitchen chair and turned it around, straddling it. He rested his forearms on the back and his chin on his arms. His pale blue eyes were on mine, and my stomach muscles clenched like a hard fist. "I got an acceptance yesterday on that article I sent to *Criminal Justice Review*. That makes three articles in four months, in the top three professional journals."

"Hey, not bad for somebody who hasn't even finished his dissertation yet," I said. I laughed. "Wait until you get that Ph.D. You'll be unstoppable."

McQuaid's grin furrowed little laugh wrinkles at the corner of his mouth, but his eyes were serious. "You bet," he said. "Patterson's no dummy. He's not going to let go of his only publishing faculty member, not when he's saddled with a department full of ex-cops who hate to write. How would he explain *that* to the dean?" McQuaid's dean is an arrogant young firebrand who's always exhorting the faculty to publish and threatening to perish the ones who don't.

"There's more," McQuaid said. His eyes held mine. "I've got an offer—well, almost."

I looked into my margarita. "No kidding," I said. "Where?"

"New Mexico State." McQuaid grinned proudly, like a kid who's just won the district high jump championship. "Associate prof the first year, consideration for tenure the second. Contingent on finishing the dissertation, of course. But that's no big deal. I'll be done this spring."

I cleared my throat. "Hey, I'm impressed."

"Well, it's not definite yet. I'm going to interview next week, which will give Patterson something to think about." He paused. "But if I get the graduate course and the merit committee recommends a raise, I guess I'll stay here another year or two. After that, I can write my own ticket anywhere."

I realized I was actually holding my breath. I didn't want him to go. I liked things the way they were.

"Brian's doing great in school," McQuaid was saying thoughtfully. "Pecan Springs is a good place for him, close to his grandparents. No point in dragging him around the country unless it's clearly a better deal than I've got here." He paused, pursed his lips, still watching me. "And of course, there's us."

The silence hung between us, empty, inviting me to ask if *we* were really a factor in his career planning. I raised my glass again.

"Well, hey," I said lightly, "here's to success in departmental politics. What do you want to bet that Patterson caves in and gives you that course?"

McQuaid was silent for a moment, as if he'd been hoping for a different response. Then he gave me a little grin and stood up. "Whatever Patterson decides, he's got to do it by Monday. That's when spring course assignments are due in the dean's office." On his way back to the stove, he said, over his shoulder, "Okay if I keep the car until tomorrow? Hank had to order a water pump from San Antonio."

"Fine by me," I said. "I'm not going anywhere." I got the salad, took the French bread out of the oven, poured the wine, lit the candles, and we sat down to eat. The gumbo was fine, the wine was right, and we laughed a lot at things that weren't all that funny. After dinner we stacked the dishes, put on a Pavarotti tape, and took our wine and the candles into the living room. A half hour later, we switched to Vivaldi and moved the wine and the candles into the bedroom. In bed with McQuaid, I found myself thinking—when I could think past the warm billowing of desire—that maybe I was a fool to let a man like this get away. He could make a mean gumbo, carry on an interesting conversation, *and* make love gently, warmly, passionately. What more did I want?

No, that wasn't the question, I thought a few minutes later, letting the lassitude ebb and flow through me like a warm ocean. It was what I *didn't* want that kept me from opening fully to McQuaid. Sex was one thing. But I didn't want to go halves with somebody on my life. I didn't want a child, even one as winsome as

Brian. I didn't want to be a faculty wife and live in the dust storms of faculty politics. I didn't want to leave Pecan Springs. What I wanted to do was lie here in my own bed, within the solid stone walls of my own house, feeling soft and languid and ripe, and in a few minutes, make love again.

McQuaid propped his head on his elbow and looked at me, thoughtful in the candlelight. He traced my lips with his finger. "That," he said softly, "was pretty great. Ten plus, you think?"

"No bonus points for timing?" I asked, wanting it light.

He grinned. "Maybe," he said. "I'll consider it." He bent over and kissed the tip of my nose, his hand warm on my breast. He rubbed the nipple between thumb and forefinger and the ebb warmed, began to flow again. "Hey, China, remember what I was saying before dinner? About the job?"

I turned my head away. "Umm," I said. This was such a fine, full moment, bodies speaking to bodies, flesh to flesh, a language without words. Why did we have to *talk*?

McQuaid rolled over on his back and clasped both hands under his head, staring up at the rough pine boards of the ceiling. "Look," he said, "I know you'd like to avoid the issue. But sooner or later, we *have* to talk about it. We can't—"

The phone rang on the bedside table.

McQuaid sighed and put a pillow over the phone. It rang again.

I sat up. "We can still hear it. Anyway, it might be Brian." Brian was at his grandmother's for the night, which was a rare treat for us. McQuaid and I hardly ever spend the whole night together, and I never stay over at his place when Brian's there. McQuaid doesn't mind making love with a ten-year-old in the next room, but it's something I can't get used to. What's more, I don't want to.

McQuaid sighed. "Answer it," he said.

I reached for the phone. It was Meredith. "China," she said urgently. "Please come over. I need you."

The clock on the table said half past ten. "Meredith, don't you think it's a little late? How about if we make it for breakfast tomorrow." McQuaid elbowed me. Tomorrow was Saturday. We could sleep until at least eight forty-five. "Or lunch," I amended. "Lunch would be better."

Meredith's voice held a whimper. "Somebody broke into the house tonight, China."

I sat up straight, pulling the sheet against me. "Broke in? You mean, a burglary?"

"Yes. I went to an early movie. I just got home. The screen on the back door is ripped loose. The place is a disaster, papers and things all over. Can you come? Please?"

"Sure," I said. I looked over at McQuaid. "Have you called the cops?"

There was a hesitation. "Should I?"

"No need, not at the moment. I'll bring one with me."

McQuaid, bless his heart, didn't say a word. We got dressed, climbed into the Datsun, and headed for Meredith's. After my initial explanation, I didn't say much either. But when McQuaid pulled up at Jo's and switched off the motor, he put his hand on my shoulder.

"I'm sorry we got interrupted tonight, China. I'd like to get back to the subject when we can."

Talking wasn't going to change anything, now or later. There were things I wanted, things I didn't want, and the things I wanted didn't fit the things *he* wanted. It was as simple as that. But his eyes were on me. I nodded.

He let go of my shoulder and leaned across me, pulling my flashlight out of the glove compartment. It's as big as a billy club. McQuaid gave it to me for Christmas. "Let's go," he said.

Meredith met us at the front door, armed with the fireplace poker. Her face was taut, her shoulders rigid. She gave McQuaid a grateful glance. He's big and reassuring and still wears that cop look. She leaned the poker against the wall.

"Thanks for coming," she said. She glanced from McQuaid to me. "I hope I didn't interrupt anything."

"No, of course not," I lied. I looked over her shoulder. Jo's tidy living room was a wreck. The sofa cushions had been pulled out, chairs were tipped over, lampshades hung awry, curio cabinet doors and drawers gaped open. Books and papers littered the floor.

McQuaid whistled. "A burglar with a tornado complex," he said, and turned for the door, flicking on the flashlight. "I'll take a look around outside."

Meredith and I went into the den, where the same tornado had struck. "They went through the whole house, even the kitchen," Meredith said. "Whoever did it pulled out every drawer in the place." She reached out to straighten a lamp and I stopped her.

"Don't touch anything. There might be prints. What's missing?"

Meredith put her hands behind her. "Some antique silver. My grandmother's." She bit her lip. "It was only worth a couple of hundred dollars, but I suppose if somebody was hard up for drug money—" She stopped and frowned. "But it wasn't druggies, China."

I was looking at Jo's desk. All the drawers had been pulled out and the contents dumped in a pile under the lamp—old bills, index cards, scribbled notes, envelopes. "Why not?" I asked. I bent over to look at the envelopes.

"I smelled it again," Meredith said. She looked at the heap of notes and envelopes. "Perfume."

I straightened. "You're sure?"

"Yes. No." Meredith frowned down at the rubble. "Yes," she said.

"Tell me," I commanded. "From the beginning."

She closed her eyes, as if she were replaying a movie inside her head. "I unlocked the front door and came in. I turned on the hall light, and that's when I saw the mess in the living room. That's when I smelled it again. At least, I think I did." She paused for a moment, thinking. Then she opened her eyes. "I don't know," she said. "Maybe it was the shock of seeing . . . all this. Maybe it brought back . . ."

She might be right. The trauma of finding the wreckage might have reawakened her associations with finding her mother's body. On the other hand, the scent might be the only clue. It was my guess that the person who did this had worn gloves. There wouldn't be any prints.

We went upstairs, following a trail of rubble. "Mother's bedroom is a mess," Meredith said bitterly, opening the door. Jo's drawers were dumped onto the floor, clothes pulled out of the closet, shoes scattered. "Mine, too, but not quite so bad."

"Let's have a look anyway," I said. We went into Meredith's room. The drawers had been jerked out of the dresser and the floor was littered with lingerie. A blue suitcase lay open at the foot of the bed with a couple of books in it, and other books had been shoved off the nightstand onto the floor.

Meredith sighed. "It'll take forever to clean this mess up," she said.

I put my arm around her shoulders and led her back downstairs. McQuaid came in and flicked off his torch. "All clear," he told Meredith. "It looks like you were right about the burglar coming in the back. All the windows are intact, but the screen has been pulled loose from the back door, enough for the burglar to reach the hook. After that, it was a simple matter of opening the door and letting himself in."

"Or herself," I corrected him, and explained about the perfume. McQuaid gave me a doubtful look. Cops mistrust intangible clues.

Meredith frowned. "I don't know, China. I'm not sure I smelled it."

McQuaid turned to Meredith with a cross look. "Why didn't you lock the back door?" he asked irritably. "They'd probably have forced it, but at least they'd have to work for what they got."

Meredith lifted her shoulders wearily and let them fall. "This isn't the big city. I didn't think it was necessary."

"Pecan Springs has its share of burglaries," McQuaid said. He paused, adding weight to his words. "Next time, lock up."

Meredith looked at him. "Next time," she said, adding equal weight to hers, "I'll have a gun." There was an angry glint in her eye.

McQuaid produced a statistic from his course on crime in America. "Handguns are a hundred times more likely to kill or injure their owners than criminals."

"Not *my* handgun," Meredith said firmly. "I refuse to be a victim."

McQuaid might have gone further with it, but he was anxious to get me to leave. He looked at me. "Anything missing?"

"Some silver. A couple of hundred dollars worth."

"There's your answer. Kids after drug money. Have you called the cops?" McQuaid asked.

"Not yet," Meredith said. She frowned. "Will it be that guy with the wet cigar?"

McQuaid flashed a grin. "Bubba's a character, but he's a good cop. He's thorough. If there's a lead here, or a connection to other burglaries, he'll turn it up."

I found a tissue and used it to pick up the phone. Bubba himself answered my call to the police station. He said he'd send a car. I thanked him and hung up.

"China," Meredith said, "I'm not afraid of staying alone, but I'd appreciate the company." Her voice was thin and frayed—and angry, very angry. It was building in her, like a storm. "Could you stay tonight?"

Standing behind Meredith, McQuaid shook his head emphatically. *No*, he mouthed. *No*.

I sighed. Brian probably wouldn't stay over with his grandmother again for several weeks. On the other hand, Meredith needed me. It must have been nerve-shattering to come home and find her mother's house like this. No wonder she was angry. I couldn't turn her down.

"Sure, I'll stay," I said.

McQuaid's mouth tightened. I knew he thought I was staying because I didn't want to continue our interrupted conversation. Maybe so, but that was only part of it.

"Tell you what," I said, with a false heartiness, "how about if I brew some chamomile tea? That's exactly what you need, Meredith. You'll have some too, won't you, McQuaid?"

"Thanks," McQuaid said flatly. "But I'll be on my way. There's nothing I can do here except make the local boys nervous." He was right about that. There was an undercurrent of animosity between the Pecan Springs P.D. and the "academic cops" at the university.

"Okay," I said. "See you later."

"Yeah," McQuaid replied. "Later." He wasn't happy.

CHAPTER 9

The bed in the spare room was narrow and lumpy and the pillow was as comfortable as a sandbag. I tossed and turned for a half hour. Finally, I got up and sat in an equally uncomfortable rocking chair by the window, pulling a crocheted afghan around my shoulders. Outside, the sycamore tree wove a lacework of gnarled, knitted shadows against the nearly full moon. I stared at it and thought about the events of the night.

McQuaid had been gone only a few minutes when Bubba showed up, complete with soggy cigar. I was a little surprised to see him. I didn't think a minor burglary would merit the chief's attention, but maybe he just happened to be at the station and didn't have anything else to do. Or maybe he liked to keep his finger on what occurred in Pecan Springs. However it happened, there he was, trailed by a slender, nervous Hispanic deputy with a carefully trimmed mustache whom

I recognized from my frequent visits to Maria's Taco Cocina.

Meredith and I went into the kitchen and sat silently over a cup of tea while Bubba and the deputy searched the house competently and thoroughly, then made a quick check of the neighbors to ask if anyone had seen anything. Meredith didn't speak. She just kept turning her cup between her hands, her gray eyes dark and shadowed, a muscle working in her jaw.

When they were finished, Bubba came into the kitchen. "Guess that 'bout wraps it," he said, leaning against the doorjamb. He took his cigar out of his mouth and looked regretfully at the unlit end. There was a book under his arm. "This is the first burglary we've had in this part of town for, oh, couple of years now. Folks here got a neighborhood watch. It pretty much spooks the druggies. They got to have a serious habit to risk breakin' into these houses."

"I see," Meredith said, low. "So it was somebody looking for drug money."

Bubba plugged in his cigar and eyed her speculatively. "You got a different idea?"

I waited for her to tell him about the perfume. "No," she said, looking down. "No, I guess I don't."

Bubba held up the book he'd been carrying. "Found this here book in your room," he said. "In your open suitcase, matter of fact." He turned it over in his hands, chewing on his cigar. "I've heard about it. 'Course, Miss Martin, at the bookstore, wouldn't have it on the shelves. Suicide manual, ain't it?"

I looked. It was *Final Exit*, published by the Hemlock Society. The book had fueled a national debate over the right to die. From what I'd heard, it was full of detailed instructions on how to do yourself in.

Meredith's mouth tightened. "Yes."

"Is it yours?"

"It was Mother's. She gave it to me to read, but I never got around to it." Meredith closed her eyes and swallowed hard. "That's not true. I didn't *want* to read it." She cleared her throat. "Mother was . . . it was something we argued about. She asked me to . . . I said no."

Bubba tucked the book under his arm again. "Mind if I borrow it for a couple days?" I looked at him sharply. It didn't sound like a question.

Meredith shrugged. "You can keep it, as far as I'm concerned. I don't have any need for it." She chewed on her lip. "Do you think you'll catch whoever broke in?"

Bubba straightened up. "Not likely. They're probably meltin' the silver down right now. But we'll keep our eyes open. They won't be back tonight." He grinned mirthlessly and stuck his cigar into his shirt pocket. "Won't be back at all, I'd say, seein' as how they already got what they came for. But I'll send a squad car around to keep an eye on things." He gave me a glance. "You gonna be here tonight, Miz Bayles?"

I nodded with a pang of regret for my lost evening with McQuaid.

"Call me if there's any more trouble," he instructed, and left.

Meredith and I went into the den. She surveyed the damage once more, then poured herself a large scotch.

There were twin spots of anger, like forties rouge, on her cheeks, and she slammed the bottle down so hard that the glasses beside it rattled. She sat down in Jo's wingback chair and stared into the cold fireplace.

I poured a drink for myself and we drank in silence. Finally, I asked her. "Why didn't you tell Bubba about the perfume?"

She shrugged, her eyes still on the fireplace. "Why? Would it help? He might as well be looking for druggies. I meant what I said to McQuaid. I'm getting a gun. Tomorrow."

"But this was probably a one-time thing," I said. "Anyway, I thought you had a gun."

"It's still in Dallas. And that's what the cops said the first time I was broken into up there—it was a one-time thing." She laughed bitterly. "What do policemen know? Big, burly guys like McQuaid—they don't have to worry about being raped. This is a women's issue. I've got a right to defend myself against being victimized. Don't I?" She glared at me. "Well, don't I?"

I looked at her again, troubled. I wanted to ask her about the book, but her face was closed up and tight. She wasn't inviting questions, and the only answer she wanted—about the gun—I didn't want to give. After a while we both went to bed.

The moon disappeared behind a cloud, and the openweave lacework of sycamore shadow outside the window became an opaque, impenetrable screen. I frowned. I thought I knew the identity of the burglar.

Except for a few pieces of old silver, there wasn't much in Jo's house to tempt thieves. But there had been something that someone wanted. Roz thought her letters were here. It would have been a simple matter for Roz to follow Meredith to the movie, then return to the house for a leisurely search. She probably wrecked the place to cover any tracks she might have inadvertently left and make it look like a real burglary.

The moon came out again and the tracery of shadows became a moving design. I shivered under the afghan. There was something else. The perfume. If Roz had been here tonight, had she been here on Monday, too? When she showed up at my place Wednesday night, she claimed she'd just arrived from San Francisco. I'd had no reason to suspect her of lying, and she'd certainly acted the part of a new arrival. But then, acting came easily to Roz. That was how she made her living.

I clutched the afghan closer around me. There was another angle to this, *Final Exit*. On the one hand, the book seemed to strengthen the idea that Jo had committed suicide. In court, it was the kind of evidence I might use to argue intent. On the other hand, it also opened a can of worms. Meredith had access to the book. She might have helped her mother commit suicide. But she'd said she'd refused to read it, and to my ears at least, her statement had the ring of truth. Somehow, I couldn't see Meredith helping her mother to die and then going off on a lighthearted shopping spree with Ruby.

But what about Roz? Had Jo asked Roz here on Monday to help her commit suicide, or simply to be with her when she did it? But both Roz and Meredith had indicated that Roz's relationship with Jo was strained, at best. Roz and Jo had argued over the phone. Was it likely that Jo would have invited Roz to be with her at the end?

The moon flickered, went dim, and the shadows faded to black. I stared at the window. There was another explanation, and it wasn't assisted suicide. I'd brushed off Ruby's Mickey Finn idea because it seemed out of character for Jo to have a friendly drink with Arnold Seidensticker. But it wasn't inconceivable that she'd have a morning drink with Roz, particularly if she thought Roz wanted to mend fences. If Roz had been here, she could have slipped any number of pills into Jo's Hot Stuff and Jo wouldn't have known the difference. But what about the Smirnoff? I can always tell whether my Mary is Bloody or Virgin, but Jo wasn't used to drinking—maybe she couldn't.

But there was another glitch in the theory. If Roz had been in the house on Monday, why didn't she take the letters then? She would have had ample opportunity while she was waiting for Jo to—

I sat up straighter. No. There *wasn't* ample opportunity. RuthAnn Landsdowne had unexpectedly knocked on Jo's door at eleven-thirty. The knock might have frightened Roz into a hasty departure.

I shivered. The whole thing had suddenly become *possible*, and it made me feel chilly down to my bones. I could imagine Roz having the opportunity to kill Jo, and I could recreate a hypothetical method. But there was still the question of motive. Jo had been, at least by Roz's testimony, her best friend. What possible reason could she have had to kill her?

I climbed back into bed and folded the thin sandbag of a pillow into a wedge that fit my neck, berating myself for not going through the boxes Jo had left for me. Roz's letters to her—if that's what was in them—might hold a clue. Unfortunately, the boxes were in my car, and my car had gone home with McQuaid.

I turned over and looked at the clock: two-thirty. If it weren't the middle of the night, I'd take Meredith's car and go over to McQuaid's right now. But to do that, I'd have to wake Meredith *and* McQuaid, and that would mean explanations.

I stirred restlessly. First thing tomorrow, I'd get my hands on those boxes. If it was Roz who had ransacked Jo's house, I wanted to know why. What could be in a few old letters that would compel a TV personality and First-Lady-in-waiting to risk breaking and entering?

Or murder?

The thought made me so uncomfortable that I stopped noticing the uncomfortable pillow.

When I woke, the letters were the first thing on my mind. I told Meredith I had to get back home. "Leave the house the way it is and I'll come over this evening and help clean things up."

Meredith shook her head. "I can handle it, China, thanks." Her face was determinedly cheerful, but her eyes were bloodshot and angry. I had the feeling that she'd slept as much as I had, which wasn't very much. "I intend to get to the garage today, too," she added, picking up her keys. We headed out to her car. "I have to start going through Mother's things and decide what I'm going to keep and what I have to get rid of."

The sky was a dull, leaden gray that had started

seeping drizzle by the time I got home. I expected to find my kitchen sink full of dirty dishes from last night's dinner. But the dishes on the drainboard were clean, and there was a terse note on the table.

"Forgot to tell you I'm taking Brian camping this weekend," it said. There was a P.S. "I'll bring your car back as soon as Hank gets the new pump installed." There was a P.P.S. "Next time, let's eat at *my* place. I'll take the phone off the hook."

I reread the note. Maybe McQuaid *had* forgotten to tell me about taking Brian camping. On the other hand, maybe he'd decided that he'd rather spend the weekend with his son than listen to me avoid his questions about commitment. I reached for the phone and dialed. I couldn't blame him for being pissed. From his point of view, Meredith's call was rotten timing.

Brian answered.

"Hi," I said. "Is your dad there?"

"Nope. He's gone to get some beef jerky and stuff. For camping. You know," Brian said helpfully, just in case I wasn't familiar with jerky, "the stuff the Indians used to make for when they ran out of deer meat."

"Good stuff," I said. "Do you know when he'll be back?"

"When he finds the jerky," Brian said, and put the phone down. Brian's like that. When he's finished talking, he's finished.

I swore softly and tried Hank's. McQuaid wasn't there, either, and the pickup wouldn't be finished until ten. There was nothing more I could do for the moment. Like it or not, the letters had to wait.

I unlocked, opened the cash register, and started on

my routine morning chores. But I didn't get very far. Violett was my first customer, barely five minutes after I opened. I was rearranging the wreaths on the wall when she came in. I was shocked by the change in her. The rain had plastered her thin Mamie bangs to her forehead. Her face looked waxy, and a blue vein etched a fine line under the translucent skin of her temple. Her plain white blouse was rumpled under her raincoat, and there was a brown stain over the second button. I wasn't surprised when she asked me for something to help her sleep.

"I've tried chamomile," she said in an exhausted voice. "I need something stronger. I have a book about medicinal herbs and it says that valerian is what I want." She shifted, seeming to feel she had to explain. "I haven't been sleeping. I've had . . . something on my mind."

"I have some on order," I said. "I expect it in today." Valerian is an age-old remedy for sleeplessness—a tranquilizer par excellence. "Why don't you check with me early this afternoon?"

"I will," Violett said. Her hands fluttered. "I *have* to get some sleep."

After Violett left I dialed McQuaid's number and got Brian again. His father was still out scouting for beef jerky.

I had scarcely put the phone down when Constance hurried up the path, oblivious to the drizzle. She bounced through the door like a red-striped beach ball, wearing an unbelted blue smock, red turtleneck, red hosiery, and blue canvas sneakers. Her cheeks were puffed and as red as her sweater and her eyes bulged with important news. She looked as if she might explode any second and rain red-and-blue rags all over everything.

"I need your professional opinion," she said.

"As an herbalist?"

"No. As a lawyer."

The second consultation in two days—Thyme and Seasons was beginning to feel like a legal-aid clinic. "Former lawyer," I reminded her. "I'm still in good standing with the bar, but I don't do law anymore, Constance. It's hazardous to my health."

This was true. In the last year I practiced law, my blood pressure was creeping toward redline and I was living on stress pills. When I realized I was fast becoming a bonafide Type A personality, I knew it was time to run from the law. That, and knowing I was alive only because somebody else wasn't—a psycho client whose case I'd lost early in my career and who came after me when he got out of prison.

"But I need your advice," Constance said.

"You want a legal opinion, go see Charlie Lipton. He'll take good care of you." Charlie Lipton's law office was down the block, in a gentrified frame cottage painted a modest gray and green. Charlie's a competent lawyer, according to Ruby. He'd represented her in her divorce action.

"I can't talk to Charlie. I need to talk to a woman. It's—" Constance stopped with a hissing sound. "It'd be too embarrassin' to talk to a man about this . . . this *thang*."

"Why?"

"Because it has to do with, well, sex."

I raised my eyebrows. "You want to talk to a lawyer about sex? Isn't that what psychiatrists are for?"

Constance's nostrils flared. "Not *that* kind of sex. This sex is . . . well, different."

I was hooked. I like gossip as much as the next person. And you have to admit—different sex is more interesting than ordinary sex. "Okay, so tell me," I said.

Constance balanced on her toes and bounced nervously a time or two. "I've just heard, from somebody who knows, that Ms. Kotner and Jo Gilbert were . . ." Her voice squeaked, like a balloon when you pinch the neck and let the air out. Her cheeks puffed. "Were, well, lovers."

Lovers? Jo and Roz? *Lovers?*

Constance nodded several times, eyeing me to see my reaction.

Lovers. At first glance, improbable. It wasn't a question of heterosexual morality. Jo would have brushed that question aside as irrelevant: what she wanted to do, she simply did, regardless of what people thought. And as far as I was concerned, Jo had the right to determine her own sexual preference, just as I did.

No, it was a question of personality. Jo had been stern and often unyielding, a woman of strong convictions and a stronger will that she wielded with dignity and fairness. I had respected her for her strength of character, her intelligence, her independence. The idea of her with Roz—whom I felt to be shallow and egocentric, a childish airhead—was almost offensive to me. Surely there was nothing about Roz that would have attracted Jo.

Or was there?

Roz was physically attractive, certainly. Sexy, even. Maybe Roz's physical attractions—the porcelain skin, the full breasts, the sexy legs, combined with her delicate fragility and her youth—had appealed to Jo. Maybe it was a simple matter of sexual attraction, easily acceptable between a woman and a man; less conventional but certainly no less strong between two women.

And while I found Roz silly and superficial, I'd only been acquainted with her recently. Fame and fortune, particularly fortune, changed people. Maybe it had changed Roz. Or maybe—and this was even harder to contemplate—maybe it was her very playfulness, her childishness that appealed to Jo. Maybe lively, vivacious Roz gave Jo a sparkle that Jo's disciplined self-control wouldn't allow her to experience for herself. Perhaps Roz touched a vulnerable spot, opening Jo to feelings that she otherwise denied.

And what about Roz? What was there in Jo that would have attracted her? One thing came to mind immediately—Jo's unfailing strength and stability. To Roz, perhaps Jo's very maturity and settledness were appealing. Perhaps Jo cared for her, took care of her. Perhaps Jo was mother and father to her, as well as lover.

The possible relationship was beginning to seem less improbable. It was also beginning to seem a little scary. For love can turn to hate, and hate can turn to murder. I might have found the motive I'd been looking for.

"Who told you this?" I asked.

Constance's flush grew darker. "I can't say," she muttered. "A journalist doesn't reveal her sources."

"Journalist? Constance, you're not—"

"That's why I need legal advice," Constance broke in. "The story about Ms. Kotner's leavin' show business is a big scoop, but it's goin' to break in Washington and L.A. too." She cleared her throat. "If *this* story broke here—the one about Ms. Kotner's relationship with Jo, I mean—I'd have an exclusive." Her voice dropped on the last word, as if it were sacred.

"If the *Enterprise* breaks a story about Rosalind Kotner's lesbian relationship with her former landlady," I said firmly, "Arnold Seidensticker will be hauled into court so fast he'd pee his pants. You too," I added. "And wait until you get a load of the battery of barracudas Senator Howard Keenan will turn loose on you."

Constance's round eyes got rounder. "Senator Keenan? Why for the Lord's sake would *he*—?"

"Why, for the Lord's sake, of course," I said. "Isn't he the champion of the Moral Majority?" I leaned forward, emphasizing my words. "Visualize this scene, Constance. It's Monday morning. Senator Keenan—deacon in the church, experienced politician with aspirations for the White House—has just announced his engagement to Rosalind Kotner, famous television personality. Suddenly one of his aides runs into the room and hands him your front-page story. His fiancée is a lesbian. An hour later, the *Washington Post* and *The New York Times* pick the story off the AP wire. What do you think he's going to do? Come on, Constance, get *real*!"

Constance stepped back. She was silent for a moment, rerunning the scenario in her mind. Her face was pale, but she wasn't ready to give up yet. "But what if it's true? How can I be sued if I write the *truth*?"

I sighed. "Would you like a taste of the pretrial depositions?"

"Pretrial what?"

I folded my arms across my chest, pulled my eyebrows together, narrowed my eyes, thrust my chin forward, and spoke in my most aggressive cross-examination tone. "Ms. Letterman, this allegation of yours—it's quite fantastic, incredible, really. How do you know it to be true? On what occasions did you personally see the two women in question having sexual intercourse?"

"It wasn't me," Constance admitted nervously. "But my source is sure—"

"Ah, *hearsay*." I made it a dirty word. "Tell me—on what occasions does your *source*"—the word dripped irony—"claim to have seen the two women having intercourse?"

Constance bit her lip. "Actually, I don't reckon . . ."

"Hearsay," I said savagely. "Gossip. Innuendo. Slander. Libel." Dirty word after dirty word. I leaned forward, threatening. "Just who is your source, Ms. Letterman?"

Constance hunched her shoulders and buried her hands in the pockets of her denim smock. "A . . . a journalist can't reveal—"

I leaned back and relaxed, assuming my own voice again. "It'll be settled out of court by the *Enterprise*'s insurance company for—oh, say, ten, twelve million. Maybe more. Including, of course, your public apology. *And* your resignation. And what do you suppose

Cousin Arnold will do to you after that?"

Constance's cheeks looked shriveled and her shoulders were pulled in. She was deflating rapidly. "It's a sorry day for America when—"

I stopped her. "You asked for my advice, Constance? You got it. If I were you, I'd back off this story so far I couldn't even *smell* it."

"But I still think—" Constance began. Her voice was a whimper.

"What you think and what you can print without asking for a libel suit are two entirely different things," I said emphatically. "Stay away from it."

"But do *you* believe it?"

"It doesn't matter what I believe." I frowned. I'd just had a thought that made me uneasy. "Who have you told about this?"

"Nobody but you. I wouldn't want to jeopardize my scoop, would I?"

"Well, don't tell anybody," I said. Constance Letterman probably had the brains to see that she couldn't print an unfounded allegation, especially a sizzler like this one. If she didn't, Arnold Seidensticker would certainly be smart enough to quash it before it got into print. But if the person who told Constance had also told somebody else, the rumor was probably flying around Pecan Springs at the speed of light. The person who was peddling this story—whether it was factual or not was irrelevant—*had* to be stopped.

I made my voice gentle. "You know, Constance, Roz isn't the only one who could be hurt by this. Who told you?"

Constance pulled herself up, clutching the last shred

of her professional identity like a drowning person clinging to a chunk of floating Styrofoam. "A journalist can't—"

"Bullshit," I said firmly. "Even if it doesn't get into print, a rumor like this one could cut Meredith up pretty badly. Her mother's reputation is as much at stake as Roz's, even if Jo is dead." I paused, thinking. "In fact, maybe that's the purpose behind this little rumor. Maybe it's designed to disgrace Jo and discredit the Anti-Airport Coalition."

"Oh," Constance said, fluttering, "I don't think Violett would—"

"Violett? *Violett Hall* told you this?" I never would have guessed that shy, shrinking Violett could define the word "lesbian," let alone bring herself to use it in a sentence.

Constance's mouth trembled. "I didn't mean to . . . she told me not to . . . I wish I hadn't . . ."

"How does Violett know?"

"I asked, but she wouldn't say. I don't think it's the kind of thang somebody would *tell* her, though. I mean, I don't think it's—what did you call it? Hearsay?"

I agreed. It was hard to imagine anybody bringing up the word "sex" with Violett, much less "lesbian sex." "Maybe Violett lied," I said.

"The way it came up, I don't think so," Constance replied. "I was in my office in the Emporium this mornin', and she came in to pay the rent. She didn't look too good, like she hadn't slept. So to cheer her up, I told her about Ms. Kotner sellin' her company to Disney and marryin' Senator Keenan." She flushed guiltily. "I know I wasn't supposed to mention it 'til Ms. Kotner said so, but I didn't think tellin' Violett would . . . Anyway, when she heard, she got all funny-lookin' round the eyes. 'Rosalind Kotner is a wicked, wicked woman,' she said. She sort of burst out with it, like it was dammed up inside her. That's when she told me about the . . . the *thang* between Ms. Kotner and Jo." She shook her head. "The way she said it, it was like she didn't really want to, but it just had to come out, if you know what I mean. It was too quick to be a lie. And anyway, I don't think Violett has it in her to lie about . . . sex." She made a prim mouth. "She's got this thang about sex. She's a very religious person. She goes to church twice every Sunday and to Wednesday prayer meetin'."

"Going to church doesn't keep people from lying," I replied. "It doesn't keep them from having sex, either, thank God." I looked up as a woman came into the shop, carrying several pots of lemon thyme, southernwood, and lamb's ears that she had picked up outside. "I'd like to pay for these, please," she said, in the kind of voice that's aimed to summon the hired help from their slothful ways.

I counted the plants and multiplied times a dollar twenty-nine. "Is there anything else?"

"Yes," the woman said. I recognized her as one of Ruby's regular customers. She was a tall, striking woman with dramatic sloe eyes framed by unruly dark hair. She wore a long red cape over a black turtleneck sweater and black slacks. "I called a couple of days ago about *Aconitum vulparia*—wolfsbane. I'm looking for seeds. Do you have any?"

"No," I said, "all the aconitums are highly toxic, and I don't get much call for either the plants or the seeds. I can give you a source, though." I began to search under the counter for a catalog. Several mail-order companies specialize in odd herbs and plants like the aconitums.

"I have to go, China," Constance said. She was completely shriveled up now, totally deflated. Her eagerness about her potential story had evaporated. "Thanks for the advice."

Just to be sure, I gave her one last warning. "Take it from an expert," I said, straightening up with the catalog in my hand. "Lawsuits are no fun." She nodded and left.

The woman leafed through the catalog, took down the address and ordering information, and paid for her plants.

"What's your interest in *Aconitum vulparia*?" I asked. "It's so toxic that most people are afraid of it." The most notorious of the aconitums, monkshood, is poisonous from the root to the pollen. Native Americans used it to poison arrow tips for wolf hunts, and to treat rheumatism and the early phases of pneumonia. As a sedative and for the treatment of pain and fever, it's still one of the principal pharmaceuticals in Chinese medicine.

The woman turned her piercing eyes on me. "I collect poisonous plants," she said coolly, picked up her pots of herbs, and left. I grinned. Some people raise piranhas, others walk barefoot through rattlesnakes, and still others cultivate poisonous plants. It takes all kinds.

The woman was on her way out when McQuaid showed up. "Thank God," I said fervently.

McQuaid raised an eyebrow. "That wasn't quite what I was expecting. You found my note?"

"Yeah. Thanks for doing the dishes."

McQuaid's nod was slightly aloof. He was still smarting from the night before. "Hank's got the truck finished. Want to take me? Then you can have your car."

"Fantastic," I said. My hands were itching to get to Jo's boxes. "Let me check with Ruby." McQuaid went out to the car and I put my head into The Crystal Cave to ask Ruby to watch the shop.

Ruby was on her knees in front of the minerals cabinet, rearranging quartz crystals on a black velvet cloth. "Sure," she said to my request, "if you'll trade me an hour this afternoon. I've got an errand to run." She didn't betray any animosity about our discussion the day before. That's Ruby. *She* never carries a grudge. I guess men are just different.

"Fine," I said. "If I have to leave, Laurel's available." I didn't ask her what her errand was. I just hoped it didn't have anything to do with Arnold Seidensticker. I had enough to worry about as it was. But I thought I should tell her what had happened. "Jo's house was burgled last night," I said.

Ruby stared up at me. "Burgled! Somebody broke in?"

"That's the usual method," I replied dryly. I hesitated, wondering whether to tell her my suspicion about Roz. I decided against it, at least for the moment. If I told her that, I'd have to tell her about the letters, and from there on, the story got complicated.

Ruby's face set in hard lines. "It must have been Seidensticker," she said grimly. "I'll bet he heard that Jo uncovered something that could stop the airport. He was looking for it."

I sighed. "There isn't time to argue with you now, Ruby. I've got to take McQuaid to get his pickup. How about coming over for dinner tonight? We can talk about it then."

"Great," Ruby said. "I made a pot of chili last night, and there's enough to feed both of us and then some. If I bring it, will you mix up a batch of your terrific jalapeño cornbread?"

I nodded. "About seven, huh?" Ruby's chili took second place in the last San Marcos Chilympiad, where you can taste some of the most soul-searing chili in the world. She makes hers with home-cured venison sausage from the deer her brother-in-law provides her, and Lord knows what else. It's worth a batch of cornbread.

"My friend Mary Richards is showing some of her art at the University Faculty Show," Ruby suggested. "Maybe we could go over after dinner."

"Great idea," I said. I figured that by evening, I'd be ready for a little R and R to get my mind off things.

It took about fifteen minutes to deliver McQuaid to Hank's, where his blue Ford pickup, complete with new water pump, was waiting. Back at my place, I put the boxes on the kitchen table and turned the burner on under the copper kettle. I felt the need of a mug of strong tea.

The boxes were bound with duct tape, and tied together with string. There was a note on top. "For China Bayles," it said. As I cut the string, peeled off the tape, and opened the first box, I felt myself shifting into the defense-attorney mindset: setting up hypotheticals, framing questions, working methodically through possible answers. Meredith hadn't turned up any personal papers, so if Jo had kept Roz's letters, they were almost certainly here. And if Roz and Jo had been lovers, as Violett claimed, their correspondence probably did more than just hint at their relationship. That could explain why Roz was anxious to get her hands on the letters—so anxious that she might have risked breaking into Meredith's house to search for them. On the other hand, maybe it wasn't much of a risk, compared to what could happen if the letters fell into unfriendly hands. Obviously, the fiancée of a Senator who was being touted as a presidential candidate wouldn't relish rumors about a lesbian affair.

On top of the papers in the first box was a note in Jo's handwriting. "China," it said, "I'd rather Meredith didn't read these. Otherwise, do as you think best with them." I laid it aside. If the letters contained references to Jo's affair with Roz, I wasn't surprised that she didn't want Meredith to read them. The fact of the affair, if it *was* a fact, probably also explained why she had kept her daughter at arm's length, out of her life. She hadn't wanted Meredith to know about Roz.

The first box was full of rubber-banded packets of letters still in their envelopes. In Jo's tidy fashion, a slip of paper with a name written on it was tucked under the rubber band of each packet, identifying (I assumed) the correspondent. I took the packets out of the boxes and laid them in front of me on the table. There were five packets. The thickest was labeled "Roz."

The second box was heavier than the first. In it were six spiral-bound notebooks, their pages filled with Jo's writing. Her journals. I flipped through the top one quickly. The last entry, dated about three months before, was on the last page of the book. Somewhere there must be another journal—the *current* one. But where?

I put the lid on the box and set it on the floor. If the letters turned up nothing, I'd read the journals to see what references Jo had made to her relationship with Roz.

The teakettle was boiling. I poured water over a spoonful of lemon herb tea in my favorite earthenware pot and left it to steep while I settled down at the kitchen table. But when I opened the packet tagged "Roz," I found something unexpected. A document folded into a paper sleeve. Roz's will. When I quickly scanned through the usual boilerplate to the named beneficiary, I discovered that in the event of Roz's death, everything of which she died possessed passed to her "beloved friend and faithful life's companion, Josephine Gilbert."

I folded the document and put it back in the sleeve. There wasn't any way to tell whether this will had been superseded by a later one; after all, Jo had just rewritten *her* will. But unless Roz had made a new one—and if I knew anything about people's will-making habits, I'd bet she wouldn't do it until she was actually married—Jo was Roz's sole beneficiary. And even if she'd made a new will, *this* one was ample evidence that her feelings for Jo went deeper than casual friendship. If I were Roz, I'd be as anxious to get my hands on this as I was to get my letters.

I laid the will aside. The letters were arranged by date, oldest on the bottom and the most recent on top. I counted quickly. There were forty-two, covering a period of about four years. Better than half were clustered in the first year, with the rest spaced out over the next three. There were only two letters in the last few months. I couldn't know how many letters Jo had written to Roz. No doubt Roz had already destroyed them.

I picked up the oldest letter and unfolded it. The paper was pink (naturally), slightly fragrant, and worn at the creases, where it had been folded and unfolded many times. I read it once quickly, and then again, more slowly. Yes. Their relationship had not been simply a friendship. The letter was full of endearments, not in themselves evidence, of course—my aunt Mildred liberally sugars her letters to me with "dears" and "sweethearts," and we haven't seen each other since I graduated from high school. But beyond that, there were unabashed and explicit references to lovemaking, to nights spent together, to the longing of parted lovers. It was an eloquent letter, overflowing with declarations and entreaties. To Roz's lover, it must have been intimate testimony of unreserved, enduring affection. To an objective reader, it was a foolish letter. It was sufficient, by itself, to destroy. By itself, it could wreck any hopes that Roz might have of becoming the Senator's wife and, in due time, the nation's First Lady.

I poured an earthenware mug of lemony tea and

sipped it, feeling as if I had just peeked into somebody's bedroom while they were getting it on. I didn't have to read any more of the letters to know how Roz and Jo had felt about each other when Roz left Pecan Springs for fame and fortune in the Big Apple. But their feelings had evidently changed. I had to read some of the later letters to know whose feelings had changed, and how. I took the last two off the top of the stack.

The next-to-last letter was dated six weeks ago. It was brief, only a couple of pages, and cool—not frigid, but not terribly friendly. Roz had obviously cooled. Had Jo? Without her letters I couldn't be sure, but reading between the lines I suspected that she hadn't. I was more sure of it when I read Roz's last paragraph:

> I must ask you once again to send my letters back. I realize that you want to keep them for sentimental reasons. But what I said to you over the phone last night is true. I don't intend to continue our relationship. Whether you accept it or not, Jo, there's nothing more between us. I have been seeing someone else—a man—and I am now quite certain that something will come of it. Please send the letters *immediately*.
>
> Roz

I was beginning to piece things together. The phone conversation Roz referred to must have been the one Meredith remembered—the argument between Jo and Roz that seemed to upset Jo. Jo must have been desperately hurt by Roz's rejection and her insistence on erasing all traces of their relationship, a hurt that she obviously couldn't share with her daughter. I put the letter back and took out the last one, dated only two weeks ago. It was shorter and more curt, written fast and hard, with savage underlining.

> I don't understand why you refuse to return the letters. If you think that by holding onto them you can convince me to reopen our relationship, you're wrong, *wrong, WRONG!!* If you think you can use the letters to destroy my new relationship, think again. Don't play games. You'll be the only loser.
>
> R.

I stared at the angry words, trying to feel the depth of Jo's pain when she read them, trying to put myself into that moment. Had she knotted up inside with a pain even sharper than the pain of her cancer? Had her hurt, her disappointment, her despairing grief been powerful enough to compel her to kill herself?

And there were darker questions. I'd once helped to defend a client in an ugly case where incriminating letters had led to blackmail, which in turn had led to the murder of someone who threatened to tell everything to the newspapers. Had Roz feared that Jo would go public with their secret? Not likely. Roz would know that Jo—however firmly she stood for her private convictions—would not publicly brand herself a lesbian in this rednecked community. If Arnold Seidensticker and his buddies found out that Jo was gay, they'd use it to discredit her efforts to stop the airport.

But what if Roz feared that Jo might reveal the truth, not to the community, but to Senator Keenan? What if Jo, in a flash of anger and terrible despair, had threatened to tell Roz's fiancé about her past, perhaps even to show him the letters? In the game Roz was playing, the stakes were extraordinarily high—the Keenan millions, a chance at the White House. What if Roz had decided she couldn't trust Jo to keep her mouth shut? What if—?

And there I was, right back to where I'd been the night before. Only now, I had a motive and the proof—the letters—to back it up. A motive for murder. What was I going to do about it?

After a moment, I bundled the letters and put them back into the box. Then I tied both boxes together and carried them into my bedroom. In the walk-in closet, I pushed the wicker laundry hamper aside. Behind it, there's a piece of loose paneling that conceals an opening into the space under the stairs where I keep a few things I don't want to risk losing—like the nine-millimeter Beretta my father gave me years ago, when he'd taught me to shoot. The only time he ever spent with me was on the range, and I prided myself on learning well, to please him, to show him that girls could be as good with guns as boys. I'd used the Beretta only once since then. When I think about it now, the fact that I used it in self-defense doesn't really matter. Somebody is dead—somebody very sick—and it was my gun that did it. My finger that squeezed the trigger, deliberately, smoothly, just the way my father taught me. I wasn't sure why I kept the Beretta. To remind myself, maybe, of how easy it is to step over to the other side.

I lifted aside the paneling, shoved in the boxes, and put the paneling back up. Then I pushed the hamper across it. If Roz took a notion to ransack the place, she'd have to get very lucky to find what she was after.

Then I went back into the kitchen, poured another mug of tea, and took it to the rocking chair, where I sipped it and thought. By the time I had finished my tea, I knew what I was going to do.

CHAPTER 10

The drizzle had stopped, the gray had given way to blue, and the sun was shining. Lounging comfortably in a white wicker chair on the small patio outside the cottage, Roz was the picture of late-morning leisure. She was wearing a silky pink robe, velvet-sashed, with a pink satin rose in one velvet lapel and matching pink satin mules with pink net rosettes. She had already put on makeup and her dusty blond hair was softly arranged. There was a glass of tomato juice, no doubt spiced with her morning's ration of garlic, on the wicker table at her elbow, and she was reading Thursday's *New York Times*, which is always two days late getting to Pecan Springs.

Roz put down the paper when she saw me coming through the herb garden. "Good morning, China," she said, smiling. "How *nice* to see you." She gestured at the pink rose gracing the stone wall over her head. "I'm enjoying your lovely place."

I sat down, returning her smile. "I haven't been a very good hostess, I'm afraid. I meant to ask if you wanted to do something together yesterday evening. I hope you weren't too bored all by yourself."

"I wasn't by myself," Roz replied comfortably, sipping her juice. "I visited an old friend in Austin, somebody who goes back to the days when I was doing commercials and children's theater there. We had a great evening talking about old times."

I looked at Roz. Was she lying? I could probably find out with a few pointed questions, but I didn't want to alert her. I'd thought of a better way to make her show her hand.

"I'm glad you enjoyed yourself," I replied casually. "Unfortunately, Meredith didn't have such a pleasant evening. Somebody broke into Jo's house."

Roz's blue eyes widened. "Why, China—how awful! Did they take anything valuable?"

"Some antique silver," I said. "But there was quite a mess—books and papers all over the floor, drawers pulled out, that sort of thing. Meredith was very upset, of course."

"Do the police have any idea who did it?"

I shook my head. "The chief of police feels it was probably kids, looking for drug money. There were no prints." I hesitated. "Actually, I'm telling you because I don't want you to worry."

"Worry? About what?"

"About your letters. I was afraid you might hear about the break-in and think that they'd been taken. But that isn't the case. They're safe at my house, under my bed."

Roz's gasp was authentic. "*You* have the letters?"

"Isn't that just the way?" I said, spreading my hands. "There you were, asking Meredith, and I was the one who had them. I wish I'd known."

"You *didn't* know?"

"I'm afraid not," I said ruefully. "Sometime in the last few weeks, apparently, Jo put her journals and letters into a couple of boxes and stuck a note on them, asking me to dispose of them as I—"

Roz looked at me, her face carefully composed. "Journals?" There was a pause. "I didn't know Jo kept journals."

"Apparently she did," I replied. "There's a box full of them. She seems to have documented her life very fully, at least back through the 1970s. I guess that was before you knew her."

Roz picked up her juice glass, then put it back down again. "How . . . interesting."

"Anyway," I went on, "Meredith found the boxes and gave them to me, with Jo's note. At her mother's request, she didn't open them. That's why she didn't know what's in them. I didn't open the boxes, either, until this morning. That's why I didn't know. Sorry. It's rather a mess."

"Oh, that's all right, as long as the letters are safe." Roz swallowed, her jaw working. "You haven't . . . read them?"

I rolled my eyes. "Roz, you wouldn't *believe* how busy I've been. I kept meaning to get to those boxes, but somehow the time got away from me. I opened them for the first time just a little while ago. That's what I wanted to tell you. Ruby's coming over for dinner this evening, and we're going to an art show at the university. I won't get back until late. So I've put everything back in the boxes. They'll be safe enough under my bed until I can get them sorted. Tomorrow's Sunday, and I'll have some time to get the stuff organized."

Roz leaned forward eagerly. "I've got a better idea, China. Why don't I just come with you now and get my letters? That'll be one less batch of stuff you'll have to sort."

"Gosh, thanks, Roz," I said. "It's a generous offer, and it *would* make my job easier. But I'm afraid there's a problem."

"What is it?" Roz asked faintly.

I straightened up. "You see, since Jo left instructions to me to dispose of her papers as I see fit, the court views me as her literary executor." That statement would stand up in court, but what was coming definitely *wouldn't*. "I have the impression that she thought her papers would be of public interest. As you know, she was a prominent person here in Pecan Springs, and she made a great many contributions to the community. I just contacted Dr. Alice Dale, the director of the CTSU library. She's enthusiastic about our designating the university library as the repository for Jo's letters and journals—in fact, *all* her personal papers."

Roz's face turned ashen. "The *library*?"

I put on a pleased look. "Yes, isn't it wonderful? Alice says the papers will go to the Notable Women of Texas Collection, where they'll be available to the public. Meredith is thrilled with the idea, and when I called Mayor Perkins—" I clucked my tongue, laying it on thicker just for the hell of it. "Well, of course, you understand what an honor this is for Pecan Springs. The mayor hopes that Jo's friends will create an endowment to see that the papers are properly cataloged and displayed. She's asked me to approach *you* for the first contribution to—"

Roz's knuckles were white as she clutched the arm of the wicker chair. "But my letters! What about my letters?"

I leaned back, relaxed, very much the lawyer. In fact, I'd had to do some research on a topic rather similar to this for one of the legal education seminars that lawyers have to attend every year. "You know, the law is a funny thing. It splits hairs. With regard to letters, courts hold that they are copyrightable, and that the author of a letter has exclusive rights in it."

"There you are. Exclusive rights."

I held up my hand. "The recipient, however, owns the physical document—the paper and ink with which the letter was written. The courts have held that the recipient may show the letter to others or deposit it in a library or archive and set the terms of access."

Roz uncrossed her legs nervously and then recrossed them, showing a bit of well-cared-for thigh. One pink satin mule fell off a shapely foot, but she made no move to retrieve it. "Terms of access? What does that mean?"

"Jo, or in this case, her representative, can decide who the library permits to see the letters. You, as the owner of the copyright, can copy the letters for your collection. And of course you have first right of publication—"

"Publication? But what if I don't *intend* to publish them? What if I'd rather burn them?"

"I'm afraid you can't burn them," I said regretfully. "They are the property of Jo's estate. But you can prohibit their publication. Their verbatim publication, that is."

"What do you mean?"

"The copyright holder can deny anyone the right to quote from the letters. But scholars or writers who have access to Jo's material can use the information in it. The factual content is not copyrightable, you see—only the expressive content." I smiled, showing all my teeth. "That's what belongs to you, Roz. The expressive content."

Roz pulled herself together. "I don't want anybody using that personal information," she said. "I'll sue."

I shook my head. "Then you'll lose. You might consult Salinger v. Random House Inc.," I added helpfully. "Court of Appeals, Second Circuit, early 1987, I think it was. I can dig up the citation if you're interested. In that case, the Court held that Ian Hamilton, the biographer of novelist J. D. Salinger, was entitled to use the facts he learned in certain personal letters written by Salinger and donated by their recipients to Harvard, Princeton, and—"

"But . . . but what about privacy?" Roz asked. Her desperation was so thinly veiled that I might have felt sorry for her if I weren't convinced that she was our burglar. And if it weren't for the suspicion that she'd had something to do with Jo's death. "Don't I—doesn't Jo have a right to *privacy*?"

I dismissed her question with a wave. "Meredith and

I discussed it this morning, and we both agree. There might be a skeleton or two in Jo's closet, but we think it's important for the lives of public figures—especially women—to be made totally available, without reservation. Don't you agree?"

Roz was twisting her fingers in her lap. "Even if someone else gets hurt?" Her question was almost a whimper.

I paused. "Of course, that's a consideration. But scholars are objective. The facts, whatever they are, will be presented with great impartiality. I'm sure no one who knew Jo or loved her has *anything* to fear. Anyway, neither Meredith nor I can think of anyone who would be particularly hurt. Can you?"

Roz evaded my question. "It sounds as if you've already made up your mind."

"To donate the papers to the library? Well, yes, actually I have. But it's not just my decision," I added cheerfully. "Meredith is certainly in favor of it, and the mayor, and Alice Dale." I gave her a comforting smile. "Your letters will be in very safe hands. They are a valuable resource for scholars to study and—"

Roz gave a weak nod.

"I can see how pleased you are," I said. I stood up. "Now, if you'll excuse me, I have to get back to the shop. As I said, I'll be out until rather late this evening. But I'll be home all day tomorrow, if you'd like to look at the letters and decide which ones the library should copy for you."

Roz stood up too. "Thank you," she said. She seemed to be holding herself together with a great effort.

I went back to the shop. Ruby was signing the delivery ticket for the herb order that had just come in. I checked the register total to see what the sales had been like while I'd been gone. "It looks like we didn't have a thundering herd of customers."

Ruby ticked off the sales on her fingers. "Two books, some rose-scented soap, and the last of that basil vinegar, over there on the corner shelf." She pointed.

I took note of the empty spot. "Guess it's time to make some more vinegar." Making and bottling herb vinegars is one of my favorite evening tasks, and I love looking at the rows of sparkling bottles on the shelves. It must be the same satisfaction that country women have when they look at the rows of canned green beans on the cellar shelves. "Thanks for minding the shop, Ruby."

"My turn this afternoon," she reminded me. "I'd like to leave at three."

I hesitated. "Would it be okay if I phoned Laurel and asked her to come over? I've got something to do, too."

"Sure. It's not like we've got customers coming out of our ears."

I pulled my brows together. "Listen, Ruby, about the show tonight—"

Ruby looked annoyed. "You're not folding on me, are you?"

"No, but the plans have changed a little. I'm afraid I have to skip Mary's show, and I need your help."

"Help with what?"

"For after-dinner entertainment, we're doing a stake-out."

"A stakeout?" Ruby asked warily. "Who are we staking out?"

"You'll see," I said. "Come at seven. Wear jeans, huh? And a dark shirt." If I'd had my druthers, I might have wished for McQuaid as a stakeout partner. He's had a lot of experience with this sort of thing, and he's got about sixty pounds more brawn than Ruby. But McQuaid was camping with Brian. Ruby and I would have to handle it together.

Ruby was looking dubious. "What are we going to *do*?"

"I've baited a little trap," I said cheerfully. "We're going to wait for a rat to break and enter."

But before tonight's stakeout, I had to take care of something else. Laurel came at three to watch both stores for the last couple of hours before closing. I opened the herb order and took out the valerian that Violett had asked for.

Valerian smells like a locker room. It should be stored in a tightly lidded container, away from anything that absorbs odor. Away from cats, too. Most cats think it's even sexier than catnip, and go moderately bananas over it. But valerian is a strong natural sedative, loaded with something called valepotriates that relax muscles, calm nervous energy, and release tension. Unfortunately, there's a misleading similarity between the name of the herb and Valium, which is a potent and addictive synthetic drug made from petrochemicals. It's surprising how many people still believe that the two are related. I knew first-hand about the dangers of Valium, because it was one of Leatha's drugs of choice. *Valeriana officinalis* is entirely different. If insomnia was Violett's problem, she was right to ask for it.

I sacked a couple of ounces of the herb and stuck the sack in my purse. Then I said good-bye to Laurel and headed next door, to the Craft Emporium. When I got there, I found a CLOSED sign hung on Violett's Doll House. I went in search of Constance, whom I located in her broom-closet office under the grand staircase. There are brooms still in it, hanging on the back wall, and there's a mop bucket under the plywood shelf that serves as her desk. The shelf is always littered with curls of adding machine tape and mounds of bills that seem to grow higher every day.

Constance was never cut out to be a businesswoman, and her relationship to the Craft Emporium is one of harried struggle. When I think of her and the Emporium, I imagine a frazzled chipmunk trying to push a large, balky white elephant. Constance has spunk, but she's met her match in the Emporium's leaky roof, sagging floors, and unreliable plumbing. Not to mention its itinerant tenants whose cash flow is like a West Texas creek—intermittent in good times, dried up in a drought.

As Constance moved her pudgy elbows, a drift of papers and pink phone slips fluttered to the floor. There was a chocolate stain on her blue denim jumper, and her red turtleneck was wet under the arms. The broom closet isn't air-conditioned, and it was hot and stuffy. Her perm had frizzed out all over her head, and she'd taken her shoes off and propped her fat, red-stockinged feet on the mop bucket.

"Have you seen Violett?" I asked.

"She looked like death warmed over. I sent her home." Constance fixed me with brightly avid eyes. "You know she had a nervous breakdown once?"

I raised my eyebrows. "Violett? No, I didn't. When?"

"Just after old Mrs. Hall died. Violett took care of her mother for, oh, nine-ten years maybe, not gettin' out of the house except to go to church and the grocery store. The only other thang she did was make dolls. When the old lady died, she went all to pieces. Real basket case."

I made a sympathetic noise. It sounded as if Violett had been thoroughly victimized by life's circumstances.

Constance picked up a stray piece of adding machine tape that had just snaked from the pile, then she wrenched her attention back to the conversation. "She was totally out of it for a few days, hysterical, throwing thangs, carryin' on—mostly about sex."

"Violett?" I was surprised. Meek, mild Violett was one of the least violent people I'd ever met. It was hard to imagine her getting up the energy to sneeze, much less throw something.

"Really, you wouldn't have known the poor thang. Out of her gourd. Even the minister was embarrassed, and of course he hears *ever'thang*, people's sins, lust, shopliftin', all that. Finally, a couple of deacons hauled her off to the state hospital in Austin. She was a whole lot quieter when she got back, didn't talk about sex, didn't talk much at all, actually." She pursed her mouth. "She didn't even want to do her dolls. But after I told her she ought to open a shop and fixed up the nursery for her, she got better. Those dolls are her life. The dolls, and those cats and birds of hers. They're like her children." With an exasperated glance at the offending adding machine tape, Constance impaled it on a wicked-looking spindle.

I frowned. "What's this about sex?"

"Well, like I started to tell you this mornin', Violett's got this obsession."

"How do you know?"

"Well, back when she was havin' her nervous breakdown, I was the only one who offered to sit with her." She gave a short, scornful laugh. "And me a Presbyterian. Wouldn't you think those deacons' wives would've been Christian enough to at least give an afternoon to the poor soul? But no, it was me, so I got treated to her ravin's for the better part of a week, before they hauled her off to Austin. Mostly what she carried on about was sex. Growin' up, she was her father's little girl. After he died, she was stuck at home with the old lady, with nothin' but the Bible and her dolls for company. Mrs. Hall wouldn't let her look sidewise at a man. Wouldn't even let her have a teevee." I could have said that not having a TV might be a healthy thing for one's sex drive, but I didn't. "Her ravin's were mostly about Miss Ima's boyfriend," she added with relish.

I raised both eyebrows. This was getting juicier by the minute. "Miss Ima had a *boyfriend*?" I asked. Ima and Erma Mason, twin sisters, both in their eighties, are Violett's closest neighbors. Miss Ima is vivacious and sprightly enough, but I hadn't heard anything about a boyfriend.

Constance moved her elbows and a few more pieces of paper drifted into her blue-denim lap. " 'Course, it was only old Sam Peavy. He comes over every couple of weeks to mow the grass and help Miss Ima and Miss Erma keep up the roses. But Violett took it into her head that Ima and old Sam were committin' sins of the flesh. I doubt Miss Ima gave a hoot what Violett said. She's had quite a checkered past. But it was *very* embarrassin' for poor Erma, because it was spring and the windows were open and she could hear every last word of Violett's carryings-on. You know Erma, so proper and genteel. It worried her no end that the neighbors might think there actually was somethin' between Ima and Sam Peavy. Especially her neighbor on the west, who's a Jehovah's Witness."

I reflected. If it weren't for the letters, Violett's story about Roz and Jo could be a figment of her hysterical imagination, like the story about Ima and her lawn-mowing lover. However, there *were* the letters.

Constance combed through the papers on her lap and found another adding machine tape. She glared at it balefully. "What I'm tellin' you is that Violett looked ever' bit as bad today as she did when she was havin' her nervous breakdown. That's why I sent her home."

"I guess I'd better stop by and see her," I said. "I've got some valerian she ordered. It might help."

But the herbs were only an excuse. I had to persuade Violett not to talk to anyone else about Roz and Jo—which was exactly what she might do, if she was as unstable as Constance thought. Meredith had enough to handle without having to deal with gossip about her mother's love life. But more importantly, there was Roz. If she was capable of slipping Jo a deadly combination of sleeping pills and booze to keep her quiet, what would she do if she found out that Violett was wholesaling her sex life to the public?

Constance hoisted herself out of her chair, and the papers drifted from her lap to the floor. "If you're goin' to Violett's, will you tell her something for me?"

"Sure. What is it?"

She pointed at a calendar on the wall. The first of the month had been circled in red. "You don't need to make a big fuss about it, but would you remind her about the rent? She brought it in this mornin', but when she heard about Roz and the Senator, she forgot to give it to me. I never like to let my tenants get behind on their rent."

I was tempted to tell her I didn't collect rents, but I wasn't sure she'd know I was joking.

I biked over to Violett's. Her house is in an older part of town, a tract of one-and two-story frame homes dating from before the First World War. The houses are shabby now, patched roofs green with moss, guttering gone, porches sagging, iris borders overgrown with yellow dock and quack grass. They're lived in either by their elderly and feeble owners, as decrepit as their property, or by renters who don't give a damn. The streets are poorly paved and full of potholes, or aren't paved at all. Either way, it's potential disaster for bike riders, so I had to pay attention to where I was going.

I knew where Violett lived, but I still had trouble finding the house. It was hidden behind a scrubby oak clump at the end of Juniper Street, a narrow lane with red cedar thick on either side. There was another house on Juniper once, but it burned down and now there's nothing left but a limestone chimney inhabited by bats and quarrelsome sparrows. Violett's only neighbors, Ima and Erma Mason, live on the next street over. Their backyard abuts Violett's backyard. I'm familiar with this part of the town's geography because the Mason sisters invite the garden club to meet in their yard once a year when their roses are in bloom. Two years ago, I was invited to teach the ladies to make rose potpourri. Ever since, when the roses bloom, Erma and Ima invite me to take all I want.

I parked my bike on the gravel lane and walked down a narrow brick path, laid in an ancient herringbone pattern and matted with grass. Violett's house was a two-story frame structure crouching behind an impenetrable tangle of agarita, fire thorn, and old rose canes. The white paint had long ago scaled from the weathered gray siding, the porch steps were splintered, and a gray shutter hung loose at one corner. A half dozen cats were lounging comfortably on the front porch—several plump orange tabbies, a couple of fluffy gray Persians, a shabby Manx, and one quite large, arrogant-looking Siamese. They all scattered except for the Siamese, who sniffed my jeans inquiringly and put a front paw firmly on my foot as I knocked at the door.

"Watch it, cat," I muttered. Some people are great cat fanciers. Me, I'm usually neutral. But this one seemed altogether too sure of himself. He blinked his blue eyes at me and put the other front paw on my foot.

On the third knock, the front door opened a crack and I heard Violett's voice, thin and reedy. "Thank you, no," she said. "I don't need any."

"It's China Bayles, Violett. I've brought your herbs."

"Oh," she said. Then, reluctantly, "Well, come in."

The door opened and I followed the cat into the semi-darkened living room, which smelled of furniture polish, dusty drapes, and stale cooking odors. Violett stood clutching a navy cardigan around her. I could see why Constance had sent her home. She had the look of someone teetering on the edge. Her hair was in strings, her eyes deeply shadowed; lines etched her mouth. There was a tic at the corner of her right eye.

Although I'd never actually been in Violett's house, the interior didn't surprise me. I could guess that the room we were standing in looked just as it had when her mother was alive. The walls were papered with large bouquets of mauve cabbage roses, faded to pinky-gray and green. The windows were draped with a heavy mauve brocade and curtained with white sheers that filtered the light. A high-backed purple plush sofa, heavily antimacassared, its seat cushions covered by a dusty rose chenille throw, stood against the left wall. Over the sofa hung a portrait of a haloed and bearded Jesus, hands clasped, gazing prayerfully in the direction of God. On the opposite wall, above an oval table with a large red-letter Bible open on it, hung several cheaply framed photos: a short, slender man with dark hair parted in the middle and slicked back on both sides, holding himself with rakish and daring bravado; the woman taller and heavier and more powerful, hair drawn severely away from her forehead, lips pursed, chilly, joyless. Several of the photos included, as a kind of afterthought, a spindly, solemn child with imploring eyes.

With a start of recognition, I glanced from the pale, faded child in the photos to the pale, faded woman standing nervously beside me. Violett's arms and legs were less spindly, but her whey-colored face was still solemn and her dull eyes implored—what? Affection? Recognition? An opportunity to be herself, to grow away from the meek, obedient daughter her mother had raised? But she'd never had a chance, trapped in this house by her mother and by her own sense of duty.

A movement caught my eye, a cat jumping up on the sofa, and I noticed the others drowsing like furry pillows on the sofa and chairs, one of them curled up around the pink bear that Violett had rescued from the tourist. Another cat sat on the small claw-footed maple-veneer coffee table in front of the sofa, giving itself a bath on the *People* magazine that featured Roz. It was an interesting tableau.

Violett tilted her head, listening. "He's about to sing."

I looked around. There was no one else in the room, no television, not even a radio. But I could hear a musical twittering and in a corner by a window I saw a covey of cages filled with birds—parakeets, cockatiels, finches, lovebirds. Every cage was lined with fresh newspaper, the cups were filled with water and seeds, and little bundles of lettuce were stuck through the bars. In one cage, a yellow-green canary raised its head and began to warble a lush, full-throated song, embroidered with trills and grace notes. The cascade of melody was so surprising that it made me catch my breath.

"How lovely!" I said.

"Isn't it?" Violett's eyes brightened like a mother whose child has been praised by the school principal. "His name is Petey."

"How many birds do you have?" I asked. I could have counted, but I'd probably miss some.

Petey's song seemed to have lifted Violett's spirits a little. "Twenty-two," she said. "And eighteen cats. At least at the moment. They keep coming, you know, and I hate to turn them away." She gave me what might have been a fragment of smile. "Some people have children. Would you like to see my dolls?"

I nodded, following her into the dining room, which was obviously her doll factory. The dining table and floor were littered with cloth scraps, ribbons, laces, and yarn. An old-fashioned treadle sewing machine in an oak cabinet, its wheel worn silver, sat at right angles to the table. Shelves along one wall held bolts of cloth, bags of stuffing, hanks of yarn, and dolls in various stages of completion. Shelves along the other wall held a dozen or more antique typewriters, all highly polished and carefully dusted.

"Those were Daddy's," Violett explained, seeing my

curious glance. "He collected and restored them. He let me dust them. Of course, I still do."

"Did you type his letters, too?" I asked, and then was immediately sorry because it sounded so tacky.

But Violett didn't notice. "No, I wanted to learn to type and get a job, but Mama was dead set against it. Anyway, he didn't write letters. Mama didn't either." She bent over and picked up the Siamese, who had wandered after us into the room. It squirmed uncomfortably in her arms, gave a sharply rebuking meow, and Violett put it down. "After I was born, Mama couldn't have any more," she added, as if that explained why her parents had no one to write to. "Mama always said it was a shame I couldn't have been a boy. But Daddy liked me a lot." She smiled a small, secret smile and touched one of the typewriters. "Sometimes he liked me even more than he liked Mama."

I shivered, feeling a sudden rush of sympathy mixed with horror. I could imagine Violett as the solemn, spindly legged young girl who had by her birth thwarted her stern, joyless mother's hopes for a son. And who had been liked a lot by her bold, rakish daddy.

I cleared my throat and pulled the sack of herbs out of my purse. "Here's the valerian you wanted."

Violett took the sack. "Thank you," she said. "I'll get your money." And then, remembering to be polite, "Maybe you'd like something to drink."

The kitchen was long and narrow, and had clearly once been a back porch. One wall was filled with green-painted cabinets under a white-curtained window. A green formica-topped table with chrome legs stood against the opposite wall, with three chrome-plated chairs. On the table was a yellow plastic rose in an empty vinegar bottle wound with red and yellow yarn, a wooden spice caddy with five glass bottles with red-and-yellow lids, and a wind-up alarm clock with a cracked face. The Good Shepherd hung on the wall over the table, beside a round wooden plaque painted with the same grace I remembered Gram saying over meals. "God is great and God is good. Now we thank Him for our food." The words brought Gram back sharply, bright white hair pinned in a loose knot with tortoise-shell combs, softly slurred New Orleans speech at odds with her sharply cut face and sharper blue eyes. It's odd how much clearer my grandmother's face is in my mind than Leatha's face, which always seems gray and blurry and out of focus.

The cat jumped up on one of the chairs, where he licked a paw and regarded me attentively. He was a large cat, lean and muscular, with an air of great poise and authority. His sleek body fur was fawn-colored, but his face, ears, feet, and tail looked as if they had been brushed with charcoal. His pale blue eyes were startling in his dark face.

Violett smiled at the cat, her first genuine smile. "Come, Pudding," she crooned, "does Mama's little sweetheart want his treat?"

Bored with it all, Pudding yawned, displaying two giant fangs.

Violett went to the refrigerator and took out a carton of cream. As she poured it into a bowl, the cat abandoned his indifference. With great dignity, he descended from the chair and stalked over to the bowl, tail twitching. He poised himself in front of it, bunched his black feet under his tawny belly, and began to lap cream with a pink tongue.

I suppressed a smile. Imperious, arrogant, in total command, the cat was definitely not Violett's little sweetheart. I wondered how he felt about being called Pudding.

I waited while Violett took a canned soft drink out of the small refrigerator. She divided it carefully into two glasses and put one down in front of me, without ice. Then she disappeared into what looked like a pantry. I heard the padded thump of a hamper lid, and she came out with her purse.

"How much do I owe you for the herbs?" she asked. When I told her, she counted out the coins and put those on the table too. Then she sat down across from me and sipped her soft drink.

I skipped the preamble and got right into it. "Constance told me what you told her about Roz Kotner and Jo Gilbert."

Violett pressed her lips together. "She promised not to tell."

I ignored that. "I'm curious to know who told you."

Violett's glass made a wet ring on the table. "Nobody." She got up and wiped the table carefully. Then she took two green-and-pink crocheted coasters off a shelf. She gave one to me and put the other under her glass. "I saw them myself."

I pulled in my breath. "Saw them?"

"In Jo Gilbert's kitchen. Through the window. They were kissing." She screwed up her mouth as if the thought, the words, were horribly foul. But she said it again, mouthing it, not ready to let it go. "*Kissing*."

"When?" I asked. "A long time ago? Recently?"

"After she left. She was back on a visit. I was walking home through the alley, the way I do when the weather's nice."

"Was that all you saw?"

She threw me a bitterly righteous glance. "Wasn't that enough? I could tell what was going on. Anybody could, anybody who had eyes. It was what the Bible warns us about in Genesis, chapter thirteen. 'But the men of Sodom were wicked and sinners before the Lord exceedingly.' The women, too," she added. "Just like *them*."

I leaned forward and took Violett's hands in mine. Her fingers were cold, stiff, like brittle twigs. "Violett," I said softly, "what you saw should be forgotten. You know how gossip is in this town—if people start talking, Jo's daughter could be hurt."

Violett jerked her hands back. "What do I care?" she asked angrily. Her voice coarsened and cracked and her anger brought color to her ash-gray face, firmness to her shoulders. "The daughter's none of my lookout. But Rosalind Kotner . . ." Tears appeared in her eyes, spilled onto her dry cheeks. "People ought to know what she's done. What she's done to me."

I frowned. What did Rosalind's affair with Jo have to do with Violett? "To you? What's she done to you?"

The anger blurred into something else—grief? loss? Her face wrenched with pain. "She made me a promise," she whispered. Her voice died and she began to tremble. The stiffness drained out of her body, as if she were dissolving. "But she broke it."

I leaned forward, trying to hold her gaze. "*What* promise, Violett?"

Violett's eyes slid away from mine. She hunched her shoulders, pulling her sweater together with one hand, mumbling something inaudible. She was suddenly an old woman, lost and alone in an unfriendly world.

"Tell me, Violett," I said softly. "You can trust me. I want to help."

Violett looked at me for a moment. Then she shook her head, thin-lipped, her face immobile. "I don't need your help to get what I'm owed," she said jerkily. "I don't need anybody's help. I know a way."

"Oh?" I made my voice even, casual. "Tell me about it."

Violett didn't respond. The cat finished his cream, walked to the vacant chair, and jumped up lightly. He tucked his front paws under his brisket and began to purr with a deep, throaty rumble. Violett watched him, her hands clasped in her lap, fingers knit tightly. After a moment she spoke. Her voice was calmer, more deliberate, but grudging, as if she were measuring the words. "I know something nobody else knows." She shot a glance at me. "Besides the kissing, I mean."

"What's that?" I was pulling answers out of a hostile witness. But this was a witness who wanted to tell what she knew, or what she thought she knew.

There was a long pause, and the room was so quiet that the cat's purr sounded very loud, louder than the refrigerator and the ticking clock on the table. Violett looked up at the Good Shepherd, back down at her hands. Her knuckles were white. "She was in town," she said, "the day Jo Gilbert died."

My stomach lurched. "How do you know?"

"I saw her."

"Where?"

"On Live Oak, a couple of blocks from the Emporium."

"When?"

"A little before nine. I know because I was on my way to open the shop, and I always get there at five to." Her voice was brittle. "She was driving that fancy red rent car."

I thought for a moment. If Violett's claim were true, it put Roz in town on Monday. And while it didn't put her at the death scene, it blew Roz's credibility and confirmed at least some of my suspicions. But *was* it true? Or was Violett lying in order to implicate Roz in Jo's death, to get some kind of twisted revenge on the woman who had violated her moral and ethical codes?

I took a different tack. "So what if you did see her?" I asked, making my voice tougher. "There's no law that says Roz Kotner can't come back to Pecan Springs when she feels like it. She could have been here to visit old friends."

Violett shook her head stubbornly, still not looking at me. "She told people she didn't get here until Wednesday. She lied. And Jo Gilbert wasn't the type to kill herself. That woman had something to do with it."

"With Jo's death?"

"Yes." She met my eyes directly, almost challenging. "Are you going to tell her what I said?"

I frowned. "If you have firsthand knowledge about

a crime, Violett, it's my responsibility to advise you to go straight to—"

Violett cut me off. "I'm not asking for legal advice. I'm asking, are you going to tell her?"

And then I understood. Violett was trying to get something out of Roz. She had the idea that if I gave Roz her story—a story that, if it didn't incriminate Roz, at least put her in the embarrassing position of explaining why she had lied—Roz might give her what she wanted.

"No," I said firmly. "I won't run your errands. If you want Roz to know what you saw that morning, or anytime, *you* tell her."

Violett's eyes dropped. She was silent for a moment. Then she picked up the sack of valerian. "How am I supposed to use this?"

"Steep it for five minutes in water that's just off the boil," I said. I leaned forward and put my hand on her arm. "Violett, please promise me you won't go spreading gossip about Roz and Jo. It'll only hurt Meredith, and there's no telling how Roz will react."

But I couldn't get another word out of her, and after a few minutes I said good-bye and left. The Siamese followed me out to my bike and sat, studying me inscrutably, as I rode away.

CHAPTER 11

It was nearly five by the time I got back to the shop. Ruby wasn't back yet, so I sent Laurel next door to close the Cave, while I locked up and checked out my register. When I finished, I made a quick survey next door, paid Laurel for three hours of store-sitting, and went home through the connecting door. I poured myself a sherry and sat down at the kitchen table to think things through, beginning with Violett's claim that Roz had been in Pecan Springs on Monday.

Violett's statement wouldn't be difficult to verify. The airlines usually refused to give out passenger information, so there wasn't much point in pursuing that tack. But I could call Helen Jenson, a good customer and friend who owned Jenson's Travel, and ask her to check the flights into both Austin and San Antonio and tell me when Roz had arrived. I glanced at the antique schoolhouse clock that hung over the refrigerator, its pendulum swinging gently. The clock said five-twenty, but it was always ten minutes slow—not bad for a hundred-year-old clock. I should do so well at a hundred. But the agency would be closed already. Anyway, it was Saturday. On Saturday, Helen leaves the agency to Linda Bowles, her second-in-command, and drives ninety miles to Waco to spend the weekend with her elderly mother. I frowned. I wouldn't be able to get any information from the agency until Monday morning.

If practicing law for fifteen-plus years taught me anything, it was that there was more than one way to skin a cat. Roz had rented a car, mostly likely at the airport, and the car was parked behind the cottage. If it wasn't locked, I might be able to find the car rental agreement, which would document the day and time she'd rented it.

Not wanting Roz to see me, I took the long way—a right at the corner by the Craft Emporium, a half block, then another right down the alley. The red Buick Century was parked behind the cottage, against its windowless rear wall. I tried the doors. Locked. It looked like I wasn't going to get my hands on that rental agreement. But there was something else I could get. I copied the name of the car rental company—Ace Car Rental, in San Antonio—from the decal in the rear window. I also copied the license plate number. Then I went back to the house—the long way again—dialed information in San Antonio, and got the number for Ace. So far, so good. But then I struck out.

"I can't give you that information," a curt male clerk told me. "Our computer has been down all afternoon. Try again tomorrow morning." The clerk sighed the resigned sigh of someone used to dealing with recalcitrant computers. "Or tomorrow afternoon. Sometimes it takes a while to get it up again."

"How about checking your paper files?" I asked.

The voice laughed nastily. "No offense, lady, but I've got people lined up from here to the Alamo waiting for cars, and no computer. And you want me to check a *file*? Try tomorrow." The line went dead.

I put down the phone and poured myself another sherry. Short of breaking into Roz's car, I couldn't at the moment verify Violett's statement. But I could hypothesize. Roz had a motive—a strong motive—to silence Jo. If the Mickey Finn theory had any merit, she also had the means: a hefty dose of barbiturates and vodka added to Jo's Hot Stuff. And if Violett was telling the truth, Roz had the opportunity. My structure of guesses and hunches was pretty flimsy, shored up by purely circumstantial evidence and built on too many ifs. But it was beginning to look like a case a D.A. might be able to live with.

Somebody banged on my kitchen door. It was Meredith, dressed in her new blue jogging suit and running shoes. She had one hand on my doorjamb and was bent forward from the waist, gulping for air, her face blotchy, her eyes red and tearing.

"Are you okay, Meredith?" I asked, startled. "What's the matter? Charley horse?"

"No, I'm not okay," she gasped. "And no, it's not a charley horse. I've been running hard." Her shoulders heaved as she sucked in air. "We got'ta talk, China."

I pulled her into the kitchen. "Don't tell me you've been burgled again," I asked, alarmed. Another break-in at Jo's would shoot holes in my theory. Roz knew the letters were *here*.

Meredith shook her head and collapsed in a chair at the kitchen table. She stretched out her legs, her arms limp at her sides, chest heaving. "No," she said. She closed her eyes. "I still can't believe this, China. It's just too incredible. This mousy little woman came over to see me a few minutes ago. She claimed that Mother and Roz—"

Mousy little woman? "Violett Hall?" I asked.

Meredith opened her eyes and pulled herself up in the chair. "Yes, that's her. Violett Hall. China, this woman says that Mother—"

I held up a hand, silencing her. I got the sherry and another glass, poured her one, and topped off my own. I put her glass in front of her and sat down on the other side of the table.

"Okay," I said, putting my elbows on the table. "Now, what did Violett tell you?" Meredith chugalugged the sherry and put the glass down. "She said that Mother and Rosalind Kotner had a . . . a lesbian affair. For years and years." She looked straight at me. "Is it true, China?"

"What makes you think I know?"

"You were her friend. You must have known." She tightened her mouth, but her chin trembled. "Is it *true*?"

I had to play it straight. Whatever Jo's reservations about telling her daughter about Roz, Meredith needed to know the truth. Anyway, there was no point in lying. "I don't have any direct knowledge of their relationship, Meredith. I moved here after Roz left, and I only saw them together a few times. But there were letters in the boxes your mother left for me to dispose of. Those letters—the few I read, anyway—were pretty explicit about the relationship. There was also a copy of Roz's will, under the terms of which she left everything to your mother. Judging from that evidence, I'd say that Violett's telling the truth."

Meredith sat silent, struggling with the idea. "I suppose that explains why Mother cut me out of her life. She didn't want me to know." She gave a sharp, embittered laugh. "It's crazy, China."

"What's crazy?"

"My mother loved controversy. Show her a boogeyman—somebody like Arnold Seidensticker with his airport—and she'd go after him, damn the torpedoes. She wasn't afraid of a fucking thing. She was a feminist from the word NOW." The laugh again, even more bitter. "And all the time she was afraid to come out of the goddamn closet. The biggest feminist issue in her life, and she *ducked* it."

"Well, maybe," I said. "But this town doesn't award a medal to somebody who leads an alternative lifestyle. She had to live with these people, work with them. She needed their cooperation."

"We're not talking about this town," Meredith said. Her voice was brittle as thin glass. "We're talking about her *daughter*. I can forgive her for not wanting to come out to the people around here. I just can't forgive her for not coming out to *me*."

"Maybe she thought you wouldn't approve," I said gently. "Maybe she wanted to protect you. Maybe she wanted you to keep loving her." I stopped, struck by a disconcerting thought. Until I was fifteen or sixteen, Leatha tried to cover up her drinking, keep it a secret from me. I'd thought she hid it because she was ashamed of seeming weak beside my father's towering strength. But maybe my mother, like Jo, had wanted to protect her daughter, wanted her to keep loving her. I slid uneasily away from the thought. I'd built up a reserve of energizing, sustaining anger against Leatha. It was useful. I wanted to hold on to it.

Meredith put her hands between her knees and hunched her shoulders like a hurt child. "I'm surprised that it mattered to Mother whether I approved or not," she muttered, tight-lipped. There was a long silence. Then she sighed. "Well, she would have been right, damn it."

"You'd have disapproved?" I asked, surprised.

"Not the lesbian part. If Mother wanted to take a woman lover, that was her business, not mine. I only wanted her to be happy." She shook her head angrily.

"No, it's *Roz*. That's what I can't stomach. She's power hungry. She's got an ego that won't quit. New York, kids' TV, a toy empire—that's not big enough. What she wants is the Keenan money, the Keenan name, the White House." She shook her head again, misery drawn on her face. "My mother was tough. She was smart. I just can't understand why a woman like that would choose *Roz* for a lover."

I was silent for a moment. "Sometimes we don't choose," I said. "Sometimes we're chosen." My words surprised me. They sounded like Ruby's. But I had the feeling they were close to the truth. Whatever Jo's reasons for loving Roz, they must have been utterly compelling. They must have risen like an artesian well out of a source that she couldn't control as she controlled the ordinary events of her life.

Meredith gnawed her lower lip. I waited, but she didn't say anything. After a minute I asked, "Did Violett tell you anything else?"

"She said that Constance Letterman knows, and that pretty soon the whole town will know." Meredith's voice was flat and dull. "I tried to tell her that this would sabotage the things Mother was fighting for. But Mother isn't important to her. It's Roz. That's the one she's out to get, any way she can."

I pushed. "Anything else?" Had Violett told Meredith about seeing Roz in Pecan Springs on the day Jo died?

"Well, yes," Meredith replied slowly, "but I was so . . . so churned up by the other that I didn't think about it. She said she saw Roz here on Monday."

I could understand Violett's logic, although her purpose—or what I thought was her purpose—was a little obscure. I wouldn't take her story to Roz, so she'd gone to Meredith, telling her about her mother's lesbian relationship and planting the idea that Roz had been with her mother when she died. Enraged and hurt, Meredith would carry the story to Roz, and Roz would see that Violett was the person who held the key to her future. It wasn't blackmail, exactly, and I had no idea what Violett hoped to get out of it, other than the satisfaction of seeing Roz pay for her moral transgressions. But Violett was on dangerous territory. If Roz could kill her former lover, what qualms would she have when it came to Violett?

Meredith frowned, and I could see that she was making the connections, beginning to build her own case. She was quiet for a moment, then: "That perfume I smelled just before I found Mother—do you suppose it was Roz's? Was she in the house that morning?"

I winced. I'd just as soon Meredith didn't pursue this line of questioning. "I don't know," I said.

Meredith sat forward on her chair, elbows on her knees, arms clasped. "I didn't notice her perfume at the memorial service," she said in a low voice, more to herself than to me. "But that was outdoors. And when we went to dinner that night, she wasn't wearing her own perfume. I remember you saying she'd showered with lavender soap."

I didn't reply.

"But if Roz was here on Monday, why didn't she say so? Why did she lie?" She raised her head and looked at me, working it out. "And if it was Roz's perfume I smelled on Monday, was it the same perfume I smelled after the burglary?" Her voice was harsh. "Was it *Roz* who broke into the house? But why? What was she after?"

There wasn't any point in trying to stop her. She was thinking too fast, clicking away question after question, gathering momentum.

"And if Roz was here on Monday, was she with Mother before she died? Or *when* she died?" She half rose out of her chair, her eyes wide, her face putty-colored in an intensity of anguish and despair. "Jesus, China, did Rosalind Kotner *kill my mother*?"

I put out my hand and gently pushed her down again. Meredith's questions had pulled her into the heart of it. I wasn't prepared for that. I was afraid she'd want to take some kind of action—what, I wasn't sure. I had to slam on the brakes, keep her from going further.

"Listen, Meredith," I said carefully, "everything you say could be true. But we don't *know* that it is. We don't have enough facts to go on. We'd be jumping to conclusions if—"

Meredith wasn't listening. "I think she did!" she cried. She strained forward, every muscle tight, her eyes bright with a feverish clarity. "I think she came over to the house, mixed pills and vodka for a great double whammy, and poured in enough spicy tomato stuff to cover up the taste. She did it to keep Mother from telling people that they'd been lovers. *That* would queer her chance at the White House!" She laughed bitterly at her own tasteless joke, her voice rising. "Queer her chance—get it?"

I raised my hand. "Hang on, Meredith," I said. "Do you really think Roz would worry about Jo spilling the beans? She'd know Jo wouldn't risk damaging the Anti-Airport Coalition."

It worked—for a minute. Meredith sat back, looking remarkably like her mother. Then she straightened up.

"Mother wouldn't have told the world," she said. "But she had something fierce in her, and she'd learned how to land a punch where it did the most good. If she was angry at Roz, or hurt, she might have threatened to tell Senator Keenan and back it up with the letters. And *that* would have fixed Roz's wagon." She barked a laugh that was so much like Jo's that it made me shiver. "Yes, that would have appealed to Mother's sense of justice. And if Roz knew anything about Mother, she must have known that's precisely what Mother would do. So she killed Mother to keep her from going to the Senator!"

I shifted uncomfortably. Listening to my own argument as Meredith worked through it, energized by her passion, I knew that the case against Roz, circumstantial or not, was very strong. But this conversation was getting out of hand in a hurry. All Meredith needed was to fit one more piece to the puzzle and—

She got it. "The letters!" She jumped out of her chair and paced furiously around the table. "Once Roz shut Mother up, she still had to get her hands on the letters. That's why she broke into the house!"

I sighed. "Oh, come on." I loaded the words with sarcasm. "Don't tell me you *really* believe that the fiancée of a presidential candidate would risk breaking into—"

"Of *course* she would!" Meredith punched the air with her fist. "Goddammit, don't you see? Those letters must be terribly incriminating. Once she has them, she'll be home free." She stopped pacing and swung around. "I want those letters, and Roz's will. We have to lock everything up someplace—Mother's safe deposit box, maybe. We *can't* let Roz get her hands on that stuff!"

I couldn't give her the letters. Number one, they were the bait to my trap. Number two, there was Jo's instruction not to let Meredith read them. I could finesse the first: if I handled things right tonight, Roz would never know whether the letters were actually here or not. I couldn't finesse the second, even though

Meredith knew about the relationship. I had read only three of the letters, but I knew what private emotions they touched.

Meredith was pacing again. "I *know* Roz killed my mother," she muttered. "I *know* it, China. But it's no good just to know it. I have to *prove* it."

I rolled my sherry glass between my hands. With any luck, tonight would get me the proof Meredith was asking for. But if I told her what I was up to, she'd want in on it. As wired as she was, she'd blow the whole thing. She'd get herself or Ruby hurt. She'd get me hurt.

I pushed the glass away and folded my arms on the table, courtroom-style. "Accusing someone of murder is a very serious business," I said. "You only *think* Roz is involved with your mother's death." Meredith started to sputter and I held up my hand. "But you don't have proof, and there isn't any easy way to get it, at least, not tonight. I suggest that you go home and let this thing simmer a day or so. A friend of mine owns a travel service. On Monday we'll ask her to check Roz's flight schedule."

"Monday!" Meredith said. "Roz could be out of here by tonight—by tomorrow!"

"I doubt it. She's waiting to get her hands on those letters. Anyway, what if she leaves? That's what extradition is all about. If she's guilty—"

"*If* she's guilty!" Meredith slammed her fist on the table. "What the hell do you mean, *if*? Rosalind Kotner killed my mother—your friend—and you *know* it! How can you sit there and let her get away with it?"

"Meredith, Meredith," I said quietly, shaking my

head. "I don't know anything of the kind, and you don't either. Now, I suggest—"

"Yeah, I know," Meredith said. "Be a good girl and go home and watch television. Sit on my ass and twiddle my thumbs." She could barely contain her disgust. "Some friend you are, China Bayles. Some *lawyer*, too. So what's the deal? You're still on the crook's side? You want to see Roz Kotner get away with murder?"

"I'm just trying to keep you out of trouble." I picked up the sherry bottle and gestured toward her empty glass. "I advise you to calm down, have another sherry and—"

"You can take your goddamned advice and stuff it. I'm Jo's daughter. *I'll* take care of my mother's business." She stalked out the door and slammed it so hard that the dishes rattled in the cupboard.

I put down the bottle and sat morosely. Boy, had I screwed *this* one up. I'd wanted to calm Meredith down and keep her from doing something she might regret—something *I* might regret. Instead, I'd gotten her angry, charged up. What would she do with that anger? Would she go to Roz? And what would *Roz* do? Maybe I'd better add Meredith to my list of people to worry about.

But I also had to worry about what *I* was going to do. I sat there for a moment, thinking. Then I reached for the phone. I needed somebody to listen critically to my version of what had happened, somebody who could help me ask the right questions, head toward the right answers. I needed McQuaid. It was only last night that we'd made love, but it seemed like weeks. Maybe he could come over tonight and have chili and cornbread with Ruby and me. Maybe he could join our stakeout team. Maybe—

With a muttered curse, I dropped the phone. McQuaid had gone camping with Brian, probably deliberately, to put some space between us. I was on my own.

CHAPTER 12

I did what I often do when I've got something to think about. I cooked. When Ruby arrived a half hour later, I was putting the cornbread into the oven. It's a terrific recipe, made with cheese and corn and home-grown jalapeño peppers. I bake it in my cast-iron skillet and cut it into wedge-shaped pieces that are brown and crispy on the bottom, steamy and corn-sweet inside, with flecks of red and green pepper. I always enjoy making it, but tonight I have to admit that my attention wandered. I forgot the peppers.

Ruby had followed my instructions. She was wearing a black turtleneck sweater with the sleeves pushed up, skinny black denim jeans and black suede boots, matching my own black sweater and dark jeans and sneakers. She was carrying a heavy pot filled with venison chili. She thumped the pot onto the back burner of the stove and turned on the flame. Then she straightened up, hands on hips.

"I've figured it out!" she announced, triumphant. "China, I have *solved* the mystery. And the answer is so incredible that you will never guess it—not in a million years. Not in a *trillion* years."

I reached automatically for the sherry. Then I pulled my hand back. I'd already had several sherries and I needed to be able to think tonight, not just slosh around. So I went to the refrigerator and got out a couple of bottles of sparkling water. "Does this have to do with Arnold Seidensticker?"

Ruby took her glass and sat down at the kitchen table, looking uncomfortable. "Only indirectly. I mean, it started out about Arnold Seidensticker. But it ended up about—" She ran her fingers through her red-orange hair, fuzzing it wildly. "What I found out changes everything, China. I mean, *everything*. It's totally incredible. You won't believe it."

I know Ruby. When she gets into this state, there's no reasoning with her. "Okay, P. I. Wilcox." I sighed, resigned. "Tell me what I won't believe. Only make it fast, huh? We've got to talk about what we're going to do tonight."

Ruby jumped up to pace around the table, hands stuffed into the pockets of her jeans. "First, I have to confess that I really *did* think Arnold Seidensticker killed Jo. Or maybe Lila. I was trying to think how to pin it on them and I got to thinking about that Bloody Mary mix—Hot Shot. Meredith said they didn't have any, so I figured I'd find out where Arnold or Lila bought it."

"Needle in a haystack," I said, "unless the bottle had a store price label." I'd wasted time on scavenger hunts like that myself, beating the bushes for evidence that never turned up. You could search until you dropped, and still come up empty-handed.

"I thought about the price label," Ruby said, "but Bubba took the bottle, so I didn't have that to go on. But it turns out that Hot Shot is what you might call a gourmet brand of Bloody Mary mix. The chains don't carry it, which is lucky."

"Yeah," I said, wishing she'd speed it up.

"So I started making the rounds of the liquor stores. But I didn't have to go far. I found it at the second place I went to. Bart's Liquors." Ruby stopped pacing. "And get this, China. The clerk—a kid, actually, just graduated from high school last June, still living at home with Mom and little sis—remembers selling a quart of the stuff on Monday morning. It was his first sale of the day, about two minutes after nine. *And* he remembers who he sold it to!"

"I sincerely hope it wasn't Arnold Seidensticker," I muttered. We didn't need a complication like that.

Ruby threw up her hands. "I keep telling you, China. *Forget* Arnold. I admit I was barking up the wrong tree. No more Arnold Seidensticker. Now we're onto the *real* killer."

"Ruby," I said, "will you get to the point? We've got a lot to do tonight and—"

Ruby put her hands on the table, palms down, and leaned on them. "The reason this kid remembers the sale is that he recognized the person he made it to. You see, his little sister watches something called the StrawBerry Bear Kids' Klub every Saturday morning." She straightened up with a look of mixed jubilation and incredulity, like an amateur magician who's just pulled a live rabbit out of her hat and can't quite figure out where it came from. "The person who bought the quart of Hot Shot was our very own—Rosalind Kotner!"

I closed my eyes briefly. I'd gone the long way around to verify Violett's claim, while Ruby had taken the shortcut. Not only that, but she'd just put the means to murder right into Roz's well-manicured hands. Well, almost.

I opened my eyes. "I hate to rain on your parade, Ruby, but buying a bottle of Hot Shot doesn't prove shit. A good defense lawyer could probably convince a jury that Roz was buying it to spice up her garlic-tomato juice cocktail."

Ruby shook her head, and I remembered I hadn't told her about Roz's garlic habit. "I don't know about that," she said, "but the clerk said she bought something else." She leaned forward again and pulled out another rabbit, a big one. "She bought a bottle of Everclear."

I stared at her. Everclear is a hundred and eighty proof. It packs more whammy than anything else you can drink, unless you make it yourself. What's more, the stuff is absolutely odorless and colorless. If Roz had mixed it into the Hot Shot, Jo would've been drunk out of her mind before she figured out what she was drinking. And if it were combined with sleeping pills—I whistled.

"I knew you'd be surprised," Ruby said excitedly. "The last person you'd think of, right? I mean, as far as the rest of us know, Roz didn't get into town until

Wednesday night." She narrowed her eyes and pushed out her lips. "Now, all we have to do is figure out Roz's motive for killing Jo and—"

"I know the motive," I said quietly. I told Ruby the entire story, from last night's break-in to my clumsy attempt to cool Meredith off a few minutes before. I told her about Violett's report of the relationship between Roz and Jo, about the confirming letters, about Roz's will leaving everything to Jo.

"Oh, wow," Ruby said, when I finished. Her eyes were as big as sand dollars. "Oh, *wow!*"

"Yeah," I said. "Means, motive, opportunity—it's all here. Roz must have doctored the Hot Shot with a handful of pulverized sleeping pills. Then she surprised Jo—"

"Sure," Ruby said, sitting down on the edge of her chair. "She probably pretended that she wanted to talk things over, maybe get back together. When she got the chance, she went into the kitchen, poured Jo half a glass of doctored Hot Shot and topped it off with Everclear. Maybe she even managed to get Jo to drink a *couple* of glasses of the stuff."

I nodded. "With Jo safely knocked out, she found the vodka bottle, dumped out the contents, and printed it with Jo's fingerprints. She left it and the empty bottle of pills on the table, with what remained of the Hot Shot, also printed. And she left the note, too, that Jo had started to write to Meredith. It made a perfect suicide note."

"And when that was taken care of, she started looking for the letters—"

"But got scared off when she heard RuthAnn knocking at the door." I shook my head. "Except for that, she didn't miss a trick. Every prop was in place. It was a first-class job of staging a suicide."

"Amazing," Ruby said, awed.

"Unfortunately," I said, "our case is entirely circumstantial. Which means that without a witness or a confession—"

"But that's what we're after tonight, right?"

I nodded. "I hope getting caught breaking into my house will rattle her so much that she'll spill the whole story."

Ruby rubbed her hands. "That's the way it happened in the old Nancy Drew books. Nancy nabs the crook and the crook spills the beans."

"Yeah," I said. "But that was before Miranda. The D.A. won't touch Roz's confession if the defense can argue coercion or entrapment. So we've got to be careful." I stood up and went to the kitchen desk where my Macintosh lives, along with other important things like cookbooks and recipes and manila folders full of craft clippings. I pulled a Sony minirecorder out of the drawer and put it on the table. "If she confesses, I want to get it on tape."

Ruby stared at the tape recorder, suddenly sobered. "Listen, China," she said slowly, "is this the kind of thing we ought to be tackling alone? How about giving McQuaid a call? Maybe he'd like to hang out with us tonight."

I shook my head. "McQuaid's gone camping with Brian." I gave Ruby a sidelong look. "If you want to get somebody in on this with us, we could ask Bubba."

Ruby's green eyes widened. "Bubba? No way. He'd

be a total disaster. Anyway, he wouldn't take us seriously. He'd say we're just a couple of weird broads. When we've got evidence, *then* we call Bubba."

"That's what I thought." I turned on the tape recorder to make sure the batteries were up.

Ruby cleared her throat. "If we can't have McQuaid, what about your gun?" When there'd been a spate of shop break-ins, I'd told Ruby about the Beretta. That is, I told her I had it, and that I knew how to use it. I hadn't told her why I wouldn't.

"I doubt if Roz will be armed, and I don't think a gun would serve any useful purpose."

Ruby looked disappointed. "I wasn't suggesting that you actually *shoot* it—just wave it around a little. Look authoritative."

I made a noise. "People who wave guns around get themselves into a shit-pot of trouble."

Ruby gave it up. "What time does all this Junior G-Man stuff take place?"

"I told Roz we were going to the art show," I said. "So I guess we'd better leave about eight-thirty. We can park on Guadalupe somewhere and sneak back. It'll be full dark a little before eight. My guess is that she won't try anything until then."

Ruby sniffed. "I'm glad you programmed in plenty of time for dinner," she said. "That cornbread smells terrific."

I had to apologize for forgetting to put the peppers into the cornbread, but Ruby's venison chili lived up to its reputation for firepower. We each had seconds. Then I checked the bedroom to make sure that everything was in order. Before Ruby got there, I had arranged packets of letters on the bed, as if I'd been interrupted in the process of sorting. Roz's letters and the journals, however, were still safely tucked away under the stairs.

Then I stuck the tape recorder and a small pocket torch into my brown leather shoulder bag. We went out the kitchen door—the one that faced toward the guest cottage—laughing and making a great show of leaving, pulling the door shut without checking the lock. I glanced toward the cottage. The Buick was in the alley behind the cottage, and the cottage lights were on. Roz was watching, I hoped, for us to leave.

Ruby and I got into my Datsun, drove around the block, and pulled up on Guadalupe. Not speaking, we climbed out of the car and cut across the Emporium's skimpy backyard. The house itself is so large that it takes up most of the lot, leaving a little patch of weeds that Constance occasionally mows with an old-fashioned push mower that a tenant once gave her in lieu of the rent. The stars were out in a black velvet sky, and the moon hadn't risen yet. It was dark, especially in the shrubbery around the Emporium's rickety back porch, where we stationed ourselves.

I couldn't see the guest cottage because the Emporium's dilapidated garage blocked the view. But we were only a few yards from my kitchen door, which was in full sight, as was the bedroom window. I had left a night-light burning in the kitchen and another in the bedroom, so Roz wouldn't have to stumble around in a dark house. The night-light in the bedroom gave us a shadowy view.

I settled under a shaggy juniper to wait. Ruby squatted down beside me. I could feel her trembling slightly.

"I wish McQuaid were here," she whispered. "A little muscle would be reassuring."

I agreed with Ruby about the muscle, even though I thought that we could handle Roz, who was smaller than both of us and probably out of shape. Anyway, I was hoping there wouldn't be any rough stuff. "Yeah, well, remind me to invite him next time we do something like this," I said.

"He'll probably invite himself when he hears how much fun we had. I can't imagine an ex-cop missing a chance to strut his stuff." Ruby squinted at her watch. "How long have we been here?"

"About two minutes."

We sat, eyes growing accustomed to the dark, for another ten minutes. Juniper needles were sifting down the back of my neck, my fanny was cold, and my right foot had gone to sleep. I shifted to get the circulation going again. I could hear tinny music from the direction of Lillie's Place further down on Guadalupe, where Ruby and I hang out fairly regularly. Lillie's is an interesting Texas-style bar, frequented by a miscellany of rednecks, cedar-choppers, and cowboys, with a few intellectuals from the university thrown in to leaven the lot. It's owned by a guy named Bob, who is also interesting and always pleasant, if sometimes a little quirky. The bar is named for Lillie Langtry and plastered with posters and pictures and fake "Jersey Lily" memorabilia put up by the bar's former owner—a woman—to attract tourists. Sometimes the tourists come and sometimes they don't. The rest of us are pretty regular, though. I could hear Willie Nelson singing "Mamas, Don't Let Your Babies Grow Up to Be Cowboys." I fantasized a takeoff: "Mamas, Don't Let Your Daughters Grow Up to Be Stakeout Artists."

"God, I hate that song," Ruby said. "It was Ward's favorite. Every time we'd go up to Austin to country dance at the Broken Spoke, he'd bug the band until they played it." She sighed mournfully. "I'll bet he still does—only now he takes *her*, not me."

"Ruby," I said gently, "lay off the self-pity and be quiet. Okay?"

Ruby straightened her shoulders. "Yeah. I don't have anything to feel sorry about. *She's* the one who got the turkey. Me, I'm doing great, just fantastic. Did I tell you about this real cute guy who asked me for a date? His name is—"

"Shh! Listen!"

We both heard it. The rustle of footsteps, the crackle of tiny twigs. And I smelled it—the brisk, tangy scent of thyme.

"She's coming down the path!" Ruby whispered. A dramatic Nancy Drew whisper.

But Roz couldn't be coming down the path—there weren't any twigs on the path. For some reason, she was creeping through the thyme bed along the side of the Emporium's garage. What was she doing there? She'd seen us leave—why didn't she just come up the path to the kitchen door?

A minute or two later, the rustling stopped. Unfortunately, the garage blocked my view. I waited another minute, then stood up, half stooping under the juniper. "I'm going over by that yaupon holly," I whispered to

Ruby, "to get a better view. You stay here. Don't make a sound."

"Screw that," Ruby whispered back. She rose to her feet. "I'm coming with—"

Suddenly all hell broke loose. A gunshot shattered the silence. It was followed by an ear-piercing scream that was punctuated by a second shot. Then footsteps raced toward the alley. More screaming, loud and shrill.

I took off in pursuit, with Ruby close behind. But whoever it was had a start. By the time we reached the alley, there was no one in sight. Only the screaming, high-pitched and hysterical, going on and on and on.

CHAPTER 13

The screams came from Roz. She was crouched on knees and elbows on the cottage floor, her hands clasped over her head as if she expected shell fragments to rain down. She was dressed for an air raid, too—black slacks, black sweater, her blond hair covered by a dark scarf. It was also perfect breaking-and-entering garb.

"Roz!" Ruby shouted. She grabbed Roz and pulled her to her feet, shaking her. "Roz! It's okay. You're fine. You're safe."

Roz's eyes were squeezed shut. She was still shrieking, high-pitched and shrill.

"Quit!" Ruby commanded, and slapped her, hard.

Roz's eyes popped open and her scream switched off as if a circuit breaker had tripped. She swiveled her head from Ruby to me. "I . . . I thought you'd left," she said in a childishly thin, gasping voice.

"We did," I said. "What happened?"

"Somebody tried to kill me. They just *missed*! If I'd been standing up straight I would be dead right now!" She opened her mouth as if she were going to scream again.

Ruby shook her again. "It's over, Roz. Whoever did it is gone. They ran down the alley."

Roz pulled away from Ruby and groped unsteadily toward the liquor cupboard. She picked up a nearly full bottle of scotch, but her hands were shaking so badly that she couldn't open the bottle.

Ruby went to her rescue and poured her a stiff shot. Roz gulped it and held out the glass. I shook my head warningly at Ruby. She put the bottle back on the shelf, led Roz to the loveseat, and made her sit down. "I'll make some coffee," she said, and headed to the kitchen.

I sat down beside Roz. "Where were you standing when this happened?"

"Right there," Roz said, pointing to a spot a little to the right of the coffee table, toward the fireplace. Her voice was stretched like a too-tight violin string. "Then I bent over to get something out of my purse and . . ."

Both our eyes went to Roz's purse, which was lying on the coffee table. A credit card lay beside it. This time, Roz wasn't trusting that the kitchen door would be unlocked.

"I . . . I was checking to see that I had my . . . credit card," Roz said lamely. "I . . . was on my way to the liquor store for some more scotch."

Yeah, sure. I didn't look at the open cupboard, where the scotch bottle was nearly full. "So you were standing by the coffee table," I said, "and you bent over . . ."

"And the first shot came," Roz said. "Right over my head." Her voice rose, wobbling. "If I'd been standing straight, I'd be dead. If I hadn't dropped onto the floor, the second shot would have got me." She wrapped her arms around herself and rocked back and forth against the cushions, shivering uncontrollably.

"Coffee coming up," Ruby called from the kitchen. "Black? Cream?"

"Black's good," I said, and Roz nodded. She was starting to cry again, but more softly.

I went to the casement window. It was open and gave a good view of the thyme bed and the Emporium's garage not a dozen feet away. I looked down at the limestone window sill. A piece had been freshly chipped out of the outer edge, the limestone glistening white, where a bullet—the second one, most likely—had struck the sill. I opened the door and went outside, being careful to stay on the stepping stones along the cottage wall.

Across the alley, old Mr. Cowan's back door opened and a square of light fell out onto his grassy yard. I heard the brisk, scolding yap of his Pekingese, Lady Lula. "What's goin' on out there?" a quavery voice called. Mr. Cowan is spry for his eighty-five years and his hearing is pretty good, but he obviously wasn't in a hurry to investigate.

"It's okay, Mr. Cowan," I called. "It's just me—China Bayles, your neighbor. There's been some shooting, but nobody's hurt."

Mr. Cowan wasn't pleased. "Neighborhood's goin'

to hell, if you ask me." The door closed, silencing Lady Lula's irritating yap, then opened again. "Want I should call the po-lice?"

I considered. The last thing I wanted was Bubba poking around, asking a lot of questions. But this was clearly a case of attempted murder. I could be in big trouble if I *didn't* call the police.

"Yes, thank you," I said. "We've got our hands full over here."

Mr. Cowan's door slammed.

With Bubba on the way, I had only a few minutes to look around. I pulled the torch out of my shoulder bag, flicked it on, and turned toward the thyme bed. Along the garage wall, the fragrant plants were trampled into the soft earth, showing clearly where someone had stood. I shone my light onto the ground. That's when I saw it—a clear, unmistakable shoe print, deeply impressed into a patch of bare earth. The print was a distinctive zigzag.

I flicked off my torch and stood for a moment in the dark. That Z was remarkably like the print of Meredith's new running shoes. The mark of Zorro.

Meredith? That was crazy! Meredith wouldn't do something like this.

Yeah, well, maybe not so crazy. Last night Meredith had announced she was getting a gun. This afternoon, she had come to the conclusion that Roz had killed her mother. I turned on the torch and knelt down to inspect the shoe print again. Yes, there was no mistake. It looked very much as if Meredith had tried to kill Roz.

I frowned. To kill Roz—or to scare the hell out of her? I straightened up and looked into the living room through the open casement window. The range was close, no more than four yards. Roz had been a standing target, easily visible in the lighted room. The assailant had shot and missed as Roz bent over to pick up her credit card. Then, as Roz dropped to the floor, the assailant had fired again. That bullet had taken a chunk out of the stone window sill and ricocheted off. Meredith had said that she'd taken an NRA course. If she'd shot to kill, Roz would be dead by now. It looked to me as if Meredith had only tried to scare her.

I went back into the cottage. Roz was hunched on the loveseat, shaking hands cupped around a mug of coffee. Ruby looked at me. "Should we call the police?"

"Mr. Cowan's taking care of that," I said. I went to the fireplace and examined the mantel, a foot-thick beam of solid oak. On the far right end, about an inch from the top, I found what I was looking for, a neat round hole about the size of my little finger. The first bullet was embedded in the mantel, and it wasn't going to come out without a lot of digging. I'd leave that to Bubba.

I studied the stone wall and rough pine ceiling, gauging where the second shot would have hit after it ricocheted off the sill. There was a fist-size patch of plaster missing from a spot on the wall opposite the window, exposing the stone beneath. I glanced at the floor. Among the dust and plaster shards was a battered slug. I bent over and studied it, not picking it up. It was what was left of a lead bullet, probably a thirty-eight, flattened and deformed.

Two squad cars skidded to a stop in the alley. Doors

slammed. Fifteen seconds later, Bubba marched into the living room with his hand on his gun, cigar stub clamped in his jaw. "Somebody get shot?" he asked.

Roz opened her eyes and made a little whimper.

"Someone shot at Ms. Kotner," I said, stepping forward. "Twice. Both misses."

Bubba shoved back his Stetson with a thick, meaty thumb and regarded me. "If it isn't Miz Bayles. You're a busy lady."

"The shots came through that open window," I told him. "The first bullet seems to be embedded in the mantel. The second ricocheted off the stone window ledge and ended up on the floor behind the loveseat."

A policeman came to the door, the same mustached Hispanic who was with Bubba the night before. "All clear out here, chief," he reported. "Musta got away down the alley." He gestured. "Somethin' out here you should see."

"Be out in a minute," Bubba said. He stepped to the mantel and inspected the hole in the wood, then went behind the loveseat and hunkered down on his heels to look at the spent bullet. Then he stood and went to the window and peered out.

"Out there in that patch of weeds, huh?" he asked me. "That's where the shots came from?"

"Thyme," Ruby corrected him. "It's an herb, not a weed." It was a nice effort, but I doubted if Bubba cared about the botanical distinction.

Bubba growled something under his breath. The cigar worked its way across his face and his black brows pulled together like the eyebrows on an animated cartoon figure. "From out there to in here—pretty close range," he said. "Ask me, the person doin' the shootin' was a lousy shot." He turned to Roz. "You Miz Kotner?"

Roz summoned what dignity she could. "I am."

Bubba lifted his hat and scratched his head. "Ain't you the lady that does tee-vee? Saw you at the service t'other day."

"That's . . . right," Roz said stiffly.

Having sorted things out, Bubba gave a satisfied nod. "Well then, Miz Kotner, suppose you tell me what happened."

"I was on my way to the liquor store," Roz said, not looking at me, and then went on to tell Bubba what she had told me. By the time she finished, she was crying again.

"Then what?" Bubba prompted. "What happened after the shootin'?"

"They came," Roz said, gesturing at Ruby and me. She lay back against the loveseat as if she were exhausted. "They got here right after it happened."

Bubba turned to Ruby. "Where was you and Miz Bayles when the shootin' was going on?"

"We were going to an art show," Ruby replied. She didn't even look at me. "We were just leaving when we heard the shots."

"You didn't see nobody?"

"We *heard* somebody," I said, "in the thyme bed. But whoever it was got to the alley and was gone by the time we could follow. So we came in here to see if Roz was hurt."

"It was lucky we *were* here," Ruby said. "Whoever it was might have shot a third time."

Roz moaned and squeezed her eyes shut.

"Stay put," Bubba grunted, and stepped outside. I went to the window. The other cop signaled him, and the two of them bent over the shoe print. But when Bubba came back into the cottage, he didn't mention it. Instead, he pulled out his pocketknife, one of those six-bladed Swiss Army types that can handle an entire troop of Boy Scouts on a week-long campout, and went to the mantel. While I watched, he gouged a hole in the wood and extricated a misshapen hunk of lead. He picked the other bullet up off the floor and wrapped both in his handkerchief and stuck them in his pocket. Then he turned to Roz.

"What's your guess on this, Miz Kotner?"

"My . . . guess?" Roz asked faintly.

Bubba gave her a patient look. "Who's got it in for you? Who wanted you dead—or wanted to scare you?"

Roz sat straighter. "Several people hate me enough to kill me," she said. "But I'm sure that none of them would want me *dead*."

Bubba scowled. "Meanin'—?"

"Meaning that I've made a number of enemies—it's hard not to, in my business—but none of them can afford for me to be dead. I'm worth too much." She spoke with an odd mixture of pride and bitterness. "Nobody wants to kill the goose that lays the golden egg."

Bubba sighed and took out a small notebook. "How about givin' me some names."

Roz frowned, concentrating. "Well, there's my producer, Matthew Harmon. I just turned down his contract offer and Jane says he's very upset. But my secretary told me that he's in Toronto for a few days."

"Jane?"

"Jane Dorman, my agent. She's not exactly happy with me right now, either, but she's spending the weekend at her cottage in Vermont. She called me from there this morning."

Bubba's cigar came up. "Anybody local?"

Roz started to say something, then paused. Then she shook her head. "No, no one. I knew only one person well, and she's . . . dead."

Bubba flipped his notebook shut and stuck it into his pocket. "Guess that's it for now," he said. "When we get it wrapped up outside, we'll be goin'."

Roz sat up. "You're not leaving! I need *protection*!"

Bubba looked at me and a brief smile twitched his thick lips. "Looks to me like you got plenty protection. Miz Bayles is here."

"But I need *police* protection!" She held out her hands in entreaty. "Somebody tried to *kill* me tonight! You're not just going to walk away from that, are you?"

Ruby intervened. "Don't forget," she said delicately, "that Ms. Kotner is a well-known performer. If anything happened to her here in Pecan Springs . . ." She left the sentence dangling, but the implication was clear.

Bubba's cigar worked from right to left. If there was anything he *didn't* want, it was to have a national celebrity—a kids' TV favorite, at that—assaulted under his very nose.

"Well," he allowed, "reckon I could send a patrol car down the alley ever' little bit."

Roz's smile was dazzlingly grateful. "*Would* you?" she asked. "That would make me feel so much safer."

"Yeah," Bubba said. He glanced at me. "You stayin'?"

"I don't think that's necessary, if your men are patrolling. But I'm close by," I added to Roz. "If you want me, all you have to do is yell." Given her pitch and range, I was sure to hear.

"I will," she said. "And thank you," she added to Bubba, who was walking out the door. "I appreciate the offer of the patrol."

Bubba tipped his hat, more courteous now that he'd reflected on the down side of another attack on Roz. "Don't mention it, ma'am," he said. "G'night."

I turned to Roz, who was headed for the scotch bottle. "If everything's okay, Ruby and I will be on our way. I guess we'll have to scratch the art show tonight."

"Of course everything's not okay," Roz said sharply, glancing up at the patch of exposed stone where the second bullet had struck. "It wouldn't be okay if somebody shot at *you*, would it?" She poured herself a drink. "But I guess there's nothing more to be done tonight."

"I guess," I agreed. "Just yell if you need anything." As we left, I waved at Bubba and the patrolman, bent over the footprint. Making a casting, I thought. I wondered how many people in Pecan Springs had bought Sears running shoes recently.

"So we have to reset the trap," Ruby said as we went into my kitchen.

"Yeah," I said. "I figure that Roz is too out of it to

make a pass at the letters tonight." I cut two wedges of cold cornbread and put them in the microwave. In my opinion, warmed-over cornbread is better than cake. "But I'll understand if you don't want to do another stakeout, Ruby. This one didn't exactly go the way we figured."

"I can handle it," Ruby said. "If McQuaid's back, though, maybe we can include him."

I nodded. My thought exactly.

Ruby sat down at the table and propped her chin in her hands. "So who do you think fired at Roz?"

I poured a couple of glasses of milk and got the butter out of the refrigerator. I cook with margarine mostly, and save the butter for when it makes a difference. On cornbread it does. "What would you say to Meredith?"

Ruby's copper-colored eyebrows shot up into her hair. "Meredith? That's idiotic! What makes you think *she* did it?"

I explained about the gun Meredith had said she was going to buy, her state of mind when she'd stormed out of the house, and the shoe print. While I talked I got the wedges of cornbread out of the microwave and buttered them. Ruby took one, and I took the other.

"You think she did it?" Ruby asked incredulously when I finished my story. "You think *Meredith* did it?"

"I think it's possible," I said. "When she left here, she was mad enough to do just about anything, including taking a couple of threatening shots at Roz. If Bubba knew what I know, he'd think it was possible, too. In fact, Meredith would probably be at the top of his suspect list."

"But those shoes aren't unique," Ruby said. "She got them at Sears. There must be hundreds of people running around leaving that crazy tread print behind them. And a whole lot of them must live in Pecan Springs."

"Maybe," I said. "But there aren't hundreds of people wearing Sears' shoes and living in Pecan Springs who also have it in for Roz Kotner."

Ruby frowned. "It sounds bad, but I just can't believe that *Meredith* could be guilty of . . ." She heaved a long sigh. "But before this afternoon, I wouldn't have believed that Roz could be guilty of murder, either. I guess it's possible." She thought of something else. "You mentioned Roz's will. If Roz died and left all her money to Jo, but Jo is dead, would Meredith inherit?"

"The state of Texas treats that situation differently than some other states." I closed my eyes and tapped into a memory from some long-ago exam. "If the beneficiary is related to the testator, and in the absence of specific alternative instruction, the legacy passes to the beneficiary's heir. If the beneficiary is not related to the testator, the legacy does not pass. The testator is considered to have died intestate."

Ruby reached for her milk. "Is that lawyer talk for no?"

"Yeah. If Jo had been Roz's sister, and if Roz hadn't given other instructions, Meredith could inherit. Jo wasn't Roz's sister, so that's the end of that. But the situation is different in different states, and most people don't know the law. It's also possible that Meredith believes that she is now Roz's heir. It's also possible that if Bubba finds out about Roz's will, he might think Meredith stands to inherit."

"Is he likely to find out?"

"Probably not. I don't think he'd ask about a will unless Roz were actually dead. And she's not."

Ruby finished her cornbread and licked the butter off her fingers. "Do you think Bubba suspects Meredith?"

"How could he? He hasn't seen her shoes. They made a cast of the print, but it won't help him unless he gets his hands on the original."

"What about the gun? *If* Meredith bought one, I mean."

I thought. "I suppose it depends on what shape that mantelpiece slug is in. The lab can match a bullet to a gun if there's enough left to work with. But those were soft lead thirty-eights, and the one I saw on the floor was pretty badly deformed. It's my guess it won't yield a successful ballistics test. Anyway, we don't know whether or not Meredith has a gun."

Ruby paused. "So? What are we going to do?"

I gave her a crooked grin. "What's this *we* shit, kemo sabe? You don't have to get mixed up in it." The lawyer part of me cautioned that Ruby and I could get into big trouble for obstructing justice. But the friend side of me said it was time to check in on Meredith. I glanced at the clock. "It's just ten," I said. "Maybe I'll drop in on Meredith tonight."

Ruby gulped the last of her milk. "I'm already mixed up in it. I'll go with you."

We both went.

* * *

Meredith's gray Mazda was parked in the drive. I put a hand on the hood. The engine was cold. It hadn't been driven that night. But that didn't mean anything. Whoever shot at Roz had been on foot.

The light was on in the living room and I could hear the sound of the ten o'clock news as we walked up on the porch. Meredith answered on the second knock. She was wearing the same blue jogging suit she'd had on earlier—and her running shoes.

"Hi," she said. She opened the door wider, looking from Ruby to me. "Long time no see. Come on in."

We followed Meredith into the living room, which had been straightened after last night's mess. Ruby glanced at the sofa, and I knew that she was thinking that it was where Jo had died only a few days before. But she sat down on it without saying anything. I sat down too, feeling awkward and tense, the muscles knotted up at the back of my neck. I was out of practice for this kind of thing. But even in the old days, this wouldn't have been fun. I liked Meredith. I hoped like hell she hadn't done what I was afraid she'd done.

Meredith switched off the TV, sat down in the rocking chair, and propped her feet on the coffee table. I glanced at the soles of her running shoes. If there'd been any earth clinging to them from her waltz through the thyme bed, it was gone now. The soles were as clean as if they'd been scrubbed.

"What's up?" Meredith asked. She zeroed in on me. "Have you changed your mind about helping me get proof?" She turned to Ruby. "I assume she's told you."

Ruby nodded, very serious. "You think Roz killed Jo."

"Think!" Meredith said angrily. She slapped the arm of the rocking chair with the flat of her hand. "I *know*. All I want is a little help from—"

"What have you been doing tonight, Meredith?" I asked.

Meredith stared at me. "What the hell do you think I've been doing? I've been cleaning house. And while I was at it, I was trying to figure out how to prove—"

"Did you come straight back here from my place?"

Meredith frowned. "Well, no, not *straight* back. When I left you, I was pretty mad. I was tempted to go to the cottage and tell Roz what Violett had told me. But I didn't."

"How come?"

"Because I didn't want to tip her off. I haven't figured out what to do yet. When I do, I'd like to have surprise on my side."

"So if you didn't go to Roz's, what did you do?"

She shrugged. "I stopped at Cavette's for bread, then came back here. I tried calling Roz's office in New York, on the off chance her secretary might still be there. I wanted to find out where Roz was on Monday. But all I got was the answering machine. After that, I tried the airlines, but I couldn't pry any information out of them. I guess your friend at the travel agency is our last hope. Or maybe McQuaid could dig it out for us." She looked at me, frowning. "How come the questions?"

I cleared my throat. "Last night, after the break-in, you said you were going to get a gun."

"Yeah." Meredith tossed her head. "And I got one,

too. I went down to the gun shop at the corner of Brazos and Eleventh and bought a thirty-eight revolver, just like the one I have at home. Want to see it?"

Ruby and I exchanged a wordless glance, and I nodded.

Meredith pushed herself out of the chair and went to a small table. She opened a drawer and pulled out a gun and handed it to me. It was a short-barreled thirty-eight, respectably heavy and solid—and cold. "I'm not bloodthirsty," she said. "I just want to be able to take care of myself."

I held the gun up and sniffed it. There was an acrid smell of burned powder, and I could see powder residue on the front of the cylinder. I depressed the catch and swung the cylinder out. Fully loaded—five live rounds.

I handed the gun back. "It's been fired recently."

Meredith put the gun back in the drawer. "Of course it's been fired. Do I look like a bimbo who'd buy a gun without trying it out? There's a range behind the shop. I shot a couple of rounds to get the feel of it."

"You reloaded?"

"Yeah. I bought it for protection. An unloaded gun isn't going to do me a lot of good." She frowned. "What is this?" she asked. "The third degree?"

Beside me, Ruby leaned forward. "What about tonight?" she asked intently. "Did you use the gun tonight?"

Meredith looked at Ruby, then at me. "No, of course I didn't use it tonight," she said, in the tone of one speaking to idiots. "I fired it this afternoon. I brought it home. I loaded it and stuck it in the drawer." Her patience was wearing thin. "What *is* this?"

I cleared my throat. "Somebody shot at Roz tonight."

Meredith stared at me. "Shot at *Roz*? You're kidding! Who would—" Her gray eyes widened. "You think *I* shot at her?"

"There was a print of a shoe like yours in the dirt outside the window where the shots were fired. The gun that was used was a thirty-eight."

Meredith shook her head wonderingly. "I still don't—Shot *at* her? So she wasn't hurt?"

"No," I said.

I kept my eyes on her. I've questioned a lot of people, and I pride myself on knowing when somebody is lying. I was reasonably satisfied that Meredith was telling the truth. Not a hundred percent sure. You can *never* be a hundred percent sure. But sure enough to relax a little.

Meredith lifted her right shoe and looked at the sole. She put her foot down. "Well, it wasn't *my* shoe, I can tell you that. It wasn't my gun, either." She paused. "Who do the police think did it?"

"Bubba didn't let us in on his thinking," I said. "But as far as I can tell, he doesn't have any bright ideas. Yet."

"Bubba *never* has any bright ideas," Ruby said.

"Don't underestimate him," I warned. "He knows his business. Anyway, Roz seems to think that most of the candidates aren't local." Roz had paused slightly when Bubba asked her if any Pecan Springs people might have it in for her, but there was no way of knowing what had gone through her mind at that moment.

"Well, you can count me out," Meredith said. "If I was going to shoot somebody tonight, would I have bought a gun here in town this afternoon? That would really be stupid."

I agreed. That *would* be stupid, and Meredith wasn't. But Bubba didn't have any way of knowing how smart or how dumb Meredith was. If he found out about the gun—no, make that *when* he found out about the gun—Meredith was going to be on his suspect list.

Meredith pushed her lips in and out, thinking. "Is it possible that Roz staged the attack herself?"

It was a possibility I hadn't considered. But when I thought back on the second shot, the one that had ricocheted off the window ledge and into the room, I had to shake my head. "At least one shot came from outside the window."

"And we heard the footsteps outside after Roz started screaming inside," Ruby said. "She couldn't have been both places at once. Anyway, what would she gain by staging an attack?"

None of us could come up with an answer to that one.

"Well, I don't intend to lose any sleep over Roz," Meredith said. "If somebody does her in, I won't shed any tears. In fact, it'll save me a lot of trouble." She glanced sharply at me. "That doesn't mean I'd try to kill her," she added. "If I have my way, Rosalind Kotner's next starring role will be in court—on trial for murder."

CHAPTER 14

I'd been home ten minutes when there was a tap on the back door. It was Roz. She was still wearing her black breaking-and-entering costume. There were dark circles under her eyes and sooty furrows of mascara on her cheeks. She also wore the sweet perfume of scotch, but she didn't look drunk. She looked distraught.

"Can I come in?" she asked. She was shivering slightly, although it wasn't cold. "I need to talk."

"Yeah," I said, without enthusiasm. I'd had a long day, there'd been several surprises, all of them nasty, and I was ready to head for a hot bath and bed.

But I fired up the copper teakettle instead. "Decaf okay?" I asked. I gave up the other kind when I left the law. I hadn't known until I quit how caffeine hyped me, what a crutch it was. The first couple of weeks were sheer misery. I dragged around feeling fatigued and spiritless until the toxins got flushed out of my system. Since then, I've learned to be wary of caffeine even in its sexiest, most seductive form, chocolate.

Roz nodded, hardly hearing my question. She glanced at the straight-backed kitchen chairs and opted for the rocker beside the kitchen window. When she sat down she went limp, like a marionette whose strings had come unstrung. She rested her head against the carved oak back and closed her eyes. That's how she sat for the next few minutes, until I touched her shoulder and put a mug of steaming decaf in her hand. I pulled up a chair opposite the rocker and put my feet on the wooden milking stool I found at an antique store in New Braunfels. It's probably ninety years old and the green paint has been rubbed off by countless behinds in the course of doing the milking. But it makes a great footstool, table, plant stand—whatever I'm in need of at the moment.

"What do you want to talk about?"

Roz sipped her decaf for a minute or two. Then she said, in what I'd come to think of as her real-Roz voice, "I know who shot at me tonight."

"Who?"

"I can't tell you just yet, because I have to figure out what to do." She raised candid blue eyes to mine over the rim of her cup. "I'm sorry, China. I don't mean to be obscure. I just mean . . . this person thinks I owe her something, and maybe I do. But I've got something more important than that on my mind."

I raised my eyebrows. Something more important than stopping the person who had threatened her life? But it didn't sound as if she suspected Meredith. The bit about owing something reminded me of what Violett had said this afternoon. Did Roz actually think Violett Hall would take after her with a gun?

Roz pulled my attention back to the conversation. "But that's not what I came to talk to you about," she said. She put her cup on the window sill. "I came to tell you the truth about Jo and me, and why you can't—you absolutely *cannot*—give Jo's letters and journals to the library."

I stared at her. This was the last thing I'd expected.

"You see," Roz said, with the air of someone making her last confession, "Jo Gilbert and I were more than just friends. We were lovers." She paused. I made a noise that could have been surprise, and she went on, speaking with slow, careful deliberation. "To tell the truth, I was pretty unsettled when I first met Jo. I was still a kid—I had acting talent and a good regional performing background and work, TV commercials, children's theater, stuff like that. But I didn't know where I was going, or what I wanted. I was just sort of drifting. Then Jo came into my life and kind of . . . well, took it over. She helped me find confidence in myself, help me develop a sense of who I was and in what direction I wanted to go."

I made an encouraging noise. I didn't want to say anything to stem the flow of words or divert it.

"It's hard to explain how things got started between us. Anyway, that's private. You don't need to know. After a few months of trying to figure it out, we decided it was good for both of us and we stopped fighting it."

"You weren't worried about being discovered?" I

asked. "Pecan Springs is a small town, and you *were* living together."

Roz seemed a little more at ease now, as if my response assured her that I wasn't making moral judgments. "Sure, we were worried—at first. But after a while, it didn't seem like much of a problem. Women live together for all kinds of reasons. And Jo was . . . well, you know what she was like. The pillar of the community, all that, very sort of stern, reserved. It just didn't occur to anybody that anything was going on. We were discreet, but discretion didn't seem necessary—except for Jo's daughter, of course. Jo had the idea that Meredith would be opposed, so she kept her at arm's length. That wasn't hard, since Meredith was busy with school and her career. I felt bad about it and tried to get Jo to soften up. But you know how she was. Once she got something into her mind, that was it. That was the way things were going to be, no matter what."

I nodded and sat back, sipping my decaf. So far, so good. Roz's story fit with the way I had doped things out.

Roz began to rock, signaling a new chapter. "But then things changed. I got a lucky break. One of the guys I was working with in children's theater in Austin had a friend in New York. An agent, Jane Dorman. The guy did a test video of some of our kids' stuff and sent it to New York. Jane put us together with a producer who was looking for what we were doing, and that was it." She shook her head, musing. "I still can't believe it, sometimes. It was a one-in-a-million chance at the brass ring, and I got it. The rest you can read about, if you haven't already."

"What happened with you and Jo?"

Roz raised her shoulders, let them drop. "The same thing that happens when anybody gets zapped with a big chance. It pulled us apart. I asked her to come to New York—over and over I asked her. Sometimes she'd come for a few days, a week. But she despised New York, hated apartment living, traffic, noise, pollution. The city was a symbol for everything she *didn't* want in her life. After a while it got harder and harder to hold the connection. And it was a lot more dangerous than it had been before, when I was nobody." She smiled a half smile. "I'm a *children's* star, you know. It wouldn't be good for public relations if people found out that once upon a time StrawBerry Bear had a lover. A woman lover."

"Yes," I said, "I see."

"So I broke it off with Jo. It wasn't easy for either of us, but we both knew it was a good idea. And she was ready, too. It was so tough for her, not being able to have a real life together." She darted a quick glance to see how I was reacting. "Anyway, Jo always wanted the best for me, wanted me to be happy. When I told her that Howie and I planned to be married, she was absolutely *delighted*, offered to help with the wedding, that sort of thing. She wanted to send the letters back right away, but I said no, hold on to them, I'd pick them up the next time I was in town. I knew she was ill, you see. I figured I'd fly down for a day or two to visit her, cheer her up, and get the letters. I had no idea she was so depressed that she . . ." She swallowed hard.

"I've been feeling so *guilty* about her death, China. I feel like I'm responsible."

I shifted. "Responsible? How do you mean?"

Roz looked down, looked up, looked down again. "She said she wanted me to marry and be happy. She said she was ready to let go of what we'd had together. But she must have been more hurt than I realized about the end of our relationship." Tears welled in her blue eyes, threatening to spill over, and her lip trembled. "I feel as if I drove her to suicide, as surely as if I'd been here and given her the pills. That's why it hit me so hard when I found out what happened. I may be responsible. I hate myself for that."

I thought fast. Roz's story was a masterly blend of truth and fiction. I knew Jo hadn't been delighted about Roz's upcoming marriage, or willing to end the relationship amicably, or eager to give over the letters. I had satisfied myself that Roz had been there on Monday, that she'd had both the means and the opportunity to poison Jo. The trouble was, I didn't have any hard evidence—yet. I didn't have the rental car contract or her plane tickets. I wanted like hell to confront her with what I knew—Violett's account, the clerk's story about the Everclear and the Hot Shot—but it just wasn't enough. The chances of pulling a confession out of her were just about nil. And even if I did, it wouldn't be worth much. A good defense attorney could shoot it down.

So, even though I hated myself for playing along with her game, I was stuck—for the moment. I pulled out a smile and pasted it on my mouth. "I'm really glad you've told me all this, Roz. It helps me to put things into perspective."

Roz nodded. "I wish I'd come clean in the beginning. But Jo didn't want Meredith to know about us, and I thought she had the letters. I'm sure Jo wouldn't have minded your knowing, though, especially since she trusted you enough to give you my letters for safekeeping." She reached forward and put her hand on my arm in a sisterly gesture. "If it'll make things easier for you, China, I'll take them tonight."

I shook my head regretfully, falling back onto my earlier lie. "I understand what you're saying, Roz, and I agree—these letters definitely won't be going to the CTSU Library. But I have to talk to Alice Dale first. I'm sure you understand."

Roz gave me a measuring look. "You *are* going to return the letters to me? Tomorrow, perhaps?"

"Probably not tomorrow. The first part of the week is the best I can do. I'm Jo's literary executor, and I really feel I have to handle the job right." I gave her my most engaging grin. "That comes from spending a big chunk of my life as a lawyer, I guess."

Roz sighed, resigned but accepting. "I suppose." She rose from the chair. "Now, if you'll excuse me, I'm very tired. It's been a long day."

I saw her to the door and watched her walk down the path to the cottage. It had been a long day for me, too, crammed full of surprises, not the least of which was Roz's partial confession. I had to hand it to her—she was a superb actress. If I hadn't known what I knew, I might have fallen for her story. I might even have given her the letters.

I skipped the nightly hot bath ritual and went straight to bed. I had the feeling of suspended elation I used to get when I was coming up on closing arguments and summation, ready to test myself and the case against the jury's final verdict.

I had no idea how absolutely final a verdict it was going to be.

I woke at seven the next morning—Sunday—with the nagging sense that I hadn't finished something. For a minute, I wasn't sure what it was. Then I remembered my dream, a confusion of images in which Violett and Meredith and I, each dressed in athletic shorts and running shoes and with a smoking gun in hand, raced around and around the cottage. First one of us was ahead, then another, until none of us knew who was chasing whom or why. The race came to an inconclusive end when Bubba popped out of the thyme bed waving a checkered flag. Ruby would probably say that the dream was a message from my Inner Guide. I felt vaguely irritated. If my Inner Guide had something important to say, she could learn to speak English.

I rolled out of bed and onto the carpet, where I did a few yoga stretches to get my spine unkinked and my brain operating. If I'd understood Roz last night, she thought Violett was the one who had fired at her. It hadn't seemed likely to me at the time. On the other hand, Violett's recent behavior had certainly been unusual. Maybe my dream was saying something important about Violett. Maybe I shouldn't be so quick to cross her off the list. Maybe I should at least talk to her first.

I stood up and did a couple of forward stretches and a back bend. Then I found a pair of jeans and a navy blue sweatshirt that said LIFE IS UNCERTAIN, SO EAT DESSERT FIRST. I open at one on Sunday, and the morning is good choretime, so I got busy. The laundry hamper was overflowing with at least a month's dirty clothes, and I took three minutes to dump a load of sheets into the washer, add soap, and set it on white wash.

Then I tied a red bandanna over my head to disguise the fact that I should also have washed my hair, shrugged into a denim jacket, and set out for Violett's a little after seven-thirty. I figured a good, fast walk would get the last of the cobwebs out. I also wanted to confront Violett early, before she got to church and somebody treated her to a full report of last night's incident. Mr. Cowan probably wasn't the only neighbor who'd heard the fracas. I wanted to be the first to tell her, so I could watch her reaction.

As I rounded the corner, heading north on Guadalupe, I spotted Roz on the other side of the street, going in the opposite direction. She was wearing pink sweats, pink running shoes and pink socks, with a pink scarf wound turban-style around her head. She was moving quickly, chin up, arms bent at the elbow and pumping, flinging her hips from side to side in a stiff-legged, heel-toe walk. She looked like a pink ostrich in a hurry. As she passed, she glanced up and waved.

As luck would have it, I didn't have to go all the way to Violett's house to see Violett. I ran into her in front of Cavette's Grocery. Cavette's is a mom-and-pop store—actually a pop-and-son store, now in its third generation, on the corner of Guadalupe and Green. An old-fashioned market, Cavette's has wooden bins and wicker baskets of fresh fruit and vegetables lined up out front, butted up against the glass windows which are pasted over with hand-printed notices of Tupperware parties and four-family garage sales and lost dogs and baby-sitting. The Cavettes buy organic meat and produce from local growers, which means they depend less on the massive food distribution system that shackles most of us. They're a good market for my fresh herbs, too, in season. It gives me a lift to see cellophane packages of Thyme and Seasons basil and rosemary and marjoram displayed in their produce section, along with some little ceramic pots of chives I'd sold them a couple of weeks ago. I feel every bit as proud of those chives as I ever felt about a well-done legal brief. I haven't figured out whether that judgment represents an overvaluation of my chives or an undervaluation of my briefs.

Violett had just come out of the store carrying a brown paper bag. She looked much worse than she had yesterday afternoon. Her face was chalky, her cheeks sagged, her shoulders hunched. Her purple woolen sweater was buttoned crookedly and the lace collar of her navy dress was half up, half tucked under her sweater. Untidy brown hair stuck out from the green knitted cap she'd pulled on against the morning chill. She averted her eyes when she saw me, and tried to brush past.

I put my hand on her arm. "How'd the herb tea work last night?" I asked. "Were you able to sleep?"

She pulled her arm away. "I didn't take any," she

said, and then added jerkily, still not looking at me, "I decided I didn't need it."

"Violett," I said, "have you heard about Rosalind Kotner?"

"What about her?" Her voice was guarded, cautious.

"Somebody shot at her last night, through the window of the cottage."

If I'd been looking for a reaction, I got one, although it wasn't exactly what I expected. Violett took an involuntary step backward. "Shot at her with a . . . *gun*?"

"That's what people usually shoot with," I said. I frowned. "Are you okay?"

Violett's face was gray. She clutched her grocery bag like a shield. "My . . . my father had a gun. He was loading it and I came up behind him and he shot his foot." The words tumbled out fast, without any deliberation.

"That's pretty traumatic," I said with real sympathy. "How old were you when it happened?"

"Seven. My mother said if he died it would be all my fault. He didn't, but his foot was never right. That was my fault, too. Mother made him get rid of the gun." Then her second reaction hit. "Is she all right?"

"She's okay," I replied. "A little shaken, but okay."

She closed her eyes. "That's good," she breathed. "If somebody had killed her before I . . ."

The door of Cavette's Grocery opened and Mr. Cavette himself hurried out—young Mr. Cavette, that is. He's every bit of sixty-five. Old Mr. Cavette is now in his eighties and still runs the old-fashioned cash register that he started business with sixty years ago. The youngest Mr. Cavette, whom everybody calls Junior, is pushing forty-five. Junior is the meat and produce buyer. He's the one who buys my herbs.

"Oh, Miz Hall," young Mr. Cavette said breathlessly, "I'm so glad I caught you." He has ruddy cheeks and a fluffy fringe of white hair around a bald head so shiny it looks like he polishes it with Pledge. He plays Santa in the Pecan Springs Christmas Festival, and last year the Festival Association raffled off a Christmas turkey to buy him a new Santa suit. It was about time, too, because the kids were making fun of the holes in the old one.

He held out a sack. "You forgot the rest of your groceries. Eggs, mushrooms, tomato juice— Your company'd have to go hungry if I let you go home without your breakfast fixin's."

"Thank you," Violett muttered, clutching the sack.

Young Mr. Cavette looked at his watch. "Guess I'll be seeing you at church in a little while. I understand Bobbie Jean Sawyers will be offerin' us a soprano solo." He rolled his eyes. "Fine singer, Bobbie Jean, although them high notes are a little hard on my ears."

"I can't come this morning," Violett said, ducking her head with the guilty look of a child playing hooky. "But please tell Reverend Block I'll be there tonight."

Young Mr. Cavette grinned jovially. "Faithful as you are, Miz Hall, I'm sure the good Lord won't strike you dead for missin' one service." He went back into the store, the door swinging shut behind him.

"You have company?" I asked.

Violett colored. "Just . . . a friend," she muttered. "Ms. Bayles, I'm thinking maybe I should take you up on your offer yesterday. I need to talk to a lawyer. How much do you . . ." Her voice wavered uncertainly. "I mean, is it expensive?"

"If you have a legal problem, I'd be glad to give you some advice. No charge."

That seemed to reassure her. "Rosalind Kotner and I had an agreement," she said, putting the words together slowly, as if she were stringing a bead necklace, selecting each bead separately. "She paid me some money, but now she says she's selling out and she won't give me any more." She swallowed painfully. "I was thinking that maybe a lawyer could tell me what to do."

I frowned. Why had Roz been paying Violett? "I close the shop at five today—how about if I come over after that?"

Violett gave me a grateful look. "Thanks," she said. "I'll see you then." She hurried off.

I went into Cavette's and bought a half dozen fertile brown eggs, a jar of my favorite strawberry preserves, and some feta cheese to dress up my breakfast. At home, I shoved the wet clothes into the dryer, stripped the bed and the bathroom towel racks, and threw the sheets and towels into the washer. I scrambled two eggs with the feta cheese, added some basil and thyme, topped the cooked omelet with yogurt and chives, and sat down to eat and think. By the time I'd finished the eggs and a slice of toast with jam, the clothes in the dryer were ready to be folded, the washer was ready to deliver a load to the dryer—and I was still wrestling with the question of who had tried to kill Roz.

I pulled the sheets and towels out of the dryer and heaped them on the bed. If I was any judge of character (which I was), and if I had any skill in questioning a suspect (which I did), I'd say it was ninety-ten that Meredith hadn't shot at Roz. But if she hadn't, who had? Roz thought it was Violett, but Violett had appeared genuinely surprised when I told her about the attack. And Violett's fear of guns and the story behind it seemed believable. If she was lying, she was far better at it than I would have predicted. Still, Violett shooting at Roz didn't seem any more or less unlikely than Meredith shooting at Roz.

I finished the sheets and started on the towels, going back to Meredith. My reluctance to consider her a serious suspect was a right-brain hunch that my left brain was beginning to question—probably legitimately. What if my judgment was colored by our friendship, and by my love for Jo? What if I had put too-easy questions to her and swallowed her too-quick answers—simply because I *liked* her? It was a possibility I couldn't discount.

I was putting fresh sheets on the bed when the phone rang. The voice was clipped and brusque, words bitten off and spit out fast, New York style. "Jane Dorman," it announced.

"Hello, Jane," I said, sitting on the half-made bed. "I hear you're in Vermont."

Jane gave a short laugh. "Yes," she said. "I've been reading, watching the lake, relaxing. It's beautiful up here, and very remote. Not even a phone. But I've been worrying about Roz, and when I came to town this morning for supplies, I thought I'd call you."

"Worrying?"

"She's acting strangely. I don't know if she told you,

but she turned down a big contract, an *enormous* contract. Not only that, but she doesn't seem to want to return to New York. You don't have to run right out and check on her, China, but I'd feel better if you kept an eye on her. Give me a call at the office if there's something I should know."

"Sure, I can do that," I said. I wondered if I should tell her about the shooting, but I decided against it. If Roz wanted her to know, *she* could tell her. "When will you be back in your office?"

"Tomorrow or Tuesday." Jane thanked me and hung up. I sat on the bed with the phone in my hand, staring at it for a moment and thinking that Jane wasn't the type to worry about her clients' welfare unless their welfare affected hers. But she had a big investment in Roz, and she didn't know about the Disney deal. She probably wanted somebody to spy on Roz, and I was being recruited.

I got up and finished changing the bed, a job that I actually kind of like, at least now that I have time for it. There were plenty of years when I slept more often than not on six-week-old sheets. I was topping it off with Gram's last quilt, a red-and-white pattern called Drunkard's Path because it is such a weird arrangement of curves and angles, when Bubba Harris knocked at the kitchen door. I invited him in, accepted without surprise his refusal of a cup of herb tea, and asked him, cigar and all, to sit at the kitchen table. At least he wasn't smoking the damn thing.

Bubba took off his Stetson, laid it on the table between us, and got right to the point. "Miz Bayles, what d'you know about Meredith Gilbert?"

I thought rapidly. Unless Violett had floated a lot more loose talk than I thought, and unless Constance had babbled, it wasn't likely that Bubba had stumbled onto the rumor about Jo and Roz. He probably hadn't discovered the incriminating running shoes yet, either. But Bubba's thorough. It *was* likely that he had found out about the thirty-eight. Either late last night or first thing this morning, he'd rousted out the local gun shop owner and checked the store's records. When he got around to asking Meredith for the gun—if he hadn't already—he'd do a routine print check on it and turn up mine. Sooner or later I'd find myself being asked to explain how and when I had handled that particular gun. Better to take the offensive now than be put on the defensive later.

"What do I know about Meredith Gilbert?" I asked thoughtfully. "Well, I know she came to Pecan Springs to be with her mother. I know she's staying at her mother's house until she decides what to do. I also know that she was so upset by Friday night's burglary that she went out yesterday afternoon and bought a thirty-eight."

Bubba was suddenly still. He pulled his cigar out of his mouth and laid it on the table beside his hat. "You don't say," he said, very slowly. "And just how d'you happen to know that?"

"Because Ruby and I went over there last night after the shooting," I said. "Meredith showed it to me. She'd tried it out on the range at the shop."

Bubba pushed out his lower lip, pulled it back in. "The gun'd been fired recently?"

"Yes."

He picked up his cigar and rolled it between his fingers, his eyes level on mine. "D'you know of any reason why Miz Gilbert might have it in mind to kill Miz Kotner?"

I ran swiftly through the consequences of a truthful answer. Given the state of those slugs, a ballistics test could be inconclusive, leaving the possibility but not the certainty that the bullets had come from Meredith's thirty-eight. Besides the gun, there were the shoes, clean but probably also inconclusive. There were probably a dozen similar pairs within a six-block radius. If I handed Bubba a motive—especially the powerful motive I had in mind—he would be greatly tempted to haul Meredith in for questioning, perhaps even charge her. And although my left brain accepted the fact that Meredith *could* have tried to kill Roz, my right brain maintained that she hadn't. As far as I was concerned, the jury was still hearing arguments. Bubba could hunt up his own motive.

"No," I lied, "I can't think of a reason. Meredith *knows* her, of course—Roz Kotner was her mother's friend. Roz and Meredith and I went out for dinner on Thursday evening. But a motive . . ." I shook my head. "You've got me, Chief Harris. Have you asked *her* that question?"

Bubba stuck his cigar back in his face and hoisted his bulk out of the chair. "Not yet, but I'm fixin' to." He picked up his hat. "How about you, Miz Bayles?" he added, with perfect Columbo timing. "You got a motive?"

"No," I said. "I do *not* have a motive. I'm not in the

habit of shooting at guests who are occupying my cottage. It's inhospitable."

Bubba jammed his hat on his head. "Don't reckon you'd tell me if you did," he reflected without animosity, and started for the door. He paused. "Oh, by the way, I been readin' that book."

"Book?"

"*Final Exit.*" He paused. "Miz Gilbert ever ask you to help her kill herself?"

"No," I said, "she didn't."

"Think she might've asked her daughter?"

"Meredith's already answered that question, I believe."

He pulled his cigar out of his mouth and stuck it into his shirt pocket. "Yep," he said. "She has." He started toward the door again.

I didn't get up. "Let me know if I can be of any more help."

Bubba turned with his hand on the knob, his hat pulled down over his eyes. "Guess I don't have to tell you that two on-the-scenes in two nights is pretty much a record for a person in this town. Even for a slick ex-lawyer like you." His look was bland. "Coincidence, huh?"

"Yep," I said.

Bubba gave his pants an irritated hitch and left.

For a moment, I debated whether I should call Meredith and warn her that the cops were on the way. But if I did and Bubba found out, he'd assume that Meredith had something to hide, or that *I* had something to hide, or both. In fact, if Bubba was the smart cop McQuaid insisted he was, and if he had the idea that

Meredith and I were in this together, he might have dropped in to panic me, betting that I'd alert Meredith. Nope, no phone call. Meredith would have to handle Bubba without any help from me. And Bubba's interest in the book worried me. I thought I could see where he was going with it, and I didn't like it.

I put in another load of laundry and made a quick tour of the living room with lemon oil and a dust cloth. In between, I placed two calls. The first was to Ace Car Rental, where a harried female voice informed me that the computer was still down and there was no chance of getting the information I wanted until tomorrow. The second was to Helen Jenson, on the off chance that she'd gotten back early from Waco and could check on Roz's flight schedule. But I struck out there too. No answer. I'd just put the phone down when it rang.

"Chief Harris was here," Meredith said. She sounded calm but worried. "He knew I'd bought the gun. I guess he found out from the shop owner."

"Did he take it with him?" Dumb question. Of course he took it with him. At this very moment, he was probably having somebody run ballistics.

"Yes, he took the damn thing," Meredith said. "He took my shoes, too. And he says he wants to keep the book a while longer." She gave a nervous laugh, high-pitched, edgy. "But he didn't take *me*, not yet, anyway. He just told me not to leave town." The laugh again, higher-pitched, edgier. "At least I know a decent lawyer."

I laughed too, making a joke out of it. "Yeah, I can

probably give you a good deal. My overhead's pretty low these days."

There was a silence. When Meredith spoke next, her voice was lower, more controlled. "Any developments on the Roz front?"

I hesitated and decided against volunteering the information about Roz's visit the night before. "My friend with the travel agency isn't home yet," I said. "And Ace's computer is still down. We'll get on it first thing tomorrow."

Meredith made an impatient noise. "I didn't shoot at Roz, but maybe I wish I had. I'm scared that she's going to skip town before we've come up with any concrete proof that she killed my mother." There was a brief silence. When she spoke, her voice was low, anguished. "God, China, I can't *stand* this . . . this sitting around, knowing the truth but not able to act on it. I need to *do* something."

I didn't know how to respond. "Well, I'm open to suggestions," I said at last. "Have you got a better solution?"

"Yeah," Meredith said. "Poison."

CHAPTER 15

It was eleven forty-five, and I was finishing the last of my housekeeping when I heard the shriek of a siren coming down Guadalupe. It turned into the alley and died abruptly.

I went to the kitchen door and looked out. An orange-and-white EMS ambulance had pulled up in the alley behind the cottage, the blue light on its cab flashing. A man and a woman jumped out. The woman ran around the cottage and banged on the front door. The man went to the rear of the ambulance and pulled out an equipment bag. By the time he got to the door, I was there too.

"No answer," the woman said. She was a slender, dark-haired woman with regular features, a firm jaw, and dark-rimmed glasses. She wore navy slacks and a gray uniform shirt with a shoulder patch that said CITY OF PECAN SPRINGS, EMERGENCY MEDICAL SERVICE. Her gray plastic nametag said that she was A. GARZA,

SENIOR MED. TECH. She carried herself like a woman in charge of decision-making.

"What's going on?" I asked.

"Medical emergency," the man said. He dropped the equipment bag, tried the knob, and pushed at the door with his shoulder. His brushy crew cut was the color of weathered brick and his face was pockmarked with ancient acne scars. His nametag said he was P. D. SCHWAMKRUG, MED. TECH. It was the kind of name that sounded like it should be printed in Gothic letters, with lots of curlicues. "Door's locked. How do we get in?"

"Follow me." I ran to the south side of the cottage, the man and woman on my heels. "What's wrong?"

"A woman called in a medical emergency, dropped the phone, and left an open line," Garza said. "The 911 operator dispatched us here."

I pushed open the French doors and stepped into the darkened bedroom. "Roz," I yelled. "Hey, Roz!"

No answer. I glanced around. The bedroom was empty, the bed unmade, its blue coverlet flung back. The blue velvet slipper chair in the corner was buried under an untidy heap of Roz's lingerie, and a pair of pantyhose was draped like a silken snake over the closet door. The silence was heavy, ominous, spiced with a strange coppery odor with an undertone of garlic, as if Roz had been cooking.

The medical technicians pushed past me into the hall and I followed. The odor was sharper. The receiver of the white wall telephone an arm's reach from the bathroom door dangled by its spring-coil cord. There was a bloody handprint on the white-painted wall beside it, and beneath that a long bloody smear, as if someone, falling, had put a hand on the wall for support. Bloody footprints on the beige carpet led from the bathroom to the phone and back again. In the bathroom door was a pair of pink running shoes, soles up and bright red, like rubber stamps inked in blood. Inside the shoes were Roz's feet.

When I looked into the bathroom, what I saw made my breakfast rise in an acrid bubble at the back of my throat. Roz was still dressed in the pink sweats I'd seen her wearing earlier, but the pink was mostly red. She was facedown on the tile in a puddle of blood and vomit that had spread around the toilet and under the sink. The toilet was full of blood, there was bright red blood in the bathtub, and blood in the bathroom sink. She was clutching a blood-soaked washcloth in her left hand. The scene looked like something out of *The Texas Chainsaw Massacre*.

Garza pushed the door open all the way and stepped over Roz and into the bathroom. She knelt in the blood to feel for a pulse at Roz's throat. "No carotid," she said after a moment. "No apparent respiration." Her voice was calm and steady. "Let's put her on the monitor and see if we get any cardiac."

Schwamkrug disappeared. Garza pulled Roz's sweatshirt up and scanned her back, flopped her over and quickly inspected her chest. Seeing Roz's face, I swallowed. Her bloody mouth was open in a last anguished gasp, and her face was the color of washed-out denim. The color of asphyxiation.

"No wounds," Garza said. "I'd say bleeding ulcer."

Then she pulled Roz's head back, cleared her mouth, and began doing chest compressions.

A bleeding ulcer? I remembered Roz saying something about an ulcer. But she hadn't seemed to think the condition was serious, certainly not serious enough to erupt like this, in a spewing volcano of hot red blood.

A minute later, Schwamkrug reappeared with a black case and what looked like a small duffel bag. I stepped aside and he leaned into the bathroom, putting the case on the floor. "Any luck?" he asked.

"Unresponsive," Garza said. She did one last chest compression and sat up straight. She yanked some wires out of the case and deftly attached them, one to each shoulder, a third to Roz's chest wall. I heard a thin, continuous *bleep* and the small green scope on the monitor showed a flat line. Garza pulled two paddles out of the case and adjusted a knob. "Stand clear," she said.

I turned away from what came next, but I could hear the small clap of the defibrillator. The *bleep* didn't change.

"She's gone," Schwamkrug remarked clinically.

Garza shook her head. "Give me an airway. No, a P.T.L." Schwamkrug pulled a cellophane-wrapped package out of the duffel bag, and a cylinder of oxygen. A moment later Garza had inserted a plastic tube in Roz's throat and the oxygen began to hiss.

While Garza worked, Schwamkrug went to the wall phone and dialed. A moment later I heard him talking in low tones, first to the dispatcher, then to the hospital. He came back and spoke briefly to Garza. "Doc Bennett says to give her five minutes. If you don't get anything, he'll issue a T.O.D."

"Time of death," Garza said to me.

The next five minutes ticked out endlessly while the three of us waited: Garza kneeling on bloody knees beside Roz's bloody body; Schwamkrug with his arms folded across his chest, leaning against the doorjamb; me alternately pacing up and down the hallway and crowding into the doorway beside Schwamkrug, watching Garza's effort to hiss the life back into Roz. This pair saw death every day, and maybe they got accustomed to its faces, its smells, its taste. But not me—and this was the second corpse I'd seen in a week. One part of me was already making a list of questions. But another part, the operative part, was still coping with the sight of so much blood, with Roz's blue-denim face, with the coppery, garlicky smell of vomited death that hung in the room like stale kitchen odors.

Garza looked past Schwamkrug to me. "Friend of yours?" she asked, her voice colored with professional sympathy.

"I knew her," I said. "This is my cottage." I looked at the blood pooling in the floor. "You said it was an ulcer?"

"That's what it looks like," Garza replied. "She would have died from the bleeding in pretty short order if she hadn't asphyxiated first. She must have passed out when she was making the call, recovered enough to drag herself in here, started to vomit, passed out again, asphyxiated."

"What could have triggered the bleeding?" I asked.

"Something corrosive, maybe," Garza said. "Or maybe she developed a severe gastroenteritis, and the vomiting kicked up the ulcer."

Beside me, Schwamkrug straightened and looked at his watch. "That's five," he said.

Garza sat back on her heels. "Okay," she said. "Get Bennett." She looked at me. "I'm sorry."

"Yeah," I said, feeling a sweep of pity. "Me too." I hadn't liked Roz, and all the evidence led me to believe that she was a murderer. But nobody should have to die this way, gasping for air, choking on blood and vomit, knowing she was losing it—

My racing mind pulled up like a car screeching to a hard-braked stop. Last night there had been two shots through the window. This morning, Roz was stretched out on the floor in the final agonies of death.

Call it intuition, a hunch, whatever. There wasn't any visible evidence, but I knew, just the same. I turned as Schwamkrug went to the phone. "After you talk to the doctor," I said, "you'd better get Chief Harris over here. I think she's been poisoned."

The cop showed up at the kitchen door five minutes later. He was a chunky, broad-shouldered man in his late twenties. He wore a thick blond mustache and his brown eyes were narrowed and alert. He stood easily, arm held out slightly from the holstered .357 Magnum at his hip. The nametag on his pocket said he was Officer Petersen.

"Understand there's been a death," he said, glancing past me into the empty living room. "A poisoning?"

I didn't answer his question, just stepped back to let him in. "In the bathroom," I said.

He went into the hall, where Garza and Schwamkrug were packing up their equipment. After a few words with Garza, he stuck his head in the bathroom. A moment later, he came back into the living room. "What makes you think she was poisoned?"

I put my hands in my pockets. I didn't want to tell the complicated story twice. "Is the chief on his way?"

Petersen raised both yellow eyebrows. "It's Sunday," he said, as if that explained something. I gave him a blank look and he added, "The Cowboys are playin' the Packers."

"When you call him," I said, "tell him that Rosalind Kotner is dead."

Petersen heaved a sigh. "Look, lady, I don't mean to be offensive at a time like this, but I don't think we should bother the chief this after—"

"The woman's name is Rosalind Kotner," I said. "StrawBerry Bear."

"StrawBerry—" He looked at me for a minute, and then it dawned on him. "The lady who does the teevee show?"

"That's the one."

His brown eyes widened. "No kiddin'," he said. "Hey, my girls watch that bear every single Saturday. They know the words to all the songs." He frowned. "But I still don't think it's a case for the chief—especially seein' as how it's Green Bay."

"The chief might think so," I said quietly. "Somebody took a couple of shots at her last night. He handled the investigation himself, and when he was done, he sent out a special patrol to keep an eye on her."

Petersen looked at me. His tongue went out, licked

at the corner of his yellow mustache once, twice. Then, without another word, he turned and went through the door. A moment later, I could hear the crackle of a squad car radio out in the alley.

The medical technicians came into the living room, Garza in her socks, carrying her bloody shoes. The knees of her slacks were bloody too, and there were smears of blood on her sleeve. "I'll get on the radio and let the dispatcher know what's happening," she said. She handed Schwamkrug a clipboard. "While I'm doing that, P.D., you can get started on the report."

Schwamkrug looked pained, as if he didn't like taking orders from a woman. But when she had gone, he sat down in the chair across from the loveseat, pulled out a pen, hunched over and began to fill in blanks.

While he was writing, I stepped back into the kitchen and did a quick scan. There was no sign that Roz had eaten breakfast that morning. The stainless steel sink was empty and wiped dry, and the kitchen counter was bare except for a plain water tumbler beside the sink. Traces of tomato juice stained the sides and in the bottom I could see the residue of an incompletely dissolved powder. I bent over and sniffed it, not touching. Garlic, faint but definite. Roz must have used the glass for her morning cocktail. But what was the residue? Was she adding some sort of herbal powder to her garlic cocktail? Or had somebody put something into it—something deadly?

There was a box of tissues on the counter. I pulled one out and went to the refrigerator. Using the tissue and two fingers, I opened the door. The refrigerator was nearly empty, with that abandoned, sterile loneliness of unused refrigerators. On the top shelf was a glass bottle of tomato juice, half full, and beside it, the small bottle of garlic extract Roz had bought from me on Thursday morning, about two-thirds full. I'd handled that bottle of garlic extract at least twice, once when I stocked it and again when I sold it. Unless it had been wiped, my prints were all over it. My prints on Meredith's thirty-eight, my prints on the extract bottle. Two more coincidences for Bubba to chew on. Not counting the fact that Roz had died in the bathroom of my cottage.

I bent down and peered at the tomato juice bottle. It was hard to be sure because of the natural cloudiness of the juice, but it looked like there was a very thin layer of undissolved residue in the bottom of the bottle, like the powder in the glass. I guessed that a fair amount of something powdery had been added to the tomato juice and shaken up in a hurry, without a great deal of effort being given to dissolving it. The killer would have counted on the cloudiness of the juice to mask any undissolved powder. I'm no toxicologist, although I've picked up quite a few things during various pretrial investigations and I'm familiar with the diagnostic characteristics of plant poisoning. I knew about one poisoning that had resulted in the kind of severe hemorrhagic gastroenteritis that could have triggered Roz's ulcer. The victim—the owner of a large fruit shipping company in the lower Rio Grande Valley—had apparently failed to hold up his end of a bargain with a dope smuggling ring operating between Brownsville and Mexico City. One of his former colleagues tied him up and dosed him with malathion, a pesticide used to spray fruit. The first symptom was massive nosebleed, quickly followed by bloody vomiting and bloody diarrhea, cardiac arrhythmia, and pulmonary edema. He died within hours from respiratory failure. It wasn't my case, thank God. I preferred the kind where I could develop some personal sympathy for the defendant, even if I privately thought he—or she—was guilty as hell.

As I shut the refrigerator door, I saw a small bottle with a red-and-yellow lid lying on the floor, coated on the inside with a fine gray dust. I knelt down and sniffed it. I caught a very slight, lingering scent of garlic—no, not a scent, exactly. It was more like a bitter aftertaste, at the back of my tongue rather than in my nose. Garlic powder? This stuff had the same texture, but the odor of garlic powder was stronger, more pronounced. I stared at the bottle for a minute, while something tried to nudge its way into my conscious mind. But it didn't make it, and I straightened up.

As far as I could tell, there was nothing out of place, no sign of forcible entry, no indication that a murder had been committed here. Only in the bathroom—I pressed my lips tight together, pushing down the sudden nausea. Roz had died a horrible death. Not a death you would wish on your most bitter enemy.

Unless you thought she had murdered your mother. The words came into my mind as if I'd read them off a teleprompter. Had it been Meredith, after all? Having missed her target last night, had she tried again this morning? I remembered something else. When I'd asked Meredith if she had a better idea for dealing with Roz, she'd come back with one word.

Poison.

A few minutes later, a squad car braked to a sliding stop in the alley. Doors slammed, running feet crunched on gravel. Bubba pushed the front door open and barreled in, followed by Garza and the mustached patrolman. Bubba's eyes were narrow slits in a face the color of a piece of raw sirloin, and he was chewing viciously on his cigar. I thought about asking him the score, but it didn't seem like the right time.

"No question she's dead?" he muttered at the med techs.

Garza shook her head. "Messy business. Lot of blood."

"Great," Bubba said with enormous weariness. "Fuckin' *great.*" His eyes flicked to me, registered disgusted recognition, then back again to Garza. "What was it? Knife? Blunt instrument?"

Petersen glanced at me. "She says it was poison."

Bubba turned to Garza. "What do you say?"

Garza told Bubba what she had told me about the bleeding ulcer and the asphyxiation. When she finished, Bubba glanced at me and waited.

"Roz had an ulcer," I said, "but she didn't act as if it were terribly serious. I don't think the bleeding was spontaneous. After what happened last night, I believe the enteritis was induced, and that kicked off the ulcer."

"Possible?" Bubba asked Garza.

She shrugged. "I don't know anything about what happened last night. But yeah, it's possible. The M.E. will say for sure." The pager at her belt made a beeping sound and she looked at Bubba. "If you're through with us, we've got another run."

Bubba nodded. Schwamkrug stood up, tore out the pink copy of the report, and put it on the coffee table. He and Garza left, carrying their equipment. I wondered what kind of trauma they were headed to now. An accident on I-35? A heart attack triggered by the excitement of a fourth-down kick? I was glad I didn't have their jobs. I'd already seen enough death to last me.

Bubba jabbed a finger in my direction. "Stay put," he growled. "You're first after the corpse."

I sat down on the loveseat while he stepped into the bathroom. He came out a minute or two later, jaw working. I knew what he was thinking because I'd gone over the same ground. It was possible that Roz's death, ugly as it was, had nothing to do with last night's shooting. It was also possible that the killer had decided to come back and finish her off. He was weighing each possibility against the other, and against the work involved if he treated this as a murder investigation. Finally, with an irritated jerk of his cigar, he made up his mind.

"Notify the M.E.," he barked at Petersen, who had been standing nervously by the door. "Get Masters and his video gear over here, pronto. Get J. P. and the ID boys for prints. And tell the dispatcher to keep a tight lid on this thing. Nothin' to the tee-vee, newspaper, radio, until I say so. Got that?"

Petersen gulped, nodded, and fled.

Bubba folded his arms across his chest and looked at me. He pulled his forehead down and pushed his cigar up past his nose in a creditable imitation of Winston Churchill. I fought the nervous urge to giggle. This was not a laughing matter.

"All right, Miz Bayles," he said, "I want the whole thing."

"I don't know any more than you do," I said. I was lying, because I knew what I'd seen in the kitchen. But Bubba would find the evidence for himself. Anyway, I didn't want him to know I'd been poking around in there. "I heard the siren. I got here when EMS did, and let them in through the patio door. I didn't want them breaking down the front door of my cottage."

"You see the lady this morning?"

I nodded. "Around seven-thirty, near the corner of Guadalupe and Crockett. She was out for a walk. I have no idea when she returned or how long she was gone." I frowned. The killer must have come in while she was walking. I would have thought she'd lock up, given last night's attack. But maybe she'd locked the front door and forgotten about the French doors. Or maybe the killer had forced one of the casement windows.

Bubba rubbed his chin. "You got any idea about that garlic smell in the bathroom?"

I felt a grudging admiration. Bubba had a sharp nose and a sharper curiosity. "Every morning, she drank tomato juice mixed with a couple of spoonfuls of garlic extract. She used it as a health tonic. I assume she drank it this morning, as usual."

Bubba grunted. "Anything else?"

I shook my head. I could have told him about my conversation with Roz last night. I could also have told him about Meredith's one-word answer to my question about dealing with Roz. But I had this terrible ambivalence about Meredith. Part of me suspected that she *could* have killed Roz. The other part knew she wouldn't have. That was the part that didn't want to give Bubba any more bright ideas than he could come up with himself.

Bubba took his cigar out of his mouth and stuck it into the pocket of his uniform. There was a silence while he considered his next step. I stared at the stain that this cigar and numerous others had left on his pocket. Poor Mrs. Bubba, I thought irrelevantly. I'd hate to wash those shirts. But maybe she sent his uniforms out. I looked at the creases in the sleeves and the vertical creases down the front and felt gratified. Good for Mrs. Bubba. At least she hadn't washed and ironed *that* shirt.

Petersen came back. "Masters is on his way," he said, and added, in a lower voice, "He was watchin' the game too."

Bubba sighed. "What's the score?"

"Twenty-one three, Green Bay," Petersen replied unhappily. "Middle of the first quarter."

Bubba sighed again, the sigh of a man who has heard this one before and knows the way it turns out. He turned to me. "What about next of kin?"

"To my knowledge," I replied, "Ms. Kotner didn't have any immediate family. But to be sure of that, you'd probably better ask her fiancé. He'd know."

"Fiancé? She was engaged to somebody?"

"Yeah. To Howard Keenan."

Bubba's jaw went slack. "*Senator* Howard Keenan?"

I nodded.

"Oh, *crap*," Bubba said, with great feeling.

In spite of myself, I felt sorry for him. Not only would he have to deal with the press, he'd have to deal with Washington, too—the Senator's aides, maybe even the Senator himself. Chances were good that Pecan Springs would be overrun by outside law enforcement agencies, from the Texas Rangers to the FBI. Everybody would be Monday-morning quarterbacking his investigation. Not to mention the pressure he was going to get from the county D.A., *plus* the mayor and the City Council.

I took advantage. "Do you suppose I could go now?"

Bubba shifted from one foot to the other. "Yeah, I reckon," he said reluctantly. "But stay where I can find you if I want you." I was out the door when he thought of something else. "And keep your mouth shut," he yelled after me. "I don't want a bunch of reporters rootin' around like pigs in a sweet potato patch. You hear?"

I heard. So also, I thought, had half the neighborhood.

Outside, I breathed in the clean air, tasting it, and finding it blessedly free of the smell of garlic and blood and wet cigar. But when I started up the path to the house, my way was blocked by Mr. Cowan, from across the alley. He was leaning an arthritic, blue-veined hand on a carved walking stick, scrawny jowls like wattles, watery blue eyes avid with curiosity. Something round—a cud of Red Man, most likely—was tucked in his right cheek and his white-stubbled chin was stained with tobacco. He wore an old brown sweater with a dribble of what looked like oatmeal down the front, and a pair of baggy brown pants, the cuffs turned up several times and pinned with diaper pins. A sour-faced Pekingese glowered at me from behind his ankle.

"Somethin' goin' on," he remarked in a shrill, knowing voice. The Peke growled.

"Yes," I said, edging backward, out of reach of the dog. I don't mind big dogs so much, it's the little yappy ones that make me nervous. I have the theory—untested, at least so far—that they bite harder and hold on longer. "Ms. Kotner, who was staying here, has died." Bubba probably wouldn't approve of my telling the old man, but I didn't think he would run back home and phone the newspaper. Besides, he might have seen something.

"Same one as was shot at last night?" Mr. Cowan asked loudly. The Peke growled again, and he frowned. "Now, hush, Lady Lula. There ain't no call to take on so. This here person ain't gonna bite. Not while I'm here, anyhoo." Lady Lula hushed, apparently comforted by the old man's assurance of my good will.

I nodded. "Yes, the same one."

"Got her this time, eh?" Mr. Cowan asked with satisfaction.

"It's not exactly clear how she died," I said evasively. "But she wasn't shot."

"Neighborhood's goin' to hell," Mr. Cowan declared with a snort. He spit tobacco juice into the lavender and scrubbed the back of one hand across his stubbly chin. "Po-lice in the alley all hours of the night, people hangin' round, people gettin' shot at. Not a safe place for a law-abidin' body." He glanced down at Lady Lula. "Not safe for critters, neither. Next thing you know, it'll be dogs they're after, eh, Miss Lula?"

Miss Lula barked in a frenzy of apprehension.

I frowned. "People hanging around?" I asked. "You mean, around the cottage?"

Mr. Cowan considered my question as if he were not used to being listened to. He nodded. "Seen 'em m'self." He switched his cane from one hand to the other.

"Saw them when?" I asked urgently. "Who did you see?"

"Runnin' down the alley in them purty blue suits," he replied with consummate scorn. "Don't work hard enough during the week, I reckon. Got to run on Sunday mornin' to make theirselfs tired."

I frowned. Meredith had a blue jogging suit. Had Mr. Cowan seen her running down the alley this morning?

Lady Lula launched a swift sortie with the clear intention of nipping all potential dognappers, beginning with me. I stepped back again. "Did you see anybody besides the jogger?" I asked.

"People *allez* walkin' up this alley, pokin' around," Mr. Cowan muttered, emphasizing his words with another spurt of tobacco juice. "People lookin' in the garbage. People lookin' in windows. Damn peepin' Toms."

"Did you see anybody peeping this morning?"

Mr. Cowan frowned. "This mornin'?" he repeated vaguely. "This mornin'?" He scratched his chin, reflected a moment, spit into the lavender again. "Mebbe

I did. Or mebbe 'twas t'other mornin'." He grinned, showing toothless gums. "Happens all time. All time."

And that was the best I could get out of him, no matter how hard I pressed. I finally ushered him to the cottage door, told Petersen when he answered my knock that the old man claimed to have seen people "hanging around" the cottage, and left Mr. Cowan and Lady Lula to Bubba's tender mercies.

I went home to think.

Back in my kitchen, I put on the copper teakettle and brewed a cup of ruby-red rose-hip tea from a batch of special rose hips I'd gathered at an old farmstead a couple of miles out of town. Rose hips—good to clear the mind, good to think with. Whatever was buried in my unconscious needed some encouragement to get through. What I wanted to connect with had something to do with the scent of garlic. I cupped the steaming mug in both hands, savoring the citrusy tang and the remembered fragrance of roses, almost like an after-taste.

My right brain nudged me. It wasn't the scent of garlic I needed to connect with, it was the *taste*.

I put down the cup. No, that wasn't it. It wasn't the taste of garlic, it was the *aftertaste*.

And then I had it.

One evening the summer before last, I'd been invited to dinner in Jo's backyard. Jo was there, of course, and Roz, visiting from New York with her agent, and a half dozen of Jo's friends and co-conspirators on the Pecan Springs Park project. Roz had discovered a large ant mound at the base of Jo's favorite rosebush and insisted that something be done about it, on the spot. They could be fire ants, the bane of local backyards. Jo didn't think they were fire ants and neither did I, when I was called in to consult. But to appease Roz, Jo sent us into the garage for ant poison. We found it on a shelf beside the door, in a rusty can with the label half torn off. Something sulfate, it was—thallium sulfate, I seemed to remember. When Roz brought it out, Jo kiddingly told her to be careful of it around the food because it was toxic—so toxic that an eighth of a teaspoon would put you away forever. It was on the EPA's no-no list and wasn't available any longer. What I remembered about the episode, and about the ant poison, was that when you sniffed the stuff, you got a bitter, garlicky aftertaste.

I emptied the last of the tea in one gulp and reached for my denim jacket. The last time I'd seen that can of thallium sulfate was on the shelf in Jo's garage.

On my bike, it took all of four minutes to get to Jo's. Meredith's Mazda was gone, and I didn't hesitate. I leaned my bike against the house and went around the back, to the garage. The side door was unlocked, just as Jo had always left it. I flicked on the light and surveyed the shelf where Roz and I had found the ant poison.

The can wasn't there.

In fact, as I saw when I looked around, the garage had been neatened. The bundled newspapers, piles of old magazines, cans of paint—the clutter that I remembered was gone and the remaining tools and gardening supplies were tidily arranged on pegs or shelves or on the floor. Either Jo had had an attack of housecleaning frenzy in the weeks before she died, or Meredith had gone through in the last couple of days and cleaned everything out. I paused as something clicked. No, it wasn't Jo who'd taken care of that chore, it was Meredith. Yesterday morning she'd mentioned that the garage needed cleaning, and she intended to do it that day.

I went out, closing the door behind me. Had Meredith found the thallium sulfate when she was cleaning and recognized it as a deadly poison?

When the shooting was unsuccessful, had she turned to poison—*ant* poison?

Or had the ant poison been thrown out weeks or months ago? If so, what had killed Roz Kotner?

No answers. My right brain still dug in its heels when it came to believing that Meredith was a killer. My left brain still insisted I was losing the objectivity I'd always been so proud of, especially in the light of the mounting evidence of Meredith's guilt. I biked home more slowly than I had come.

"You're kidding," Ruby breathed, straightening up from the bookrack she was dusting in the Cave. It was already one-thirty, and I hadn't opened up yet.

"I wish I were," I said.

She shuddered. "*Poison*—"

"That's just my guess," I said. "Nobody will know for sure until the medical examiner is finished."

"Yes, but it stands to reason." Ruby was frowning. "Have you come up with any suspects?"

"I'm not the one who's doing the investigation, Ruby. The question is, who will Bubba come up with, especially given the fact that he'll be under pressure to do it quick?"

She chewed her lower lip. "Meredith?"

"She's already on his list." I reported Bubba's two visits that morning, the first to me, the second to Meredith. I repeated Mr. Cowan's scornful remark about the Sunday-morning jogger in the pretty blue suit. And I told her about the can of ant poison that no longer sat on the shelf in Jo's garage.

"Gosh," Ruby said, awestruck at the bleak litany, "things really look *bad* for Meredith."

"Yeah," I said. "Looks like she's guilty as hell."

"To somebody who doesn't know her," Ruby added.

"Even to somebody who does," I said ominously.

Ruby thought of something else. "China, what are we going to do about Jo's murder now that Roz is out of the picture? Can we still prove that Roz did it?"

"The evidence is circumstantial and presumptive."

"English, please."

"If I were the D.A., I'd want a witness. I'd want fingerprints. I'd want something to tie Roz to the crime." I paused. "Anyway, now that Roz is dead, I'm not so sure we want to prove that she killed Jo."

"Why not?"

"Because we'd have to give that information to Bubba."

"And what's wrong with that?" Ruby demanded indignantly, narrowing her green eyes. "Roz may be dead, but so is Jo. And we *have* to tell people that she didn't commit suicide. We have to clear her name."

"I'm afraid it's not that simple. To prove that Roz killed Jo, we have to establish her motive, which means revealing Jo's relationship with Roz. Do you want people like Arnold Seidensticker knowing the details of Jo's personal life?"

Ruby chewed on that for a minute.

"Furthermore," I went on, "the way things stand now, Bubba probably hasn't come up with a plausible motive for Meredith. But if he knew that Roz killed Meredith's mother, that would clinch it. And then, of course, there's Roz's will."

"But I thought you said that Meredith can't inherit Roz's money through her mother. Wouldn't Bubba know that?"

"Maybe, maybe not. But Meredith probably doesn't. Money—even if it's merely the expectation of money—is a classic motive for murder. Add money to revenge and you've got an unbeatable combination, at least as far as the D.A. is concerned."

Ruby shook her head stubbornly. "I still don't—"

I sighed. "Put yourself in Bubba's boots, Ruby. What would *you* do if the City Council and the county D.A. and a U.S. Senator were coming on hot and heavy for an arrest and you had Meredith up your sleeve?"

"Well, then," Ruby said with the air of someone who has come to a logical conclusion, "why don't you find out who *really* killed Roz? Then Bubba wouldn't arrest Meredith."

"Sure," I said. "But Violett is the only other person I can think of who might have done it and—" Violett. I'd forgotten about Violett. "I'm supposed to see her this afternoon."

"Well, go over there now," Ruby said. "Tell her about Roz's death and get her reaction. If she didn't do it, we'll have to get busy and figure out who did."

I stared at her. Out of the mouths of babes. "Will you open the shop for me?"

"Sure. I have a big job to do anyway. I need to build a new display before the media show up."

"The media?"

"Roz Kotner isn't your everyday, run-of-the-mill murder victim," Ruby said patiently. "When the newspapers and the TV reporters and the tourists find out that StrawBerry Bear is dead, they'll be flocking around. I don't mean to be crass about it, but *some* of that traffic will be hoofing past my window. I need a display that will catch their attention."

"On Roz? I didn't know you carried kids' stuff."

"I don't," Ruby replied absently, going to a shelf and pulling out a few books.

When I left, she was building a display on reincarnation.

CHAPTER 16

There were two problems, of course. It took a substantial stretch of the imagination to see Violett sneaking into the cottage a few minutes before or after our encounter this morning to dump ant poison into Roz's tomato juice. It took an even more substantial stretch to come up with a *why*. Violett thought that she and Roz had some kind of agreement that she needed to collect on. But with Roz dead, Violett was, as we say in Texas, up shit creek without a paddle.

There was no answer to my knock on Violett's door. The Siamese jumped lightly off the porch swing where he was napping and arched his back in an indolent stretch. There were half a dozen cats lying under the porch swing, but he was the only one *on* it. Obviously, he was in charge and the other cats knew their place—beneath him. He gave my jeans an arrogant sniff and arranged his two front paws on my right foot as I knocked for the second and third times.

"Not home, huh?" I asked him. I'd told Violett I'd be there after five. Maybe she hadn't believed young Mr. Cavette when he assured her that the good Lord wouldn't strike her dead for missing one service. Maybe she'd gone to the church this afternoon.

Cat—I couldn't force myself to call him Pudding—pricked dark ears forward and gave me a penetrating blue-eyed stare, assessing my intelligence. Then, with a gruff, throaty *meow*, he stepped off my foot, strode purposefully down the steps, and crossed in front of the garage. He paused at the corner of the house, looked back over his shoulder, and spoke again, peremptorily.

I, too, knew my place. I followed Cat around the garage to the open back door. I knocked and called Violett's name several times, but there was no answer.

"Should I go in?" I addressed the question to the Siamese, feeling like Alice speaking to the Cheshire Cat.

By way of answer, Cat shouldered the door open and stepped into the kitchen.

Again, I followed. The house was quiet except for Petey pouring liquid cadenzas into the musty air. Cat leaped to the linoleum-covered counter and from there stepped to the window ledge over the kitchen sink, where he sat watching me, flicking the tip of his charcoal tail. I glanced in the sink and saw several unwashed dishes—an omelet skillet crusted with egg, a single plate, two glasses that had held tomato juice. Beside the sink was a wooden cutting board, a knife, the shells of two eggs, half an onion, several cloves of fresh garlic, and a cello-wrapped tray of mushrooms three-quarters full.

I turned around. On the table was one of Violett's father's antique typewriters. Beside the typewriter was the wooden caddy of spice bottles with red-and-yellow lids. One bottle was missing. Beside the caddy was a rusty, dented can with the label half torn off. It was the ant poison from Jo's garage.

With a velvety thud, Cat leaped from the counter to the floor, walked to a closed door in the kitchen wall, and waited for me to open it. When I did, I saw a steep, narrow flight of worn wooden stairs. Cat took the stairs swiftly and turned at the top with restrained impatience, summoning me.

I hesitated. I was trespassing. I'd be in an awkward fix if Violett came in and caught me. But there was the can of ant poison on the table and Cat at the top of the stairs, muttering an imperial command. I climbed the stairs and followed him down a short, dark hallway to a closed door. With a guttural meow, he sat. This was the place. I pushed the door open and went in.

Violett lay on her stomach, diagonally across the white chenille spread, her head and one arm hanging limply off the side of the bed nearest me, over a white enameled bedpan. Blood-stained vomit overflowed the pan and puddled on the wood floor. The room was acrid with the smell of vomit and garlic.

I stepped to the bed, bent over the silent figure, and put a finger to her throat. She was breathing irregularly and shallowly and there was a faint pulse. I rolled her over on her back and pulled her head back over the edge of the bed to make it easier for her to breathe. She moaned and stirred, then was still.

The phone sat on the bedside table beside a framed picture of a blue-robed Jesus holding a sheep, a woolly flock arranged picturesquely at his feet. I dialed 911, giving Violett's address to the dispatcher and telling her that I suspected poison. "Better get the police here too," I said. As I put the phone down, I saw a long-barreled revolver on the table, lying on a typewritten note. Some of the characters were dirty and badly out of line, but the note had been typed with a sure, firm touch. I read it without picking it up.

To Whom It May Concern:

Last night, I tried to shoot Rosalind Kotner. But I missed, so I put ant poison in her tomato juice. The Lord told me to do this because she is a wicked woman who doesn't deserve to live. She thought she was outside the reach of man's law, but Vengeance Is Mine Saith The Lord.

Now His work is done. I go to be with Him forever more. His name is praised.

Violett Hall

I stared at the note. It looked like Bubba had lucked out. All the loose ends were right here. Violett had neatly and conveniently tied them all together.

But there was something about the note that troubled me. I tried to focus on what it was, but I couldn't. The whole thing was too much, emotionally, and my mind didn't want to function. I was having a hard enough time dealing with the larger picture, never mind the details. Jo and Roz both dead, Violett near death—too many, too much, too awful. What had been gained by all this dying?

On the bed, Violett moaned again, and I turned to her. Her eyes were open and glassy in her pale face and her chest was heaving. She was gasping for breath in deep, labored gulps. I yanked the bedspread loose on one side and pulled it over her, then bent down and smoothed her wispy brown hair.

"You'll be okay, Violett," I said, with more conviction than I felt. She looked inches away from death. "Help is on the way." But I wasn't sure she wanted help. She had chosen to die. And if she lived, she'd have to face the law.

She shuddered convulsively, trying to bring her eyes into focus. She tried to say something but her lips couldn't form the words. Then her eyes rolled back in her head until there were nothing but whites, and she lapsed into unconsciousness. She was still alive, but there was no telling how long she'd stay that way.

A siren wailed. I ran down the stairs, dashed through the house to the front door, and flung it open to Garza and Schwamkrug. "This way," I said urgently, ignoring their blinks of surprise. "Hurry! She's upstairs, still alive."

Garza turned to Schwamkrug. "May be a transport. Get the scoop and the stretcher." Schwamkrug headed for the ambulance. Garza followed me to the back of the house and up the stairs, carrying the defibrillator and the bag with the oxygen equipment. In the bedroom she went to work expertly on Violett's waxlike, unmoving body, following the same routine she'd followed with Roz. The monitor showed a faint, arrhythmic beeping, but the electrical shock of the defibrillator seemed to regularize it, at least temporarily. She'd already set up oxygen and an IV when Schwamkrug arrived with two aluminum slats, each about a foot wide, linked with crosswise straps.

"Another one?" he asked, taking in Violett's unmoving body and the pan of blood-stained vomit. "What is this, an epidemic?"

"Get the scoop under her," Garza said, pulling off Violett's shoes.

Schwamkrug slid one of the straps under Violett's right side, the other under her left, and fastened the straps across her. She was trussed up and immobile.

"We're ready to transport her," Garza said to me. "Can you carry the oxygen and the IV?" With me close behind, linked to Violett by two plastic umbilicals, the techs picked up the scoop and headed for the steep, narrow stairs. I imagined disaster, but they successfully wrestled her down. In the kitchen, Schwamkrug had already set up a wheeled aluminum gurney. I ran to open the front door.

In the lane, a squad car pulled up in back of the ambulance and the cop with the yellow mustache got out and started up the walk, leaving the car door open and the radio playing. I could hear Frank Gifford doing the play-by-play of the Dallas–Green Bay game. Garza and Schwamkrug, with an inert Violett on the gurney, brushed past him on their hurried way down the walk to the ambulance.

Petersen stared at their backs, then turned to me. His eyes narrowed. "You again?"

"Yeah," I said grimly, watching Violett being hoisted into the ambulance. "Same song, second verse."

Petersen followed my look. "Dead?"

"Close enough." I sighed. "You'd better call the chief."

Petersen glared. "Look, lady, the chief's still got his hands full with the *last* one you called in. When I left, he was on the phone to the mayor. This one will have to wait. I'll get a couple of patrolmen to come and secure the place until he gets around to—"

"Yeah, sure," I said agreeably. "But if I were you, I'd get on that radio and tell Chief Harris that there's been a poisoning, and that the symptoms are similar to those displayed by Roz Kotner. I'd also tell him that there's a suicide note, a can of ant poison, and a gun."

It took Petersen ten seconds to make up his mind. Then he turned and sprinted for the patrol car.

I stood for a moment, thinking about the note and about what I'd seen. Then I went back into the house. Cat was in the kitchen, polishing off the last of the cream in the blue bowl in the corner. He licked his whiskers, raised his elegant head, and stared at me, asking for more.

"Sorry, Cat," I said. "I'd hate to feed you something that had ant poison in it." I went to the sink and looked again. Yes, I'd recalled correctly. There was one skillet, one plate, and two glasses. Violett had had company for breakfast, but only one of them had eaten. Which one? I could guess.

I turned to the kitchen table and looked at the typewriter, a polished black Royal, probably dating from the thirties. It was undoubtedly the machine on which the note had been typed. I stared at it for a minute. Violett said she'd never learned to type.

I took the stairs two at a time. I reexamined the note. I'd been right the first time. There was not a single error, not a strikeover, and the spacing and weight of the keystrokes were equal—all this on an old-style, unforgiving machine. Whoever typed it had been an experienced typist.

I looked again at the gun. It was a long-barreled thirty-eight, like an old-fashioned police service revolver—*not* the same thirty-eight Meredith had shown me, now in Bubba's possession. I'd bet dollars to doughnuts that this was the weapon that had been fired at Roz. I was even more sure when I looked down and saw the shoes that Garza had pulled off Violett's feet—running shoes. I picked one up. The sole had a zigzag tread pattern. I put it down again and stood, thinking.

By the time the siren had sounded out front I was back downstairs, sharing the sofa with a lazy trio of gray tabbies. To the tune of Petey's liquid glissandos, I'd sorted my thoughts and drawn at least one conclusion—one that I didn't like, because it took me absolutely no place where today's poisonings were concerned.

Bubba shouldered his way through the door, trailed by the yellow-mustached patrolman and a disdainful white cat with a fluffy tail as big as an ostrich-feather boa. Bubba's face was grim, his hat was yanked down over his eyebrows.

"What's this bidness about a note?" he demanded. The cat wound itself affectionately around his ankles, leaving feathers of white fur on his tan polyester pants.

"It looks like a confession note," I said. "Murder-suicide."

Bubba reached for the unlit cigar in his stained pocket. "Claimin' responsibility for the Kotner kil-lin'?"

I nodded. "The note and the gun are upstairs on the bedside table. The poison's in a can on the kitchen table, beside the typewriter on which the note was apparently typed."

"Who wrote the note?"

"It's signed with the name Violett Hall," I said. "That's the woman the med techs just took out of here. But I don't think she—"

Bubba looked distastefully at his pant cuffs, then pushed the cat aside with his foot. "That'd be old Finney Hall's girl, I reckon," he said. "This was his place, the old son-of-a-gun. He was one to kick ass and take names, 'cept where his wife was concerned. 'Round home, I heard, she did the ass-kickin'." He looked around at the tidy living room, the antimacassars and tabbies on the sofa, the Jesus picture, the birds in their cages. "What's Finney Hall's girl got to do with the Kotner woman?"

I stood up, scattering cats. "Look, Chief Harris," I said, "maybe I should just tell you how I happened to find Violett Hall and why I don't think—"

But Bubba decided there'd been enough chitchat. "Stay put," he commanded for the second time that day. "I'll be back." He disappeared toward the back of the house, followed by the other policeman.

I sat back down. I could hear footsteps moving

around in the kitchen, then tramping heavily up the wooden stairs. There was nothing to do but wait. The white cat with the feather-boa tail jumped on the coffee table and blinked at me. It was sitting on the magazine picturing Roz on the cover, enthroned like a queen on a pyramid of pink StrawBerry Bears. I nudged the cat aside and picked up the magazine. When I turned to the article, I saw that someone had neatly clipped it out.

I stared at the cover photo for a minute as something began ticking at the back of my mind. Then I looked around for the stuffed bear I'd seen the day before. I found it on the floor, half under the sofa. StrawBerry Bear. Probably half the little girls between the ages of four and eight wanted one, and the other half owned one. It was the mass-market answer to their fondest wish.

But when I held the bear in my hands and looked at it closely, I realized that this wasn't a mass-market bear. Its clothing and hat were obviously handmade, not of the cheap materials used by most toy manufacturers but of fine cotton, with handcrafted ribbon flowers painstakingly hand-stitched onto the handmade straw hat. When I took off the hat, there was an embroidered label inside it: VIOLETT HALL, and a date—the same year that Roz had gone off to New York in search of fame, carrying an original bear who turned out to be worth a fortune. And then I knew, with a jolting clarity, exactly what it was that Roz had taken from Violett.

A minute later, I heard footsteps clomping back down the stairs. Bubba came into the living room, followed by Petersen, who went on through and out the door, presumably to radio for a photographer and a fingerprint team. The white cat jumped off the coffee table and followed him.

Bubba wore an immensely satisfied look. "Well," he said vigorously, all but rubbing his hands, "guess that about wraps this baby up." To celebrate, he tossed his old cigar in the wastebasket beside the sofa and took a freshly wrapped one out of his shirt pocket.

I stood up again. "So you're satisfied that the note is genuine?"

"Sure as hell am," Bubba said. He unwrapped the cigar, crumpled the cellophane into his pocket, and licked the length of the cigar before he stuck it in his mouth. "Murder-suicide." He sounded as if he were rehearsing his presentation to the D.A. "Violett Hall got it some way into her poor weak head that Miz Kotner was a bad person. She began to believe that the Lord wanted her to do something about it. She tried first with the thirty-eight, but she's no Rambo. So she found a can of ant poison—probably some old Finney Hall had stashed in the shed out back—put a couple ounces in one of them spice bottles on the kitchen table, and doctored Miz Kotner's tomato juice with it. Then she began to have second thoughts and it seemed like the Lord had another job for her. She typed the note, took the poison, and went upstairs to die. And she would've, too, if you hadn't come along." He frowned at me, ready now to get back to the information I had tried to volunteer early. "Just why *did* you come along, Miz Bayles?"

I stuck my hands in the pockets of my jeans and

balanced myself on the balls of my feet, leaning forward slightly. It had once been a favorite courtroom stance. "I ran into Violett this morning shortly before eight, in front of Cavette's Grocery," I said. "You can confirm that with young Mr. Cavette, who spoke with both of us. She asked if I would see her this afternoon about a legal matter on which she wanted my advice. I was supposed to arrive at five. I came early. When there was no answer to my knock, I went around back and knocked. I let myself in, found her on the bed upstairs, and called EMS." I shifted my weight. "I find it difficult to believe," I added carefully, "that Violett Hall tried to kill herself."

Bubba eyed me, understandably reluctant to entertain any notions that might contradict the murder-suicide theory that neatly wrapped up both crimes and got him off the hook with the D.A., the mayor, the Senator, the Texas Rangers, and the FBI. And God. "Oh, yeah?"

"Yes," I said. I didn't think that anything short of hard physical evidence would persuade him, or any cop, for that matter. That's how they're trained. But I had to have a try. "Number one, someone was here this morning with Violett. It doesn't make sense that she'd trot over to dump poison in Roz Kotner's tomato juice, come back here and cook breakfast for a friend, then poison herself. The psychology is all wrong."

"How do you know someone was here?"

"Violett told me when I saw her this morning. She told young Mr. Cavette, too, and she bought extra groceries. Further, there are two glasses in the kitchen sink."

Bubba shrugged. "Could be she lied. Mebbe she wanted to cover her tracks. I checked the kitchen. There's only dishes for one—eggs and mushrooms, looks like, with garlic. If she bought extra groceries, doesn't look to me like her company touched 'em."

"Perhaps," I suggested pointedly, "her company didn't feel like eating. Perhaps there was something toxic in the omelet, and the killer used the garlic to mask any taste."

"Mebbe," Bubba said, with a look that said *Sure as the Pope wears pantyhose.*

I sighed. I had the feeling that the rest of my evidence was going to meet the same objections, but I went on. "Another thing. Violett is terrified of guns. I doubt that she could bring herself to touch one, let alone fire it."

Bubba sighed a long-suffering sigh. "How d'you know that?"

"She told me."

"Ah," he said, arching his eyebrows significantly.

I ignored the eyebrows. "What's more, Violett doesn't know how to type."

"You don't need to know how to type to operate that old clunker on the kitchen table," Bubba said. "I could type on that thing, and I'm just a hunt-and-peck man."

"But look at the note," I argued. "No errors, no strikeovers, every keystroke even. The person who typed it was an experienced typist." I knew I wasn't getting anywhere with all this, but I've never been able to leave anything out of final arguments. You never know what evidence might sway a jury. Bubba wasn't exactly a jury, but I needed to convince him. "And there's the shoes."

"Funny you should mention shoes," Bubba said, sure of his ground on this one. "It so happens that we got a clear print outta that weed patch next to your cottage. Those sneakers upstairs—pretty good match, looks t'me like."

"Maybe. But Violett doesn't wear sneakers. She wears sandals, at least lately. She's got some sort of foot fungus, and wearing shoes makes it worse."

"Yeah, well, that don't mean she couldn't put on a pair of runnin' shoes for a half hour and go out to do a certain chore—'specially if she figured she'd have to get away fast."

"I doubt if she *owned* a pair of running shoes. Violett didn't go in for jogging."

"Then who do them shoes upstairs belong to? And how about the gun? And the note? If she didn't type it, who did?" He grinned. "You got any bright ideas, Miz Bayles?"

Regrettably, I didn't. "But I *do* know," I said, summoning the last piece of evidence in Violett's defense, "that she wouldn't commit suicide without providing for her animals." I gestured toward the covey of cats and the flock of caged birds on the window sill. "Anybody in Pecan Springs will tell you she worries more about them than she does about herself. They're like her kids."

Bubba shook his head. "Won't wash, Miz Bayles. Way it looks now, I've got more'n enough to take this to the D.A. He'll be mighty pleased to get it wrapped up, believe me."

"I'll bet," I said dryly. "Maybe the two of you can catch the fourth quarter."

Bubba looked hurt. "Now, that ain't called for. I'm just doin' my job."

I sighed. Yes, he was. Just doing his job. And doing it with competence and dispatch, too. On the physical evidence, Bubba was right, and any other cop would have come to the same conclusions. That's what's so scary. That the evidence can lead to such terribly logical, terribly *wrong*, conclusions.

Bubba gave his pants a yank. "I'm on my way to the hospital to look in on Miz Hall. If she can't answer questions, I'll put an officer in her room so that somebody's there when she *does* talk. Believe me, if she's innocent, she'll have plenty of time to say so."

"Assuming she's still alive."

"Assumin'," Bubba replied agreeably. "I'll have to ask you to leave too. I'm goin' to have this place sealed up." He strode to the door, looking like a man whose afternoon had turned out far better than he'd expected.

"Hey, wait," I said. "What about the cats and the birds?"

Bubba frowned. "What about them?"

"Somebody's got to get in here to feed them. Why don't you let me take care of it. I like animals." That was stretching a point. But I was keen on having access to Violett's house.

Bubba hesitated. "Well . . . I guess that'd work. You got a key?"

"No, but I'll see about getting one. Let your people know I'll be around to handle the livestock."

Bubba nodded. I followed him down the walk,

watched him speak to Petersen, and then get in his squad car and drive off. Petersen stayed behind, obviously waiting for reinforcements.

I stood for a moment, thinking. Then I got on my bike and rode down the wooded lane. I made a right turn, rode a block and made another right turn. At the end of *that* lane was where Ima and Erma Mason lived, with a backyard that butted up against Violett's backyard. If anybody in the neighborhood had a clue about what had gone on at Violett's since last night, the Mason sisters would. It was worth a try.

CHAPTER 17

Miss Erma is a frail, waifish-looking lady in her early eighties with a dowager's hump on her left shoulder and wispy white hair cut raggedly to the tips of her ears. She gets around with a walker, slowly and painfully, but that doesn't stop her from working in her garden. She was out there now, dressed in brown pants with a patch on one knee, a dark green smock, and a canvas hat folded over her ears and tied under her chin with a man's blue silk necktie. She was leaning over her walker as if she were leaning over a fence, snipping chrysanthemums with a pair of unwieldy garden shears. She peered at me over her bifocals for a minute or two before she recognized me.

"Oh, Miss Bayles," she said. "Hello." She glanced up at the rosebush on the fence. "I'm afraid you're a little late for roses. There aren't any left to speak of. But if you'd like some chrysanthemums, help yourself. I'm just cutting them to have something to do." She sighed and dropped several flowers in the basket hung on the walker. "My dear mother always cut chrysanthemums, you know. She had them in vases all over the house from the minute they started blooming until the frost came. And they last such a long time too. That's why we always have them on Mother's grave at the cemetery. But Father hated chrysanthemums, so we always put something else on his grave. He was quite partial to—"

"Thank you, Miss Erma," I broke in, "but I didn't come about the roses. Something has happened over at Violett Hall's and I thought you might be able to help me."

Miss Erma's canvas hat had tipped forward over her nose and she pushed it back with a thin, translucent hand on which the veins stood out as if they'd been drawn with a blue pen. "I believe you want to talk to Miss Ima about that," she said. She raised her voice. "Ima," she called with unexpected strength. "*I*-ma! Come out here! Somebody wants to see you."

A moment later, Miss Ima appeared on the back porch. Even though she and Miss Erma are twins, the passing years have wrenched their physical likeness some distance out of alignment. Miss Erma is bent and fragile with a tendency toward a vague and confused garrulousness. Miss Ima, on the other hand, is sturdy and ramrod-straight, with a clipped and precise speech, a habit of sharp observation, and a cultivated sense of personal style. As she came down the steps, one hand on the wooden safety rail, she was wearing a baby-blue two-piece pantsuit constructed of some kind of knobby fabric and buttoned down the front with big gold buttons. A long blue-green chiffon scarf was furled around her throat, around her carefully curled white hair, and around her throat once again, where it was secured with a large gold pin in the shape of a dragon. She wore baby-blue canvas flats in the same shade as her pantsuit. Miss Ima likes to dress up.

"So Violett's gone and got herself in trouble, has she?" she asked sharply, when I had repeated what I had said to Miss Erma.

"I'm afraid she's been taken to the hospital," I said. "I wondered if you or your sister might have seen something that would help to—"

"*Hospital.*" Miss Erma sniffed. "Well, I don't wonder." She gave her sister a meaningful look. "I do believe you were right, dear, although I hate to say it. A woman her *age*. And a churchgoer, too."

Miss Ima adjusted the dragon at her throat, patted her scarf, and gave a gratified sniff. "I won't say I told you so, Erma. But the next time I tell you what I see, p'rhaps you won't be so quick to contradict."

I looked at Miss Ima. "Then you saw something that—"

"Saw something!" Miss Ima's amused laugh was a glassy tinkle that ran up the scale a half octave and back down again. "My dear young woman, of *course* I saw something. But when I told Erma, she was so shocked that she just didn't want to believe me." She shook her head. "Erma hasn't seen as much of the world as I have, you know," she confided in a lower voice. "She shocks easily."

"Well," Miss Erma said tartly, "I've had plenty to be shocked *about*, Ima. The past is never totally dead, you know. It keeps coming back to haunt."

Miss Erma must have been referring to what Constance called Miss Ima's "checkered past." As I'd heard the story, Miss Ima had joined the WACs during the Second World War and gone off to France, while Miss Erma had stayed in Pecan Springs. Miss Ima was rumored to have had a high old time in the Sin Capital of the World. The rumors, in fact, were of Miss Ima's making. She had written several revealing postcards home, which were shared by the postmistress with her most intimate friends and subsequently most of Pecan Springs. Indeed, gossip had it that she had taken a French lover several years younger. Whether or not these things were true, something Miss Ima did caused much consternation in the Mason family and opened a rift between the two sisters that lasted until their mother died. But since they had each inherited half of the family home and it was out of the question to sell, they apparently decided it was sensible to make up their quarrel and move in together. I wondered if Miss Erma considered Violett's ravings about Miss Ima and Mr. Peavy an instance of the past "coming back to haunt."

"What *did* you see?" I asked.

Miss Ima leaned forward. "We've always gotten on well with the Halls, you understand," she said, "although I must say that old Mrs. Hall was a mean, abusive woman. The way she screamed at her husband, why, no wonder he died. He probably did it just to spite her. And that poor child used to go to school with switch marks on the back of her legs so that she looked like a—"

"Now, Ima," Miss Erma put in primly, "don't speak ill of the dead. You'll be dead too, one of these days, and you don't want people dredging up *your* old sins."

Miss Ima frowned. "Whatever her *mother's* faults," she said, amending her report, "Violett Hall has always been a good neighbor."

"That's *right*," Miss Erma said, clacking her garden shears. "Not any bit like those ruffians across the street. All those broken-down cars and trucks and dogs and drinking all hours and young women running around with barely anything covering their naked behinds." *Clack-clack*. "And next to them are those people who leave their Santa Claus on the roof until it's time to send Easter cards. How'd *you* like red lights blinking every night for six months and when you mention property values they just laugh like it's some big joke. And then there's those horrid German shepherds—"

Miss Ima reached out a hand to stem the flow. "Erma, dear," she rebuked gently, "we're not talking about the people across the street. We're talking about Violett."

"So am I," Miss Erma said staunchly. "I'm saying that she's not any bit like the people with those red lights on their roof, like a bordello." *Clack*!

Miss Ima nodded. "Violett's always been quiet and a good neighbor—"

Miss Erma hitched her walker toward a cluster of red chrysanthemums. "Except for those cats," she said. "I don't mind the birds because they don't get into the garbage, but why a person would want more than two or three cats, I can't figure. I swear, Violett's cats are every bit as bad as the dogs on the other side of the bordello." She leaned so far forward that I was afraid she might tip the walker over and fall facedown in the chrysanthemums. "There are three of them, German shepherds, and they—"

"—a good neighbor," Miss Ima went on, raising her voice, "a born-again Christian—"

"—run loose around the entire neighborhood," Miss Erma continued shrilly, "and that woman who owns them, anytime you try to tell her that her dogs are doing their naughty business in your grass, she throws God in your face. But that's those Jehovah's Witnesses for you. Now, Mother was always a Methodist. The Methodists have more tact when it comes to God." *Clack-clack-clack.*

"—and she kept the backyard mowed," Miss Ima finished, lowering her voice now that she was no longer in competition with her sister. "That's why hearing about the car in her garage last night was such a shock to Miss Erma."

"Shame to say it," Miss Erma concluded. *"Shame."*

I breathed a sigh of relief. We'd gotten down to specifics at last. "Did you recognize the car?"

Miss Ima frowned. "Can't say as I recognized it, exactly. But that garage door was hanging open the way it always does, and I got a real good look. I've told Violett over and over that she ought to get Mr. Peavy to come and fix that door. He's right handy with things like that. Hanging open, it just invites tramps and dogs."

Miss Erma frowned. "Better not mention Mr. Peavy to Violett, Ima. She's not a bit balanced where he's concerned." She looked at me. "I don't suppose you heard—"

"The car," I said desperately.

"An old brown one," Miss Ima replied. "I told Erma it looked like that car of Freddie's."

Miss Erma gave her walker a futile hitch. One aluminum leg was mired in the dirt and I went to help her pull it out. She gave me a quavery smile. "Men are so foolish about their cars, don't you think, dear? At least Freddie was, back when that one of his was new. He had a real hissy fit when Maude backed into the light pole and dented the bumper."

"What kind of car did Freddie have?" I asked, hoping to nail something—*anything*—down.

"I'm not so good on car names," Miss Ima said. "A Custer, maybe. A light-brown Custer. You know, George Armstrong."

"Buster," Miss Erma corrected loudly. She clipped a red chrysanthemum and dropped it into her basket. "It was a two-tone brown Buster that Freddie had. I remember *exactly*. He never did get that bumper fixed, and every time he got to tippling, he'd throw it in Maude's face. It'd been me," she added acidly, "I wouldn't've let him talk to me that way, 'specially after he ran into the gravel truck the afternoon he took Celeste McGraw out for a ride."

"You didn't happen to get a license number on this brown car, I suppose," I said to Miss Ima.

Miss Ima's plucked white eyebrows were indignant. "A license number? Why, that would be *snooping*!"

"That's too bad," I said. "It's possible that whoever

put that car in Violett's garage did her harm. If I can find out who—"

"I don't remember any numbers," Miss Ima said thoughtfully, "but I do recall a *letter* or two. And of course there was that bumper sticker."

"What were the letters?"

"Bzz."

I looked at her.

"B-Z-Z," she said patiently. "Bees. I don't remember the last of it, but that was the first part. B-Z-Z. Bzz. Like bees."

"What about the bumper sticker?"

Miss Erma shifted her walker back onto the grass. "I saw one the other day," she said. She looked at me. "Maybe you know what it means, dear, seeing as you were a lawyer once, weren't you? It said 'Lawyers do it legally.' Do what, I wonder."

I cleared my throat. "I'm afraid I don't know," I replied.

Miss Ima had an explanation. "I guess it means that anything lawyers do is legal."

Miss Erma wasn't entirely satisfied. "If that's what they mean, why don't they just come out and *say* so? Really, I don't understand what gets into people. Talk, talk, talk all the time but don't say what they mean."

I was beginning to get a headache. The bumper sticker wasn't worth it. Even though I had only a fragment of the plate, I could probably get a make on the car when the Highway Department opened for business in the morning. But I wanted to wrap it up, so I gave it one more try.

"What about the bumper sticker on the car in Violett's garage?" I asked Miss Ima. "I don't suppose you remember what it said."

"Of course I remember." Miss Ima gave an impatient snort. "It said 'Rent A Wreck.' Now, isn't that the most ridiculous thing you ever heard? Don't people have enough wrecks of their own without renting other people's wrecks?"

Miss Erma dropped her shears in the basket along with the snipped chrysanthemums and jockeyed her walker a hundred and eighty degrees to the left. "Just goes to show," she said, her breathing labored with the effort of dragging the walker through the ankle-high grass. "People'll put anything on cars to get attention these days. Why, just the other day I saw—"

"What time did you see this car in Violett Hall's garage?" I asked Miss Ima hastily.

"I like to walk late in the evening. Makes me sleep better. I saw the car at nine-thirty. I know, because I checked my watch under the streetlight."

"Tell her what else you saw," Miss Erma prompted, leaning heavily on the walker, which was tilting to the right.

"It wasn't a what, it was a *who*," Miss Ima said. "I saw him through Violett's living room window."

"A man?" I asked, frowning.

"Shame to say," Miss Erma said.

Miss Ima nodded. "He and Violett were standing in the living room, talking."

"Couldn't've been Mr. Peavy?" Miss Erma asked hopefully.

"He was tall and thin," Miss Ima said. "Mr. Peavy is short and fat."

"How do you know it was a man?" I asked. "Did you see his face?"

Miss Ima shook her head. "Just his back. Couldn't see him real well. But he was one of those long-haired types."

Miss Erma sighed. "Them's the ones I just can't figger. Why a man would let his hair grow down to his—"

"That's everything?" I asked Miss Ima. "The car in the garage, the person you saw through the window—"

"A man," Miss Ima said. "I always call a spade a spade, no matter how much it shocks Erma."

"—behind," Miss Erma concluded triumphantly.

That was it. I resisted the offer of a cup of tea and more conversation, got back on my bike, and rode around the block to Violett's.

The investigating team had arrived and was at work. I asked for word of Violett and was told to call the Adams County Hospital, where an edgy charge nurse informed me that her condition had deteriorated and would I please not call back for at least an hour because she had other patients to tend to. I asked for and was given permission to search for a key—clearly, none of the cops had the slightest interest in looking after the animals and were glad to palm the job off onto somebody else. It took only a few minutes to locate Violett's purse in the laundry hamper in the closet off the kitchen (where she had gotten it the day before) and to find her key ring, on which there were two neatly labeled keys, one to the front, one to the back. I stuck the back door key in my pocket.

Then I did what I'd come for. I went through the

purse. In an inside zipper pocket, I found a bank passbook. The savings account balance now stood at $9,600. For four years, until last month, Violett had made regular monthly deposits of two hundred dollars. She hadn't withdrawn a penny. Two hundred a month probably seemed like a lot of money to her until she read the story in *People* magazine and learned that StrawBerry Bear was raking in millions. And then, just when she figured out what her claim was really worth, Roz must have told her she was cutting her off completely.

I glanced at the passbook, wondering whether Roz had paid by check—in which case the payments could be traced through Roz's bank—or by cash, and whether Violett had kept the envelopes in which Roz had mailed the payments. Evidence like that could help establish that Roz had made an oral contract with Violett and perhaps even to acknowledge her as StrawBerry Bear's real creator. But Roz had apparently found it inconvenient, maybe even embarrassing, to give Violett the proper credit. And when she got the chance to sell to Disney, she feared that any acknowledgment of Violett's rights would jeopardize *her* claim, or tie her up in court until Disney lost interest.

I dropped Violett's purse back into the hamper, frowning. That line of reasoning gave Roz a motive to kill Violett, not the other way around. For a moment I played with the possibility that Roz had brought the ant poison *here* this morning, sprinkled it on Violett's breakfast while her victim's back was turned, and managed somehow to accidentally poison herself. It was an interesting theory but I couldn't make it work. You don't accidentally put ant poison into your own tomato juice in your own refrigerator.

But more persuasively, there was the car in Violett's garage. Somebody *else* had been here last night and this morning. A tall, thin, somebody—a man, if Miss Ima was to be believed—who drove a brown Rent A Wreck car. I made a face. Better not tell Ruby that Miss Ima had put a man on the scene. She'd have Arnold Seidensticker back on the suspect list.

I went back into the kitchen, found a cupboard full of every imaginable brand of cat food, opened two cans, and began to dish out fishy-smelling portions among the half-dozen bowls on the back porch. But *was* Miss Ima to be believed? Just because she immediately jumped to the conclusion that the tall, thin person had been a long-haired man didn't mean it was. I put the empty cat food cans in the trash, thinking of the tall, thin people I knew who also knew Roz and Violett. Tall, thin people who drove Custers or Busters or . . .

A bell rang at the back of my skull, and my eyes narrowed. *Was it possible?* I sat down at the kitchen table and began to sort through objections, laying the case out in my mind, arranging it the way I'd arrange Violett's defense. Yes, it was *possible*, if I changed one basic assumption I'd been living with all week. But even though I thought I knew who and how, I couldn't come up with why. It was clear that the killer had poisoned Violett in order to make it appear that Violett had poisoned Roz. But why Roz, the goose who laid the golden egg? It didn't make sense.

I filled the cats' water dish and checked the bird

cages. When I left, Cat jumped off the porch swing and followed me to the end of the walk. As I got on my bike and rode away, I glanced back over my shoulder. He was sitting on his haunches, black tail curled around four charcoal feet, observing me thoughtfully.

It was four-thirty when I got back to the shop.

"What *took* you so long?" Ruby demanded. "Not that we were busy," she added. "It's been quiet as the grave all afternoon."

"It was quiet as the grave at Violett's too," I said, reaching for the Austin telephone directory. "How about closing early?"

"Do we have a suspect?" Ruby asked eagerly.

"Actually we do," I answered, thumbing through the Yellow Pages, "although I have to confess that it's sheer speculation."

Ruby gave me a mystified glance. "You're looking for a motive in the Yellow Pages?" Then she went off to lock both front doors and hang up the CLOSED signs. When she got back, I was on the phone.

"Who are you calling?"

"Rent A Wreck," I said, counting the sixth ring. "The biggest and best downscale auto rental agency in America. We're looking for a brown Duster."

Ruby frowned. "What do we want a Duster for? I had one once, and it was a bitch on cold mornings. Something about the automatic choke. It died at every corner."

Somebody snatched up the phone in the middle of the eighth ring. "Rent A Wreck," a man said in a gravelly voice, fast and out of breath. "Sorry, I was out in the lot."

"This is Officer Byerley at the Pecan Springs Police Department," I said. "We've had a report of a minor hit-and-run involving one of your vehicles. There was no damage, and the driver might not even have been aware of the accident. The car is a brown Duster, license plate BZZ, no numerals reported, bearing your decal."

"Way it goes," the man said philosophically. "Glad there wasn't much damage. The driver called in a half hour ago, wanting to be sure that somebody'd be here for check-in at six this afternoon. Party wants to catch a seven o'clock plane."

"Party's name?" I asked.

"Hold on a sec," the man said. "I'll get it."

I was gripping the phone the way I hold on to the tow rope when I'm water skiing behind McQuaid's big boat. I was holding my breath, too. I do that when I'm water skiing because I'm a lousy skier and I never know when I'm going to get dumped in the drink. I did it now because of the suspense.

A moment later, the man was back with the name. I let out my breath. I'd been right.

CHAPTER 18

Pecan Springs is located off I-35, an eighty-mile concrete ribbon that stretches straight to San Antonio sixty miles to the south and to Austin thirty-five miles to the north. I can make the trip to Austin in about forty-five minutes when the traffic is reasonable. But this was late Sunday afternoon and the traffic was slowed by construction, which funneled everybody between scarred concrete barriers. While I negotiated for a moving patch of highway with boxy Greyhound Americruisers and tanker trucks built like submarines on wheels, I told Ruby the whole story: what I had found at Violett's, what I had learned from Miss Ima, and what I had concluded about the original StrawBerry Bear, *Violett's* StrawBerry Bear. When I finished, it was five-fifteen, and we were still twenty miles from the place where I hoped we'd tag up with the person we were looking for.

Ruby cracked her knuckles for the third time. "We

don't even have a gun," she said. She glanced at me. "Do we?"

I shook my head. The Beretta was still cached under the stairs. In Texas, the law about carrying handguns is murky. I felt I could justify the gun, but if I got stopped and a cop found it, he'd confiscate it. It wasn't worth a possible delay.

There was silence in the car while a moving van rocketed past us on the left, the Datsun shuddering in its eighty-five-mile-per-hour wake. The back of the truck declared that the driver observed the speed limit and anybody who thought differently should call the 1-800 number carefully hidden under an inch-thick coating of mud. I've called in two complaints on those guys. I wonder how many other people do it, and whether it slows any of them down. Probably not.

Ruby glanced down at the gas gauge. "China," she said, "I hate to bring this up, but we've been running on empty for the last few miles."

"Shit," I said. The needle sat on E. "I don't want to stop. I'd hate to get there late." I had a backup plan—showing up at the airport just at boarding time. But that was a lot trickier than nabbing somebody at the car-rental place.

"If we run out of gas," Ruby replied reasonably, "we won't get there at all."

I sighed, seeing the wisdom in that. A huge sign off to the right proclaimed BUDA TRUCK CITY, 1 MILE. Buda is a corruption of the Spanish word for widow. It's pronounced Byoo-da by the locals. The story goes that all the men in the town were massacred by Comanches, who felt (with some justification) that the place was getting too crowded. The widows were left to carry on alone, which they did, quite capably.

I took the Buda exit and pulled into a gigantic truck stop. Monstrous eighteen-wheelers, and eighteen-wheelers towing other eighteen-wheelers, not to mention tank trucks, stock trucks, and even a caravan of Army trucks—all were lined up for the pump islands like metallic dinosaurs jostling one another at the last watering hole. Unfortunately, all the pumps turned out to be diesel.

"Maybe we'd better forget gas," Ruby said nervously, as we wove our second circuit of the complex. "It's five twenty-five."

"There's *got* to be an unleaded pump here somewhere," I said. Then I spotted it, and dodged ahead of a green Mercury intent on the same goal. The driver, a well-dressed woman with a bleached bouffant and two kids in the back seat, shot me the finger.

I pumped three gallons—no point in spending the time to fill the tank when this would get us there and back—and we were on the road. "What's the time?" I asked Ruby.

"Five twenty-nine."

The traffic was lighter and we were back to three lanes again, so I floored it. We had just sailed down the long hill that bottoms out at the Onion Creek overpass when I saw the Department of Public Safety lurking behind the oleander clump on the other side of the bridge. The Datsun wasn't doing much over eighty when we passed the trooper, while the two cars just ahead were doing at least eighty-five. But ours was the car he pulled over. He was professionally polite behind the reflecting shield of his dark glasses. "May I see your license, please," he said in a voice without inflection.

Ruby leaned toward the driver's side. "But the cars ahead of us were going a *lot* faster than we were," she protested. I gave her a sideways scowl as I handed over my license. I make it a rule never to argue with the D.P.S., especially when I'm in the wrong. Even more especially when I'm in a hurry.

The trooper's mouth turned up in what he might have meant as a smile. "Isn't that interesting," he said. "I'll be sure and watch for them next time."

As he ambled back to the squad car to radio in the registration check and write out the speeding citation, Ruby sat back. "Maybe we should tell him. Maybe he could give us an escort."

"Oh, yeah?" I said, angry at myself for not remembering that the Onion Creek overpass was reported to yield a couple of hundred dollars an hour in fines. "It's five thirty-four now. It would take us at least twenty-six minutes to give him the facts, which—even assuming we could convince him that we're telling the truth, which is doubtful—would make us just about twenty-six minutes late for our date." I shook my head. "Sorry, Ruby. We're on our own."

Ruby didn't look exactly pleased with the idea. We sat in silence. I don't know what Ruby was thinking, but I was running through various scenarios of what might happen at Rent A Wreck. I didn't like any of them. Cops-and-robbers isn't my idea of amusing Sunday recreation.

The trooper was back within four minutes. I signed

the ticket, he gave me the obligatory caution, and we were on our way again. It was five thirty-nine. I mentally surveyed all the possible D.P.S. hidey-holes between Onion Creek and South Austin and decided to take the chance. We were back up to eighty the minute we were out of radar range.

The Wyndham Hotel rises out of a concrete parking lot like a fat stone obelisk with eyes, marking the intersection of I-35 and Ben White Boulevard. With Ruby clutching the panic handle above the door as if she were a jet pilot ready to eject, I whipped the Datsun off the Interstate and onto the frontage road. There were fifteen cars lined up for a left onto Ben White. I was in no mood to wait, so I took the center lane, reaching the intersection just as the light went yellow. I floored it and made an illegal left, heading west on Ben White.

"How far?" Ruby asked breathlessly.

"Two blocks," I said, angling for the right lane ahead of a blue van. "Should be on the right."

It was in the next block, past McDonald's and the Pizza Hut. "Rent A Wreck!" Ruby said, pointing to a ten-foot red-white-and-blue neon sign that was nearly lost in the neon jungle of taller, gaudier signs. At the curb cut, I swung the wheel hard right. It was six oh three.

We drove into what had been the front lot of a drive-in movie a few years back, before cable television and the VCR. Over a road at the rear of the lot was a weather-beaten drive-under sign that said NORTH SCREEN on one end and SOUTH SCREEN on the other, and CLOSED FOR THE WINTER underneath. The Rent A

Wreck office was in a white metal trailer with an unpainted wooden deck. The trailer sat perpendicular to Ben White, about sixty feet back from the street. A taxi and driver sat out front.

I drove around behind the building and pulled up at the far end, behind an unpainted wooden lattice that screened us from Ben White. I left the motor running, shifted into neutral, and surveyed the lot in front of us. There were four or five rows of cars—maybe twenty in all—some looking like they'd seen a lot of miles, others nearly new. The only Duster I spotted was green, with a flat front tire.

"Looks like we made it," Ruby said. "Maybe the taxi's waiting for—"

"You'd better check," I said. "But don't linger."

Ruby flashed me a grin. "I'll be right back, Sherlock." She was just getting out when a brown Duster turned off Ben White.

I grabbed Ruby's arm, adrenaline surging. "Hang on. Looks like this is it."

The car drove through the lot and pulled up in front of the office, angling nose-in beside the taxi. Ruby pulled the door shut. I shifted into first, let out the clutch, and eased the Datsun forward until we could see the driver get out of the car.

It was Jane Dorman.

She was dressed for Fifth Avenue in a slim black-and-white checked coatdress with a white shawl collar and white cuffs. She wore black stockings and high-heeled patent leather pumps and carried a shiny black purse. Climbing out of the battered old car in this seedy lot, she looked like an executive-suite hooker working the wrong address.

"It's her!" Ruby said. "Do you think she's got a gun?"

I shook my head, edging the car forward another few inches. "She left the thirty-eight at Violett's," I said. "Unless she got her hands on another one, she's not likely—"

At that same instant, Jane spotted us. Her first expression was sheer surprise, then disbelief. For an instant, I thought she might tough it out, wave, smile, trip on into the office in those patent leather pumps. Then she dove back into the car, slammed the door, and shoved the key into the ignition.

Thinking to cut her off, I twisted the wheel in a hard left and pulled forward, half behind her car. But Jane shoved the Duster into reverse, floored it, tires spinning, and rammed us in the left front fender with a teeth-rattling crash, shoving the Datsun aside. Her reverse momentum carried her across the gravel lot until she slammed into the front end of a late-model Ford.

The office door flung open and a red-faced, heavyset man with salt-and-pepper hair appeared. "Hey, you!" he shouted, waving his fist at Jane. "What the fuck d'ya think you're doin'? You crazy?"

I rolled down the window a notch. "Call the cops!" I shouted. "She's wanted for murder."

The man's jaw dropped. "No shit," he said, then ran back into the office. The taxi driver was already on his radio.

Jane had shifted into first, yanked the steering wheel to the right, and headed for Ben White. A second later,

Ruby and I were hard on her tail. At Ben White, she spotted a gap in the fast-moving traffic and pulled into the right lane, westbound. We ducked in three cars behind, under the nose of a mean-looking black Blazer with dark-tinted windows and a DON'T MESS WITH TEXAS sticker on the front bumper.

"*Jesus,*" Ruby breathed, reaching overhead for the panic handle.

"Yeah, right," I said. "Pray."

A couple of blocks ahead I could see the South Congress overpass. At the last minute, doing sixty, Jane took the exit. We took it too, with nothing between us and her. There was a red light at the intersection of the access road and South Congress, but Jane didn't stop. She took a left, hard, across the overpass. I ran the light too, dodging a rattletrap Ford truck hauling a yellow Caterpillar backhoe, and stayed on her tail, pressing her hard through the next light and down South Congress, careening past surprised Sunday drivers placidly obeying the forty-five-mile-per-hour speed limit. I had my headlights on and emergency lights flashing and the horn down hard, hoping that if a cop spotted us he'd know we were chasing the Duster, not racing it. Ruby's feet were braced against the floor. She was alternately breathing out and gasping in, loudly.

Congress south of Ben White is four narrow asphalt lanes through a hodgepodge neighborhood of forties and fifties frame-and-brick motels, miniwarehouses surrounded by chain-link fences, used car lots, rundown cafes, and pawnshops. Across the railroad tracks, there's a giant retail lumber and building supplies warehouse, a dozen acres of stacked lumber, roofing, fencing, concrete tile.

"How are we going to stop her?" Ruby asked.

"I don't know," I said, eyes on the road. "Keep praying. Maybe God will think of something."

God did.

Congress makes a downhill at the Williamson Creek bridge, then an uphill. On the other side of the concrete bridge the neighborhood turns mixed residential, frame houses, liquor stores, trailer parks, auto repair. At the top of the hill a flashing red light indicates a four-way stop. The hill slowed Jane from sixty to fifty, but she didn't bother with the light. She was barreling through the intersection when an empty yellow minivan from the Children of Jesus Tabernacle lumbered into it. At the last second, Jane locked the brakes and snapped the wheel to the right. The rear end skidded around in a cloud of black rubber smoke and slammed into the right front of the Children of Jesus. The van spun a graceful one-eighty and lurched back across the intersection and onto the front porch of the South Austin Family Medical Clinic, narrowly missing a ragged long-hair on a beat-up old bike that was hitched to a cart filled with aluminum cans. The Duster swerved right and bounced over the curb and onto the sidewalk, the passenger side scraping a stone retaining wall.

"Now we've got her!" Ruby cried.

But Jane wasn't done yet. She gunned the Duster, pulled back onto Congress, and took off again.

"Christ," Ruby said, "she's unstoppable!"

"No, she isn't," I said. "She's losing it."

Jane couldn't get much speed out of the Duster,

which was listing sharply to the right. An instant later big chunks of rubber began sloughing off the rear tire like slabs of charred elephant skin. Sparks showered from the wheel as the last hunk tore loose and the rim began to skate on the concrete. Jane lost control. The Duster lurched to the right and splintered a wooden sandwich board with MANUEL'S TRAILER SALES freshly painted on it.

I skidded up and Ruby and I piled out. Jane was out too, kicking off her black patent leather pumps. She ran to the left, into the trailer sales lot. A short, heavy-set Hispanic man with an Errol Flynn mustache and Rudolph Valentino hair popped out of a nearby trailer. MANUEL was embroidered in red on his white Mexican wedding shirt.

"Hey, I saw you hit that sign!" he yelled, shaking his fist at Jane. "You gonna pay, whore!" Jane was fast for somebody running in her stockinged feet on gravel, but she was driven by the primal urge to save her skin. She dodged to the left around a trailer with a huge BUY NOW banner draped across the front.

"You go right," I yelled to Ruby, as I swung to the left. "We'll get her between us."

"Hey!" Manuel shouted again. Now there were *three* women, not just one, running around in his lot. He jumped off the deck of the trailer and ran in our direction. "Wait'll I get my hands on you, *ladronas*! You gonna pay—or else!"

I ducked left around the BUY NOW trailer. Jane was racing across an open space, angling left toward me. But the gravel here was sharper, and it slowed her down. I was out of shape and breathless, but I was wearing sneakers. I closed the distance between us, lowered my head like a left tackle coming hard off the line, and drove my shoulder into her black-and-white checked fanny, giving it all I had. With a loud *whoomf*, she sprawled facedown in the gravel. A second later, I was on top of her and Ruby was shouting "Touch-down!"

Manuel ran up, puffing with exertion and obviously revising his estimate of the situation. There was only one thief. "Hey, good deal, you got her, the lousy *ladrona*," he said. He rubbed his hands together and grinned at me, showing one gold tooth. "You *muy hombre*. Mebbe you should try out for the Cowboys."

"Next season," I said. "Right now, maybe you could call the cops."

Jane was stirring, beginning to heave her butt under me. But there wasn't much fight left, and I figured I could hold her for a while. Or Ruby could sit on her shoulders while I sat on her behind. I wasn't worried about anybody's dignity.

Manuel bent over Jane, waggling a thick finger. "The cops, you betcha, you fuckin' *ladrona*," he said loudly, as if Jane had lost her hearing as well as her ability to move. "You know how much that sign cost me? Rodriguez painted it, and he overcharged, that sorry son-a-bitch. One-seventy-nine-fifty, not counting the paint and the plywood, which ain't good for nothin' now you smashed it up." He jabbed the finger in her face. "You gonna pay, you hear? Every *peso*."

"Want *me* to call the cops, China?" Ruby asked.

"I don't care who does it," I said wearily. "Let's just *do* it. Okay?"

As Ruby turned to head for the trailer, light tires crunched on the gravel. It was the ragged can-picker who had nearly been wiped out by the Children of Jesus.

The can-picker jumped off his bike and shoved down the kickstand. He wore an old Army fatigue jacket and a filthy vee-necked white tee, dirty jeans with both knees out, and tennis shoes that looked like they came out of St. Vincent DePaul's dumpster. "No sweat," he said. "I *am* the cops." He glanced at Jane facedown on the gravel with me on board. "She the driver of that hit-and-run?"

Beneath me, Jane moaned.

"Yeah," I said. The can-picker's face was sooty with an uneven stubble of three-day beard. His shoulder-length hair had been butchered with a dull knife and he wore the faint cologne of too many days without a bath. "*You're* the cops?"

The picker reached down and pulled a plastic shield out of one dilapidated sneaker. "Officer Pollit," he said. "Narcotics." He turned to the Hispanic. "Get a backup in here, Manuel," he said crisply. "On the double."

Manuel's black eyes had become huge, but he responded with alacrity. "*Si, señor,*" he said, and hastened off.

With a practiced gesture, Pollit pulled out a snub-nosed revolver. "You can get up now," Pollit said to me. He fished a pair of handcuffs out of his fatigue jacket and tossed them to me. "Cuff her," he said. "Please."

It was a pleasure.

The narc prodded Jane's hip with the toe of his sneaker. "Roll over on your back."

With an effort, Jane flopped over. Her hair had come loose from its chignon, the white linen collar of her chic coatdress was ripped, and there was a smear of dirt and blood on her chin where she had scraped her face in the gravel. Both knees were ripped out of her black pantyhose, and the right kneecap was darkening with a nasty purple bruise. I wondered if she'd banged it when she whammed the Children of Jesus.

"I'm arresting you on a charge of leaving the scene of an accident," Pollit said. "You have the right to remain silent . . ." He rattled off the rest of her rights from memory, fast and word-perfect. "Is that clear?" he asked when he'd finished.

Still flat on her back, Jane flashed a venomous glance at me. "Yes," she muttered. "Just keep that crazy woman away from me. She has no right—"

I looked at Pollit. "This is Jane Dorman. She's wanted for murder and attempted murder in Pecan Springs." Almost. She *would* be wanted, when Bubba and the D.A. got their act together.

Pollit arched both black eyebrows quizzically. "Oh, yeah? Who'd she murder?"

"You're crazy!" Jane struggled to sit up. It wasn't easy, cuffed as she was. Pollit motioned her back down with his gun. "She's crazy!" she cried.

"Not so crazy, Jane," I replied conversationally. "We know everything. We know you took two shots at Roz last night, and we've got a witness who places you at Violett's an hour later. We know you poisoned Roz's tomato juice and Violett's omelet before you planted the note, the gun, and the shoes. We know—"

"Poison?" Pollit said, impressed. "She involved in a poisoning?"

"*Two* poisonings," I said. "The stuff she used was pretty potent, too."

Jane gave a scornful laugh. "Poison? I tell you, Officer, this woman is crazy. In fact, this whole thing is ludicrous. I was returning a rental car when she tried to ram me. Where was I supposed to find ant poison? I don't—"

She stopped. Her tongue shot out and licked the corners of her lips. Her eyes darted from me to Pollit.

I turned to Pollit. "You hear that?" I said.

Pollit frowned. "Yeah, I heard," he said. "Ant poison, wasn't that what she said?"

Jane made a low, despairing sound.

"Good," I said, as sirens came up the hill. "Don't forget it."

When we got back to Pecan Springs, I called the hospital. Violett had died.

CHAPTER 19

After Violett's funeral, the three of us—Meredith, Ruby, and I—conspired to obstruct justice. We burned Roz's letters, her will, and Jo's journals in the fireplace in Jo's living room. They made a satisfactory blaze.

"Tell me again why this is an obstruction of justice," Meredith said, as she tossed in the last letter.

"Because we're destroying evidence that might bear on a criminal prosecution," I said, wondering briefly what McQuaid would say if I told him what we were doing. I didn't plan to tell him. We'd talked a couple of times before he took off for his job interview at New Mexico State. He was moderately upset when he learned that Ruby and I had gone trucking off to Austin after a killer without saying a word to Bubba or to him—as if he and Bubba were the sole guardians of law and order in Pecan Springs.

"The evidence we're destroying might bear on Roz's prosecution for the murder of Jo?" Ruby asked.

"That's moot, since Roz is dead," I replied. "But if I were building a strategy for Jane's defense, I'd try to pin Roz's murder on Violett, just the way Jane set it up. I'd use Roz's letters to convince the jury that Violett had a strong motive to kill Roz. She thought Roz murdered Jo, and the letters are the strongest evidence."

"Don't forget the Everclear and the Hot Shot," Meredith said. "That proves Roz killed Jo."

"*We* know about that," I said, "but Jane's lawyers probably wouldn't dig it up. It was just good luck that we found it out."

"Good luck, my ass," Ruby said indignantly. "It was my superior investigating!"

I grinned at Ruby. "Yeah," I said.

"When did you first suspect Jane?" Meredith asked.

"Not until late Sunday afternoon," I replied. "Actually, I thought I'd caught a glimpse of her on Friday evening, parked on the street behind the cottage in a dinged-up brown Duster. But it wasn't Jane's kind of car, and the driver had her hair down and was wearing something shapeless and sloppy. Roz told me that Jane had gone to Vermont, so I pushed the whole thing to the back of my mind. In fact, I didn't even think about Jane again until Sunday morning when she telephoned. She said she was calling from Vermont to ask me to keep an eye on Roz."

"But she wasn't in Vermont," Meredith said. "She was right here."

"At Violett's," Ruby said. "Cooking up an omelet."

I helped myself to some potato chips and another glob of clam dip. "What happened is that Jane phoned her secretary from here and told her she'd flown back to New York and was driving to Vermont. She asked her to pass the word along to Roz."

Ruby shook her head admiringly. "What great sleight of hand. While Roz and Violett are getting poisoned, everybody thinks Jane is a couple thousand miles away."

"Yeah," I said. "It wasn't airtight, because the airline roster on Thursday night—the night she was supposed to fly back to New York—doesn't show her name. And of course there's the rental car."

"Right," Ruby said. "She had to use her driver's license to get the car."

"But if she succeeded in pinning Roz's murder on Violett," Meredith said, "nobody'd check flight rosters or rental cars."

"And she could be pretty safe in figuring that her scheme would work," I said, licking clam dip off my fingers. "Roz was a celebrity. The local cops would be under enormous pressure to find her killer in a hurry. Jane must have figured they'd jump at a plausible murder-suicide package, just to get the case wrapped up."

Meredith frowned. "I'm not sure I know how Jane and Violett got together," she said. "They seem like a pretty unlikely pair."

"I have to admit that I'm really guessing on this," I said. "I saw Jane and Violett talking at Jo's memorial service. Violett must have told Jane at that point about her claim to StrawBerry Bear, hoping that Jane, as Roz's agent, might help her get something out of Roz. That gave Jane the bright idea of killing two birds with one stone. By that time, she'd already decided she had to kill Roz. Now she could see that she had to get rid of Violett, too."

"That's right," Ruby said emphatically. "She couldn't let Violett go around telling people that StrawBerry was *her* bear. That could cause no end of trouble."

"Exactly. So Jane decided to set it up so that Violett looked like Roz's killer. She saw Jo's sister off on her flight home to Hawaii, then headed into Austin, rented the Duster, shopped at Sears for shoes and less noticeable clothes, and checked into the Marriott, where she slept Thursday and Friday nights. She lucked out, because the Knife and Gun Show opened at the City Coliseum on Saturday. She bought the thirty-eight from a private owner who didn't bother with the paperwork or check to see if she was a Texas resident." For a dealer, that kind of transaction is highly illegal and subject to a ten-thousand-dollar fine and imprisonment. The last dealer who got caught selling a handgun to a nonresident got slapped with both. But private owners can get away with murder.

"So Saturday night's shooting was dead serious," Meredith said. "Jane wasn't just trying to scare Roz."

I nodded. "If she'd succeeded, she would've shot Violett with the same gun. Murder-suicide. When she blew the shooting, she probably decided it was too high-risk to try again with the gun. She'd been at the party the time Roz complained about the fire ants, and she remembered the poison. So she lifted it, then went over to Violett's and gave her a song-and-dance about needing a place to stay. That was about nine-thirty, when Miss Ima saw her at Violett's and mistook her for a man. The next morning, she waited until Roz had gone walking, then sneaked into the cottage and poisoned the tomato juice Roz used for her garlic cocktail. Then she went back to Violett's and cooked her a toxic mushroom-and-garlic omelet."

"What's the significance of the garlic?" Ruby asked curiously.

"The ant poison is a compound called thallium sulfate. When you sniff it, it has an aftertaste of garlic. So Jane masked it with real garlic. Smart lady."

Meredith shook her head. "I see why Jane had to kill Violett, but I still don't see her motive for killing Roz. She apparently didn't know about the Disney deal. So even if Roz was acting flaky about the contract, she still, presumably, had the potential of producing big dollars for Jane's agency."

"Remember that argument we overheard?" I asked. "It's my guess that Roz foolishly warned Jane that she was having the royalty account audited. Jane was afraid the audit would uncover some big-time embezzling. It was a powerful motive for murder."

"Sure," Ruby said. "And once Roz was dead, Jane would have a free hand with the royalty account. There wouldn't be anybody around to protect Roz's interests."

"I wonder if Jane knew about Mother and Roz," Meredith said, poking the fire thoughtfully.

I shook my head. "If she did, Roz and Violett would both be alive—or Jane herself would be dead, courtesy of Roz."

"How come?" Ruby wanted to know.

"Because Roz's affair would've given Jane the leverage she needed to declare herself a player in the Disney deal and to keep Roz from pursuing the audit."

"Which would have put the shoe on the other foot," Ruby said. "It would have given Roz a good reason to kill Jane."

"Well, there go the letters," Meredith said, watching the flames eat the last piece of paper. "I think Mother would be pleased."

Ruby frowned. "I don't understand why the D.A. didn't charge Jane with both murders. It doesn't seem right, letting her off so light."

"Sometimes the law takes what it can get," I said. "The best the D.A. figured he could do was a plea bargain—Jane pleads guilty to Violett's second-degree murder. In return, the D.A. doesn't pursue an indictment in Roz's death."

"But she's getting away with it!" Ruby protested angrily.

"Sure," I said. "That's why it's called a bargain. If I were the D.A., I might've gone for first degree on both. But I see his problem. Without a full confession—which Jane is too tough and too smart to give—the case against her for poisoning Roz is entirely circumstantial. There's also the political heat. Senator Keenan's been leaning on the D.A. He wants this thing wrapped up as fast and as quietly as possible."

"It would have been different if Violett had talked before she died," Ruby muttered. "Then Jane couldn't have gotten away with it."

"Yes," Meredith said, "but if she talked, she would

have revealed Roz's relationship to Mother. So I guess—" She didn't finish her sentence.

"What's the maximum Jane can get for second-degree murder?" Ruby asked.

"Twenty-one years," I said. "When she finishes serving that term, she'll face more time in New York—if the D.A. there turns up enough evidence to make an embezzlement charge stick." I'd talked to Roz's secretary on the phone. It sounded like the auditors already had enough to build a case.

"I think we did the right thing, deciding not to pursue the matter of Mother's murder," Meredith reflected, watching the flames die away. "It's likely that she had only a few more months to live. This way, she died painlessly, quietly, without being hospitalized again or having to be dependent on other people. Maybe Roz did for her what Mother was planning to do for herself. Final exit."

"Yes, but there's the airport," Ruby reminded us unhappily. "Jo knew something that could have stopped the airport, and the secret died with her."

Meredith laughed. "Maybe it didn't," she said. "Mother got a letter yesterday from the U.S. Fish and Wildlife Service." She took an official-looking envelope out of the top drawer of Jo's desk and began to read.

> Dear Ms. Gilbert:
>
> Subsequent to the receipt of your letter of September 25, ornithologists from the Fish and Wildlife Division conducted a preliminary survey of the acreage described. It has been deter-

mined as a result of this survey that the findings reported by you are substantially accurate, thus confirming that the aforesaid acreage is subject to likely designation as prime habitat of the golden-cheeked warbler. This office is proceeding to implement appropriate measures under the existing regulations on a priority basis. Thank you for calling this matter to our attention.

Very truly yours,
Douglas C. Arbingast
Regional Director

Ruby looked at me. "So *that's* what a little bird told Jo," she said.

"I get the general drift," Meredith said, "but exactly what is a golden-cheeked warbler?"

I grinned. "It's a rare bird that nests in a limited area. It comes under the protection of the Endangered Species Act. A developer can't cut down, dig up, or pave over its habitat without an act of Congress."

Meredith laughed. "So what this letter really says is bye-bye airport."

Ruby nodded. "That bird has already shot down a couple of big developments around Austin. When Arnold's buddies realize how much red tape they have to cut to make the airport fly, their dollars will evaporate like a mud puddle in August."

I stared at Ruby. It was the most impressive group of mixed metaphors I'd ever heard assembled in one place.

Meredith folded the letter and put it back in the envelope. "Way to go, Mom," she said quietly, and sat down by the fire again.

After a few minutes I asked, "When are you leaving?"

"Next week," Meredith replied. "I turned in my resignation, and I'm going out to Flagstaff for an interview. I've been thinking how nice it would be to find a little place in the mountains." She nodded in Ruby's direction. "We can't close the house until after probate, but the new owner's anxious to move in."

Ruby looked around. "I've got some redecorating to do: I hope you won't mind."

Meredith shrugged. "The place is yours," she said. "I'm happy, because I don't have very good memories of it. And Mother would be thrilled, especially if you fix that kitchen light." She turned to me. "What's going to happen to Violett's place?"

"Violett left everything to the Humane Society," I said, "with the stipulation that her animals be placed in good homes."

"Dottie Riddle is taking all of the cats," Ruby said, "as if she didn't have enough already." Dottie is Pecan Springs' cat lady. She has dozens of her own and she feeds countless strays around the university. "Except for Pudding, of course," Ruby added. "China adopted him. And I'm taking the canary."

I shuddered. "Cat," I said. "His name is Cat. And it's the other way around. He adopted me." It was true. I still wasn't keen on cats, but this one had decided to come home with me and I don't have what it takes to argue with him. He is a cat of great determination.

"The Humane Society can't be getting much out of

it," Meredith said. "Violett didn't have more than a few thousand dollars in the bank, did she?"

"Don't bet on it," I said. "Violett has a legitimate claim against Roz for copyright infringement. Charlie Lipton, who's representing Violett's estate and the Humane Society, has contacted Roz's lawyers and Disney's lawyers, and they're thrashing it out. I assume it'll be settled out of court—in about ten years. The wheels of justice grind exceedingly slowly."

"But they do grind," Meredith said.

"Yes," I said. "And I suppose when you get down to it, justice was pretty well served in this case."

"But not by the law," Ruby said.

"No," I said. "Not by the law."

Susan and Bill Albert publish an occasional newsletter called *Partners in Crime*, containing information about their books. If you would like to be on the mailing list, send a one-time subscription fee of $3 to *Partners in Crime*, P.O. Box 1616, Bertram, TX 78605-1616. You may also visit the *Partners in Crime* Web site at *http://www.mysterypartners.com.*